"I want to kiss you. Will you allow me to kiss you?" His eyes, his intensely dark green eyes, stared at her, his whole body immobile as he waited.

If he wanted to he could kiss her.

And this was up to her, wasn't it? He wasn't the type to leverage his title and strength and sheer Hadlow-ness of him to get what he wanted. But all of that was alluring.

She wished he hadn't asked, wished he had just taken her, claimed her mouth with his.

But that wouldn't be honest, or fair, and he might be the most abrupt and rude man she had ever met, but he was also the most honest.

And he was still waiting for an answer, his eyes not leaving her face, his hands clenching and un-clenching into fists at his sides.

That was what decided her. That clear, expressed need, that want epitomized by the movement of his hands.

"I will let you kiss me," she said in a soft voice. "Only if you let me kiss you as well."

By Megan Frampton

Dukes Behaving Badly

WHY DO DUKES FALL IN LOVE

MEGAN FRAMPTON

AVON BOOKS
An Imprint of HarperCollinsPublishers

Excerpt from *My Fair Duchess* copyright © 2017 by Megan Frampton.

First Avon Books mass market printing: August 2016

ISBN 978-0-06241282-9

Avon Trademark Reg. U.S. Pat. Off. and in Other Countries, Marca Registrada, Hecho en U.S.A.

Avon, Avon Books, and the Avon logo are trademarks of HarperCollins Publishers.

HarperCollins® is a registered trademark of HarperCollins Publishers.

16 17 18 19 20 OPM 10 9 8 7 6 5 4 3 2 1

To Scott, my own ridiculously intelligent husband, and Rhys, my remarkably wonderful, curious, and brilliant son. I love you both.

Acknowledgments

Thanks, as always, to my critique partner, Myretta Robens; my editor, Lucia Macro; and my agent, Louise Fury. You guys make my writing so much better. Thank you.

WHY DO DUKES FALL IN LOVE?

27. Because it's better than falling into a muddy ditch.

Chapter 1

"He left you with nothing?"

Edwina glanced to the side of the room, a tactic she knew full well wouldn't disguise the moisture in her eyes, especially not from Carolyn, her oldest and dearest friend. They'd met when Edwina's late husband had wanted to find a respectable, but inexpensive, maidservant, and Carolyn's agency had found the perfect person. And Edwina had finally found a friend she could actually talk to.

The room was as familiar to her as her own lodgings—and definitely more welcoming. A kettle was heating up water on the small stove, the tea things—the chipped blue cup for Carolyn, the cup with the handle that was always too hot for her—waiting until the water boiled.

Cozy, comfortable, and everything else she was not.

"No." She spoke plainly, unable and unwilling to disguise the truth of it.

Eight years of marriage to one of the most boring men of her acquaintance, and he didn't even have the decency to leave her financially comfortable when he died.

"I can help you, you know," Carolyn said in a soft voice. She got up as the kettle began to whistle and started preparing the tea.

Edwina's throat tightened. "I won't take your money." Fine words for a pauper—they both knew that if the choice came between accepting charity and letting her daughter starve, Edwina would take the money. Gertrude sat on the floor, playing with her dolls. Was she already getting thinner? Edwina's heart hurt at the thought, and she had to bite the inside of her cheek not to start fretting aloud. That would do nothing but worry her daughter, who wasn't old enough to understand.

Edwina wasn't entirely certain she was old enough to understand, either.

"I wasn't offering to give you any money," Carolyn replied in a dry tone of voice, glancing over her shoulder as she spoke.

Edwina's gaze met Carolyn's.

"Well, what then?" she asked in an unsteady voice.

"Employment," Carolyn replied, returning to her task.

"Employment?" Edwina echoed, an uneasy feeling settling somewhere in her gut. The gut that was remarkably close to her stomach, which hadn't eaten today, and had only had some porridge and some hard cheese yesterday.

So the uneasy feeling would have to ease.

"You do know I run an employment agency." Carolyn gestured to the room they sat in. "Since you have used my services."

"Yes, back when I could afford them," Edwina replied in a tone that was both wry and pained.

She took a deep breath, and looked around her. It was undeniably pleasant, if modest. The cozy, comfortable room of the Quality Employment Agency, filled with books, papers, mismatched chairs, and an enormous battered desk, where Carolyn normally sat, welcomed her, made her feel safe in a way her new lodgings did not.

"Yes, but—" and then Edwina felt both foolish and snobby, since the answer was obvious, and yet had not occurred to her because of who she was. Who she had been.

"But what?" Carolyn picked up the teacups, wincing as she felt the heat from the offending handle. She brought them over to where Edwina was seated, placing them on the desk and sitting back down in her usual spot. "You need a job, Edwina. No matter who you are. Even ladies— especially ladies, judging from my experience— need to have enough money to eat and to live. Even if their husbands were so disappointing as to leave them bereft of anything but their good name."

"And even that was sullied, thanks to George's entrusting of the accounts to his brother as soon as it seemed the businesses were getting profitable, and worthy of notice," Edwina remarked in a bitter tone. She kept her tone low, so her daughter couldn't hear. "I told him I could handle them, that I had gotten them to the state they were in, not to mention I told him how untrustworthy his brother was—and yet he said he'd never 'let a female deal with important things,' " she said in an imitation of her late husband.

"More fool he," Carolyn remarked. "If he had allowed you to continue to oversee the finances you wouldn't be in this situation now, would you?"

It was a well-worn discussion, but one that still made Edwina angry. George had been so blind to her attributes he hadn't seen she was skilled at maths, far better than anyone in his own family, especially his debt-beleaguered younger brother. He had been fine when she oversaw the accounts when they weren't important—but ironically, as soon as her skill had yielded results, he took them away from her and handed them to a man. Simply because he was a man, and his brother, and not a woman, and his wife.

And now she and little Gertrude were being made to suffer for it. George's brother hadn't done more than shrug when Edwina had told him how George had left her. He already had a wife, he said, and he couldn't afford to take her in, although he had offered a place to his niece.

But Edwina couldn't bear the thought of being separated from her daughter; she was the only thing keeping Edwina from stepping in front of an oxcart one day. That she and Gertrude might starve to death was not something she wanted to contemplate—what reasonable person would?—even though she had to.

Which brought her back to why she was currently sitting with her closest friend in said closest friend's employment agency, realizing that perhaps she had to consider employment herself.

"What can I do?" she said at last, hating how pathetic and needy she sounded. _Better pathetic and needy than dead_, a voice said inside her head.

Carolyn chuckled, taking a sip of her tea. "What can't you do? You can balance accounts, drive hard bargains with tradesmen, oversee skittish maids, sort out the temperamental discord among upper-class servants, and keep an older husband relatively comfortable in illness. Not to mention you are extremely well-read—there are benefits to having a neglectful husband—and your parents ensured you had all the education you'd need to be an adept wife, whether you married a politician, a solicitor, or even a lord."

"Or a businessman with lofty pretensions," Edwina added. "They thought they had taken care of me. I wish they were still here." She shook her head. "I do not wish to be married again, if that is the employment you are suggesting." Once was enough, and she would have said never would have been enough if it weren't for Gertrude. And it is not as though she had any other family to resort to; her parents had both been only children, and she had no relatives that she knew of.

"I am not in a husband acquisition business, Edwina," Carolyn replied in a mocking tone. "If

I were, don't you think I could afford a better office?"

They both glanced around at the tidy but shabby room. "Excellent point," Edwina replied with a grin, picking up the cup with the still-hot handle and taking a welcome sip of tea. "So what do you have in mind?"

"Thank you for your time." Michael picked up the bell on his desk and rang it once. "The type of secretary I require will need more skills than you appear to possess. You may go."

The door opened to let his butler in as Michael was sitting back down, not even bothering to watch as the candidate left, still expostulating as Hawkins led him out.

That made fourteen candidates he'd seen, and none of them would suffice.

"How difficult is it to find someone who is reasonably intelligent, organized, and doesn't make me want to fling heavy objects at his head?" This he addressed to his dog, Chester, who lay on the floor to the right of the desk.

Chester had no reply. Not unsurprising, since he was fast asleep, his limbs splayed out on the floor.

Well, he could now come closer to answering that even if Chester wouldn't, and the answer would have to be *Very hard. If not impossible.* Even his dog would have to agree.

If he didn't find someone soon, he would have to take on the task himself, since Chester had already tacitly declined the position, and while he wasn't averse to hard work, he was averse to doing things that someone else could be doing. It wasn't the sensible thing to do, and Michael was nothing if not sensible.

He knew full well that people who didn't like him—which seemed to be most of the people who met him—would also add he was arrogant, opinionated, plainspoken, and condescending. He could now put fourteen more people on the list of people who didn't like him. Not that he cared. He never had.

He'd only rarely felt the pangs of—of something, of wanting something more. But the pangs usually ebbed when he thought about having to tolerate having that intangible something in his life that could likely be as frustrating and inadequate as everything he'd encountered before.

He just needed to find a secretary. Not have to endure something that would inevitably end in disappointment.

Actually, he'd endure a secretary who didn't like him if the man could do the job.

His standards were getting lower, it seemed. He felt his lips twist into a rare smile at the thought, and he drew another applicant's letter from the stack on his desk.

There had to be somebody who would suit.

"Another applicant is here, Your Grace." Hawkins cleared his throat, something he did only when he had bad news to give. The last time had been three and a half years ago, when a fire had ravaged Michael's stables. Michael had helped drag out all but three of the horses, leaving him with scarring on his hands and a profound dislike of his butler's throat clearing.

"What is it?" Michael said in a snappish tone. Because unless the applicant was on fire himself, he didn't see the point of Hawkins being so diffident.

"It is not a man, Your Grace." Another throat clearing. "It is a woman." A pause. "A young woman."

Michael's brow rose. "And? The applicant is female, is that the cause of your distress?"

Hawkins bowed. "Precisely, Your Grace. The Quality Employment Agency assured us in their correspondence that the candidate was fully adept in all ways, but the agency did not see fit to inform us of the candidate's gender." Left unspoken, to Michael, was that Hawkins hadn't done sufficient investigation to discover just what type of agency he was dealing with. Another example of why he needed a secretary.

Michael refrained from shouting in reply. Really, people should give him a lot more credit than they did. There were so many remarkably slow people, many of whom were in his employ, it was a wonder he wasn't constantly yelling. Instead, he drew a deep breath. "Send the candidate in, then."

Hawkins knew Michael well enough not to say anything more, thankfully. "Excellent, Your Grace," he said, bowing.

"A woman, Chester," Michael said. This time,

Chester was awake, but showed no interest in conversing. Perhaps if the candidate had been a juicy steak Chester would have had something to say.

Michael sat down at his desk, reviewing the information about the candidate that nonetheless neglected to mention she was a woman.

She did indeed have everything he required, because he didn't believe a secretary in his employ necessarily had to be the same sex as he was. Despite what his butler and likely everyone else in the world believed.

If she was the best man for the job, he'd hire her. That was the sensible thing to do. And not only that, it wasn't as though there were very many places he could continue his search—clearly, if the current candidate was female, he had reached the limits of possible options. He hoped she would be a viable choice.

"Mrs. Cheltam, Your Grace."

Michael raised his eyes to where she stood in the doorway. Hawkins had seen fit to mention that she was a woman, but not that she was a wickedly, gloriously beautiful woman.

Not that that would matter any more than that she was female in the first place. Not to Michael.

She strode into the room and he appraised her as he would any work of art: thick, lustrous hair drawn back into a severe hairstyle, highlighting her remarkable cheekbones. Large, dark eyes fringed with long lashes. A nose that was strong and straight, not one of those namby-pamby retroussé noses most people found appealing.

A lush, full mouth with a beauty mark just to the left.

And that wasn't even accounting for her figure, which—like a truly skilled appraiser—he could see was curved in all the right places, her demure clothing only serving to hint more broadly at what might lie beneath.

He remained seated. She was here for a position; he didn't see the point of treating her like a usual woman, since he'd already established—in his mind, at least—that it didn't matter if she was a female or not.

Her expression flickered for a moment, then she smoothed her features and took the seat in front of his desk, settling herself into a perfect pose of politeness.

"I understand you are interested in taking employment as a secretary." Michael tapped the paper listing her qualifications. "I see you have some experience with what I need taken care of. But I would like to hear from you why you are the best choice for the job." At this rate, the only choice, given that the remainder of the applicants looked even worse than his last secretary, who'd made a muddle of everything, which Michael hadn't noticed until it was almost too late. That still made him furiously angry. Not at Mr. Crear; the man was an idiot, he couldn't help it that he didn't understand, but at himself for not assessing the situation earlier. He wouldn't make that mistake again.

"Of course, Your Grace." She visibly swallowed, then let out a soft exhale. "I have experience in accounting, keeping engagements, managing a household, and I have excellent penmanship and correspondence skills." She met his gaze squarely, raising her chin as she spoke. "I hope you will take all of my qualifications into consideration and not focus on the fact that I am a female."

He raised his eyebrows. "I have not made mention of it, have I?" He spread his hands out. "And yet it is patently obvious." Especially because she was such a beautiful female. There would be no mistaking this woman for anything but a woman. "So in drawing attention to it yourself, that would suggest to me that you are considering it, and yet wish me not to."

Her mouth tightened, and she glanced away. A faint flush stained her cheeks. "Yes. I wish you not to." She looked back at him. "Although perhaps you should, when you consider that as a woman in a position usually reserved for a man, the woman has to be better than any man would be." She lifted her chin. "I will be, Your Grace, you have my word on it." She didn't speak, just held his gaze for a few more moments, the faint flush on her cheeks intensifying as she kept her eyes steady.

He didn't stop looking at her, nor did he speak, at least not for a few moments. She was truly his last chance at finding someone to work for him, he'd already ruled out all the previous candidates, and she seemed moderately intelligent. He liked that she didn't drop her gaze. Perhaps she would be someone he could work with. At the very least, he could try.

"Agreed," he said in a short tone of voice. He

saw her shift out of the corner of his eye. He'd startled her; he tended to have that effect on people, he had no idea why. Perhaps it had something to do with his utter lack of interest in them or their problems or his refusal to put up with idiots. Or maybe that was just his assessment. Maybe they just were intimidated. He glanced down at her written qualifications. "And where did you receive this wealth of experience?" He needed to make certain, even though he'd already made up his mind.

"I am a widow," she began, her words speeding up to avoid—perhaps—the inevitable words of condolence.

Although Michael never said the polite thing, so she needn't have worried. He just didn't see the point of it. It wasted time, he'd be lying, and he didn't care anyway. He did know that few people thought as he did, but for the life of him, he couldn't figure out just why they were so determined to do things that were just not logical.

If he had ever had sympathy for anyone, he would express it. It just hadn't happened yet. Thankfully—at least according to him—he wasn't close with the few members of his family whom he acknowledged.

"And my late husband owned several businesses, and had interest in more ventures. I oversaw many of his business dealings until the year before his death."

He looked up, once again appraising her beauty. Not that it would bother him working in close quarters with her. "And why is that?"

Her chin went up again in what Michael now recognized as her preparing to say something perhaps the listener might not want to hear. He was familiar with that—he seldom said things anybody wished to hear. Which was why the list of people who disliked him was so long.

"My husband decided to entrust everything to his brother when the business began to do well." She spoke in a flat tone, but he knew firsthand what it sounded like when one was hiding one's emotions, and she was. She was practically roiling in emotion, only it was neither his place nor his business to inquire further. And usually he wouldn't care—he never did—but he did find himself mildly intrigued.

Interesting. He would have to examine that further, later on.

"So you were part of the business's success, and yet you are here now, which implies that the business was not that successful."

Her expression got fierce, and he found himself admiring her spirit. "Precisely, Your Grace. That is why I am here. After I was—after I was not overseeing things, the business faltered." She shrugged, as though it didn't matter, which Michael could tell was an absolute lie. She was here, wasn't she? "My husband's death has made it essential that I find suitable work."

Michael leaned back in his chair, steepling his fingers. Might as well tell her his decision. He loathed it when people danced around a question. "You are hired."

Her face brightened, and he, stoic though he

was, felt the impact of her beauty all over again. He could not get distracted by that, just as he could not accommodate the fact that she was a woman. "You will reside here; there is much work to be done."

And just like that, her face fell. He felt a twinge of something in his chest, but he couldn't identify the emotion. Likely because it was emotion. "No, Your Grace, I cannot." She rose. "I wish I could accept the position," and at this she met his gaze and her lips curled up into a rueful smile. "I truly wish I could, but I cannot live here."

Michael had never been told no before. It was a new experience, another one he'd have to examine later. But right now, he had more important things to concentrate on. Namely not being told no after all.

"Why not? Are you concerned about gossip? I assure you, I have no designs upon your person, despite the fact that you are a woman." It wasn't at all logical to embark on anything personal with her, despite her gender and general attractiveness— Michael despised complications, and emotions, and he knew any kind of personal relationship would result in many complicated emotions. All of them hers.

She shook her head. "It is not that, Your Grace." She swallowed and lifted her chin. "I have a daughter, and I will not be separated from her." She glanced away. "I appreciate your time."

She smoothed her skirts, which didn't seem to need smoothing, and turned to leave.

Michael didn't think anyone had ever left his presence before without being dismissed. Even more intriguing.

"Wait," he said as she was halfway to the door. She paused and turned to look at him. "Why cannot your daughter live here also?"

Her expression was taken aback. "Why would you do that? Why would you hire someone who had additional encumbrances when you could hire a man who would live here without any such requirements?"

He could have said, *Because all the men I've met with haven't been nearly as qualified or clearly intelligent as you.* But he didn't. Instead, he raised an eyebrow. "Are you questioning my judgment, Mrs. Cheltam? If you wish to take the position, and it is a requirement of you doing so that your daughter reside here as well, then that is what will happen. What do you say?"

She blinked as she considered it, then nodded, and he felt the relief through his entire body. Finally, the search was over, and he could get down to the business of getting his accounts straightened. His life back to the way he wanted it. The way he required it.

"Thank you, Your Grace. Then I accept."

"You will move here immediately," he continued. "I'll send two of my footmen with you to collect your and your daughter's things from wherever you are living. I will expect you back here within a few hours, and we will review what your duties will be."

He sat back down, feeling a slight smile twist his lips as he felt her irritation at his high-handedness wage war with her need for a position.

At last, she spoke. "There is no need to send any footmen with me, Your Grace. My daughter and I have very few possessions. I will see you in three hours."

"Make it two," he said, not looking back up at her.

"Two," she replied as she turned back around to walk out the door.

WHY DO DUKES FALL IN LOVE?

59. Because someone has to find a way to humble a duke.

Chapter 2

Edwina was shaking as she left the duke's town house, letting herself emit an enormous sigh of relief as she heard the doors close behind her.

She had done it. She had gone in and presented herself, and he had given her the position. And what was more, she wouldn't have to spend any of her precious wages on lodgings, either—she would be living there, in the grandest house she'd ever seen, let alone walked inside.

But the house was nothing compared to the duke's splendor. When she'd thought about what she might say, how she would comport herself, she had imagined she'd be facing some older gentleman. Her imagination had given him white muttonchops, a red nose, and overgrown eyebrows, of all things.

He had none of those. The reality was far, far worse. To her peace of mind, at least. He was young, likely only a few years older than she, but his demeanor was so intimidating it suited the much older gentleman in her imagination. He was tall, with a forbidding expression, and moved with an unconscious grace that made her think he did more than just sit at his desk and frown in judgment. And his eyebrows—fierce dark slashes that rose to punctuate his words—far worse than merely overgrown.

Her heart had been in her throat at the thought that she could have the position if she just let Gertrude go live with her brother-in-law, or some other place—but she wouldn't do that. Couldn't.

To say it aloud had been one of the hardest things she'd ever done, and yet she had to. Gertrude was the only reason she was doing this in the first place; it didn't make sense to just allow her daughter to be kept somewhere else, no matter how safe and well cared for she might be.

And then he'd made his proposition—no, not a proposition, not that—his alternative suggestion, and she'd wanted to fall to her knees on the thick, lush carpet of his study and cry. But she hadn't. She'd known that if she'd done that, if she even let a tiny amount of her uncertainty show, he would withdraw the offer as quickly as he'd made the suggestion.

And she was going to work for him, and what was more, work closely with him, solving problems and using her brain and not her body to make her way in the world.

She had to concentrate on that, and not on the fact that the Duke of Hadlow was likely the most intimidating person she'd ever seen.

Edwina turned the handle of the agency's door and walked in, her heart melting as she saw

Carolyn and Gertrude engaged in some sort of game on the floor. Carolyn looked up, her face breaking into a huge smile as she saw Edwina's face. "You got it, then?" she said, getting up as she spoke.

Edwina nodded, nearly too overcome to speak. Gertrude looked up also, a sweet smile on her face. "What did you get? Is it a treat?" she asked, in the single-minded focus particular to most six-year-olds, at least in Edwina's experience.

"Not quite a treat, sweetheart, but something that will allow us to get treats. Mama has gotten a job," she said, reaching out to squeeze Carolyn's arm.

"Oh," Gertrude replied, clearly disappointed.

"And we'll be living in a grand house, and the house has a dog. A very furry golden-haired dog."

"Oh!" That seemed to be much more welcome news than that they would not be starving, at least not in the near future. "What is the dog's name?"

"I don't know. We'll have to find out," Edwina added hurriedly, as Gertrude's face fell.

"You'll be living there?" Carolyn asked in a low tone of voice. She glanced to where Gertrude sat, then drew Edwina into the corner of the room, out of Gertrude's earshot.

Edwina could have told her friend that Gertrude had no interest in anything that adults wished to speak about, and would only pay attention if the words "doll," "candy," "treat," and "play" were spoken, but she didn't blame her friend for her caution.

"Yes, the duke insisted." And, she could have

added, she didn't think the man would be open to compromise.

"Well," Carolyn said in a dubious tone of voice, "that is interesting. You will be careful, won't you? I haven't met the duke, but I do know his type."

Not for the first time, Edwina wished her friend had shared the past experience that seemed to make her so distrustful of men in general, and titled men in specific.

But now was not the time to pry into closely kept confidences.

"He doesn't seem to be a type at all. Definitely his own unique man." Edwina gave a derisive snort. "And it is not as though the duke has designs upon my person. He told me precisely that when he was telling me I would live there for the position, or I would not get the position. And I have no wish to get involved with any sort of gentleman ever again. George was more than enough"—or less than enough, actually—"for me."

Carolyn raised a brow. "You keep that in mind, you need to be especially on your guard."

Edwina patted her friend's arm. "I know. I assure you, I am well aware of what situation I could get myself into if I allow myself to—well, to do the things you are worried about." She recalled the duke; how implacable, grim, and intimidating he seemed. "I don't think there is any danger of that. I promise." Even if she were so inclined—which she wasn't—he seemed as emotionally remote as any man she'd ever met, and that included her late husband.

Thank goodness he was that unapproachable. Because he was also that attractive.

"Just a few steps more, sweetheart," Edwina said to Gertrude, who was lagging behind her mother, complaining to her doll about how long it was taking them to get there.

Edwina and Gertrude had left Carolyn's office and returned to the set of rooms Edwina had rented. It had been a relief to inform her land-lady she was moving out that instant. They had only been there a few months, and already they'd learned how to best keep the mice from getting into their food, and late at night Edwina and Gertrude had been awoken by the singing of the sailors who took rooms there while onshore. Thankfully Gertrude didn't understand the words to the sea chanteys, but Edwina did, and she made sure to bolt the door as well as push a chair or two in front to keep any unwanted visitors out.

As she'd told the duke, they had very few possessions—just their clothing, a few toys of Gertrude's, and the books Edwina had kept when she'd married George. They all fit into one valise, as long as Gertrude was able to carry Honeychop, her favorite doll.

She was. Although she was not happy with having to do anything at all after the first half mile. "When are we theeere?" she said, stretching out the final word in the specific way she'd found would most annoy her mother. Or at least that's how it sounded to Edwina, but Edwina had to admit perhaps she was not the most tolerant person at the moment, given that she was toting all their possessions across London.

"It's right around the corner." Edwina could feel how damp her gown had gotten from the exertion—perhaps she should have taken the duke up on his offer to send a footman or two with her, but she didn't want to have anyone see where she and Gertrude had been living. It was already going to be an awkward thing, to be the duke's female secretary; she didn't want his staff to know just how straitened her circumstances were prior to taking the position. She didn't want to go into the house using the servants' entrance— that would set a very bad precedent for who she was, and how she was to be treated—but neither did she wish to make a bad first impression when she walked into the house.

She hoped the duke was not near the door when she entered—she did not want that supercilious gentleman to see her anything but perfectly gowned.

Thankfully, George had wanted her to look like the prize he'd thought he'd won, so while he was miserly in other areas, he was generous enough with her clothing. She'd worn her best day dress to meet with the duke—a striped gown that George had bought for her only a few months before his death. Its stripes were tan, dark red, and green, and it had full skirts and a small waist with a modest bodice. Now, however, she'd changed into her worst gown for the walk, a gray gown that was a few years out of date, styled very plainly.

It wasn't dreadful, but neither was it particularly attractive. Then again, she shouldn't be worrying about how attractive she appeared, not any longer—she was to be a secretary, not somebody's possession, not a wife whose husband only viewed her as a representation of his own success. Not a woman who had to survive on her looks. She was done with that; now she had to survive on her brain.

So if she made a bad impression, what did it matter? She would do her work well, and thoroughly, and give the duke no cause to complain, no matter what she looked like.

Thus prepared, she held her hand out for Gertrude and walked up the stairs to the duke's house, bracing herself for the new chapter in her life, but very grateful she had been able to turn the page.

Michael frowned as he glanced at the clock in the corner. It had been two hours and twelve minutes, and his new secretary hadn't returned yet. Was she regretting taking the position? Would he have to resume the search?

Please just let her be late so he wouldn't have to go through all that again to find someone else suitable. Although he did abhor lateness. But lateness was the lesser of the two evils, if one of the evils would be having to resume his search.

"Your Grace, if you would care to examine the documents, I believe you will find all the information you require."

The gentleman from the railway had been prompt, arriving some twenty minutes ago, but that had been the only good thing Michael had gleaned yet from the man. He had spent most of the time after his prompt arrival talking about expansion and opportunities and discussing in very vague terms what Michael could expect from his investment.

Apparently he would be the benefactor of modern-day travel. He congratulated himself on not telling the gentleman he was satisfied enough with being a duke. What he wanted from the meeting were not some romantic vagaries, but information. Why did people feel the need to obfuscate the facts with generalities? Generalities didn't do anything but annoy him.

He suppressed a sigh, instead looking to where the gentleman was pointing, his index finger indicating some papers on Michael's desk.

"I see." And he did see, only he couldn't focus, not with wondering if she was going to arrive. What had he been thinking, to offer her daughter a place as well? He hadn't even asked how old the girl was—not that she could be that old; the woman herself was definitely younger than thirty, so her daughter would still be young.

Not that it mattered. But a young girl. And her mother. Both living here, under his admittedly very large roof.

If he didn't wish to, he wouldn't need to bother seeing the girl at all; she would be off doing . . . something while he and her mother were working.

What would the girl be doing? He definitely

had not thought any of this through. Making such a quick decision with no debating of the merits both for and against—that was completely unlike him, and he wasn't certain he liked it.

No, he knew. He did not like it. Things needed to be orderly, to be logical, to make sense. Sense was the only thing Michael trusted. He'd settled on that course when his parents had lied to him about where his brother was, not believing a child of four could understand death. Since that day, he required—and trusted—only logic and reason. Reason made sense. Unlike death and caring for others, and trusting that people who were older were necessarily more intelligent.

That was only one of the many reasons he kept whatever family he had at arm's length. If they weren't close to him, they couldn't hurt him. And he would never allow himself to be hurt again.

But this. This impulsive action. Deciding on the spur of the moment that his secretary could bring her child to live in his house—that was nonsensical. If he had just tried harder, he could have found someone else for the position, someone who wasn't so encumbered.

In several more months of searching, perhaps.

And it didn't make rational sense to take more time for the search just because there was an accommodation in the form of a young girl.

But none of this thinking was getting the information he required. Specifically, where his new employee was. He glanced at the clock again—he couldn't seem to help it—noting that it was now two hours and seventeen minutes.

A knock sounded at the door just when he was trying to convince his brain to concentrate on the papers, not on the whereabouts of his new secretary.

"Enter," he said, not looking up.

The door opened. And Hawkins cleared his throat, damn him.

"What is it?" Michael said in a terse tone.

"Your new secretary has arrived, Your Grace."

Michael wondered just why he felt so much better than he had a few moments ago. It was only relief that he wouldn't have to continue his search, nothing more.

"Send her in straightaway," he said. He saw the railway gentleman jerk, and remembered, of course, that most people would be shocked—stupidly so—at the gender of his newest employee.

"You don't wish her to freshen up before seeing you, Your Grace?"

Michael felt his eyelid twitch, and tried not to snarl at Hawkins. It wasn't his butler's fault the man hadn't learned not to question his employer, even after being in his service for over a decade.

No, never mind that. It was his fault.

"I do not. Send her in." He accompanied his words with a dismissive wave of his hand, gritting his teeth at the thought that Hawkins's sense of propriety and what was due a duke would overcome his common sense.

A moment, and then Hawkins appeared to realize what was required. "Excellent, Your Grace," he said. Michael heard voices in the hallway, including a young child's voice, and had to wonder again just what was wrong with him that he had acted so—so rashly. Perhaps so imprudently.

And if he would come to regret his hasty decision as he'd regretted every hasty decision he'd ever made before.

"The duke is waiting for you." The butler came as close to sneering as he could without overstepping the limits of politeness. Edwina had to admire his dexterity at it, even if it smarted.

She glanced down at her gown and sighed, allowing a rueful smile to cross her lips. "I suppose he cannot wait until I am more presentable," she muttered, hoping the butler would sympathize and she could win him over sooner rather than later.

His gaze traveled over her gown as well and he met her eyes, a slightly warmer expression on his face. "The duke is a gentleman who values promptness and efficiency over everything," he said in a low tone, ensuring none of the footmen currently on duty in the hallway could overhear.

She smiled at him, thankful he'd already unbent a bit. If only she could so easily conquer the thousand or so other people who likely resided in this mammoth household, her life would be much easier. "That is good to know, I appreciate the information." She paused, but decided to ask anyway. Because if she didn't begin as she meant to go on it would be a very difficult situation. "Mr.—I'm sorry, I don't know your name."

"Hawkins, my lady."

She smiled. "It is Mrs. Cheltam, and it is very nice to meet you. I was hoping if it would not be too much of an imposition, perhaps you could ask one of the footmen to take my daughter to the kitchen to wait for me?"

His gaze darted to where Gertrude stood, currently haranguing Honeychop about the terribly long walk her mother had made her go on, as though Honeychop weren't there every step of the way. And she saw how his eyes crinkled up at the corners, just slightly, as though he were trying not to smile. "I will take her there myself, Mrs. Cheltam."

"That is terribly kind of you, Mr. Hawkins." She raised her voice to interrupt Gertrude. "Sweetheart, can you accompany Mr. Hawkins to the kitchens?"

Gertrude looked from her mother to Mr. Hawkins, clearly skeptical about the whole thing. Edwina couldn't blame her; she was as well. But it was either this or separation or starvation, and on the whole, she much preferred living in a duke's enormous town house to either of the other two options, and hopefully Gertrude would come to that conclusion as well.

"Will there be cakes?"

Mr. Hawkins bowed. "The best cakes, my lady, I know for a fact that Cook has just brought a tray out from the oven." He lowered his tone. "The duke doesn't care for cakes, or food in general, so it will be a treat for Cook to have someone who appreciates her work."

How could the duke not care about food? Edwina wondered. But he did care about promptness, and she had already spent a few precious minutes getting her daughter settled. "Where will I find the duke?"

Mr. Hawkins paused in his escorting Gertrude to the kitchen. "The duke's study, Mrs. Cheltam, just through there."

Edwina felt her insides tighten. This was it. This was the start of the next, hopefully much better, phase of her life. One where she and her daughter were fed, housed, and she wouldn't have to endure a foolish man twenty-four hours a day.

Hopefully not at all, in fact—the duke didn't strike her as foolish. Arrogant, impatient, and totally commanding, but not foolish.

That had to count for something, didn't it?

With that cheery thought, she walked to the door of the study, taking a deep breath as she knocked on the door.

WHY DO DUKES FALL IN LOVE?

78. Because a duke is, when all is said and done, still just a man.

Chapter 3

*W*ell, he could tell that his new secretary hadn't dawdled in presenting herself. She wore an old, worn gown whose color could best be described as drab, and her hair had come unpinned, with a few pieces swirling about her face.

Unfortunately, it just had the effect of making her look far more approachable, and he did not want to be thinking about approaching his new secretary on any terms. It wasn't sensible.

"Mrs. Cheltam, please come here." The railroad man had straightened instinctively, but Michael remained seated. He gestured to a chair opposite his desk, the one she'd sat in just two hours and twenty-four minutes prior. She nodded and took her seat, folding her hands in her lap.

"Mr. . . . ." and then he paused because he couldn't remember the man's name, just that he was far too vague on specifics for his liking, and he couldn't very well address him as Mr. Vague. "This gentleman was just reporting on the benefits of investing in the Right Way Railway Company. Terrible name," he added, shaking his head. "Mrs. Cheltam, you will take notes." He flicked his fingers toward the man. "Proceed. This time, please give us precise details on the venture and the various timelines for resolution."

The man's gaze shifted quickly between the two of them, the Adam's apple in his throat working visibly. He did not speak. Michael suppressed a sigh. "Unless you would care to just leave your documents here for our perusal? I can reply to your employees within thirty-six hours, if that is suitable."

Michael would have laughed at the man's relieved look, if Michael laughed at such things. Or at all. "That would be perfect, thank you, Your Grace."

He bowed in their general direction and sped out of the room, barely waiting for the door to open before bursting out of it.

Silence. Michael turned to see his new secretary regarding him. He raised an eyebrow, which seemed to make her stiffen.

He would have to do it frequently, then.

"Are you always so abrupt?" Her question, which some would have considered rude, was said in such a pleasant tone he couldn't take offense.

Besides, the answer was yes.

"Yes, I am." He leaned back in his chair. "I don't see the point of prevaricating when there is something to be said." He raised his eyebrow again. This time, it seemed she was prepared, since she didn't react. Pity. "I appreciate the same of my employees, no matter what they might say." He leaned forward, clasping his hands on his desk. "If we are to work well together, Mrs. Cheltam, I would ask you to keep that in mind. No matter what you might think the effect of what you'll say is. I assure you, I far prefer honesty to flattery, and I do not like to waste time."

She blinked, and shook her head. He resisted the temptation to lean forward even more and sweep some of the errant strands of hair behind her ears. Odd, he'd never had that thought before, and he had seen plenty of disheveled women.

"That will be acceptable," she replied in a soft, but even, tone.

He felt something ease within him. As though he'd actually been concerned about what she would say.

"I will expect you to reciprocate," she said, lifting her chin. "If you have cause for either complaints or compliments, I do hope you will offer them instead of keeping them to yourself. I will not know how to improve, or what I am doing well, if you do not tell me."

He'd never had anyone respond to his request for honesty with an equal request for honesty. Something sparked in his belly, a frisson of . . . of excitement? Of being challenged?

And here he thought he'd had all the experiences he'd ever have in his thirty-four years. His new secretary was not only new to his employ, she was providing new experiences just by being here.

Interesting.

"Of course, Mrs. Cheltam," he replied, giving her his full scrutiny and appreciating that she did not flinch from the appraisal.

Very interesting indeed.

"Good morning, Your Grace." Edwina resisted the urge to curtsey. After all, he didn't rise when she entered the room; she didn't see the point of adhering to traditional manners when he didn't. Besides which, he'd probably chastise her for wasting time.

It was the third day of her employ, and she didn't think she'd ever worked so hard in her entire life. And that included the times she'd had to pretend her husband wasn't a complete idiot.

Gertrude had made friends with Mr. Hawkins as well as Cook, a variety of footmen, and a few of the maids. She had spent the past three days exploring the duke's mansion, with several more wings to go.

Of course, Edwina would eventually have to figure out what to do with her in the long term, but for now, at least, her daughter was well taken care of, fed, and kept in clean clothing.

While her mother—well, Edwina was working the hardest she'd ever worked before, true, but she was also totally engaged, was using her brain as she'd rarely done before, and felt useful and valued. Not because of what she looked like, but because of how she thought.

She didn't think the duke even noticed what she looked like, which was a relief—she'd spent too much of her life avoiding awkward situations with gentlemen who thought that because she had a certain appearance, she was amenable to a certain type of behavior. But the duke, true to his practicality, treated her as merely his secretary, even though there was nothing *mere* about it. He was similar to George in that he valued her for one thing, and one thing only, it seemed—but the thing he valued was something Edwina had worked on, not something she had been born with.

"Good morning, Cheltam," the duke replied. He didn't look up from his desk, and Edwina settled herself in her usual spot, drawing her notepad to her. He'd dropped the "Mrs." from her name the first day of her employ. She supposed if it had bothered her she could have told him, but it was refreshing to be treated as a worker, not a woman.

"The first thing we will be doing today is review the offerings from the other railways." He picked up the teacup settled at the edge of his desk and took a sip, his movements precise and nearly elegant. As they always were.

"How many are there, Your Grace?"

He did look up at her then, frowning. "You'd best call me Michael."

"I couldn't, Your Grace." She was willing to bend propriety because he was, and it was more efficient, but saying "Michael"—two syllables— was just as time-consuming as saying "Your Grace," and far more improper.

He narrowed his eyes as though he were going to argue with her. And then didn't. "Fine. Then Hadlow will do."

Hadlow. His title, still two syllables, but not his given name or his honorific, which seemed to annoy him somehow. Perhaps because he was constantly reminded of his title by everyone who came into his presence?

Although she'd have to say that people would notice him even if he weren't a duke. He was just so—just *so*, his features so strong and sharp, his movements so precise and contained, his body hinting at power and strength and force.

When she was with him—which was most of the past few days; he never seemed to slow down—she was constantly aware of just where he was in the room, even if he was out of her sight. He seemed to exude a nearly palpable energy, and she found, to her chagrin, that she was drawn to that energy in a way that was not appropriate to an employer and his secretary.

"Do you have the notes from yesterday?"

She'd also found that his mind skipped from point to point to point in an almost dizzying way, and she had to concentrate to keep up. Even so, she could tell she was thinking too slowly for him when he grumbled or muttered or frowned when she had to ask him a question to clarify something.

Although it wasn't her fault the man couldn't seem to keep his attention on one point at a time, was it?

"I do." She rose and went to the small bookshelf he'd designated as hers. "I did not have time to rewrite the notes, so you might find them hard to read." The night before she'd had to remind him that it was six o'clock after they'd been working all day. She was grateful he appeared to have a social engagement in the evening, or they might have been at it all evening. Although Gertrude would have come to find her eventually. And Edwina did not want him to be reminded just how much he had had to accommodate his new secretary.

"Just hand them to me, I don't care what they look like." He held his hand palm up, his focus returned to the papers on his desk. She placed them in his hand with a bit more force than was absolutely essential, and had to repress a smirk at his start of surprise at the impact.

He shook his head as though to clear it and set the papers down, his long, elegant fingers shuffling them as he glanced them over. "What does this say?" His index finger pointed to something on the page, and Edwina squinted, but couldn't make it out from where she was. She took a deep breath and walked over to his side of the desk, leaning over slightly to read her writing.

"It says there will be one thousand miles of track laid the first year, with expected additions of twenty percent more each year thereafter."

"Ah."

She went to return to her side of the desk, but he grasped her wrist as she was starting to move. "No, wait. And this?" He tapped the paper with his finger and looked up at her.

And then she felt as though she were unable to breathe. The impact of him, this close, was enough to make her gasp. His intense burning green eyes, green like the darkest forest, the sharp aquiline length of his nose, the full, nearly sensual mouth just below. She had been trying not to admit just how attractive her new employer was, but this close, it was impossible to deny. And he had required her honesty, which required her being honest to herself, as well.

"Uh, that is," she said, swallowing, feeling her pulse pounding, "that says that the railway will hire approximately five hundred workers, bringing stability to all the towns along the projected lines."

He still held her wrist. She tried not to notice just how strong and warm his fingers felt.

He kept his eyes locked on hers for a few long seconds—one, two, three—then released her wrist. She felt unsteady on her feet, but just nodded and returned to her seat, picking up her pen and papers with a shaky hand. Hopefully he wouldn't notice.

Of course he would notice. He was remarkably observant, she'd already seen that. But he likely wouldn't care, even though he did notice. That gave her some measure of reassurance.

He was trying very hard not to notice just how attractive his new secretary was. He didn't have that problem with Mr. Crear, his last, unlamented secretary, nor any of the previous ones, none of whom had been nearly as efficient, intelligent, and organized as Mrs. Cheltam was.

Nor as lovely.

His fingers still tingled from where he'd held

her. He hadn't meant to touch her, it just seemed to happen. And once it had, he didn't want to stop. It had taken a concerted effort to let her go, not to just allow his fingers to rub at the soft skin of her wrist or hold her hand, of all ridiculous things.

Or other, just as ridiculous, but far less appropriate things.

He couldn't think about any of that. He didn't want a lover; those were far easier to come by than good secretaries. He should know, he'd had dozens of lovers in his years, and he hadn't valued any of them as much as he did Mrs. Cheltam in her few short days here.

It was a bonus to her working for him, wasn't it? That he could regard her beauty as they untangled his business dealings, looked into new investments, gathered information about his various holdings. He could not do anything to jeopardize his finally having someone who seemed competent. Intelligent, even.

But he wouldn't be noticing her beauty, not in a longing way, if he hadn't first recognized her intelligence. He had seen plenty of lovely women before, but none of them intrigued him as she did— the rare, likely unique, combination of appearance and intelligence was one that hit him in a way he'd never experienced before.

And she was so very efficient.

"Your—Hadlow, do you want me to finish the correspondence to your estate manager? Mr. Sheldon, I believe?"

Michael took a deep breath, clearing his mind—as

well as other parts of him—so he could concentrate. "Yes, good. I'll review the notes from yesterday, and then after that if you can retrieve the documents from the other petitioners, I'll review those." It was an exciting time to be a duke. Not that it wasn't always good to be a duke, but it had its boring moments. Strawberry leaves, people being obsequious, too many sweet cakes being thrust at one as though one was a child.

But now, when Michael felt as though the world was on the cusp of discovery, as though new and exciting things were just about to happen, and he could have a part in it—well, it was an exciting time. That he had the funds and means to participate didn't mean he would neglect his due diligence. If anything, he had to be more alert. The fate of future dukes of Hadlow depended on his managing his vast holdings properly.

His father had been much the same, although Michael had to admit his father had far less of an imagination, content to keep things as they were, never wanting to speculate on something that might not be a certain bet.

To Michael, that felt as though everything was doomed to mediocrity, and if there was one thing he did not wish to be, it was mediocre.

He wanted to leave a lasting impression on the world, to strive to make it a different, better place. It was what he had promised to himself after his elder brother, the original heir, had died. He wouldn't be content to be second-best in anything, even if he was the second son. That was why, instead of lolling about on his ducal sofa, he was engaged in progress and investigation and possible adventure.

That was why he was encumbered with the most beautiful, and beautifully efficient, secretary he could imagine.

And why he had to keep it that way, and not allow his now far too active imagination to wonder what other role she could play in his life.

"Cheltam," he said abruptly, not even realizing he had been planning to speak, "do you like this work?"

It wasn't something an ordinary employer would ask. But he knew well enough he wasn't ordinary, and neither was she—she was extraordinary, in how she seemed to anticipate his every request, how she was able to refine and distill his thoughts into something that was nearly as good as what was in his brain. He'd never met anybody who had that capacity. It made him wonder what it would be like if he were to talk to her as he had never talked to anyone before. Not having seen the need before.

But her. He wanted, no he *craved*, to know more about her.

"I do, Your—Hadlow," she said, placing her pen on the desk in a firm motion. She leaned back in her chair and assessed him as frankly as it felt he'd assessed her. Oddly, it wasn't uncomfortable. In fact, he welcomed it. "You treat me as someone whose opinion is valued—"

"That's because I value it," he said, interrupting.

A rueful smile crossed her lips. "Not many

people, especially men, would admit that. Or even think it, for that matter." He saw her blink rapidly. "It is just one way in which you are very unusual, Your—Hadlow," she corrected. "I am so grateful you offered me this position."

He didn't want her gratitude. He didn't want anyone to think he was doing something out of the goodness of his heart. He didn't think he even had a heart.

"You wouldn't be here if you weren't doing an excellent job," he muttered, almost feeling . . . embarrassed? He'd never felt this way in his entire life.

She smiled again, this time openly, causing a warmth to develop somewhere in the middle of his chest.

Maybe this was what it felt like when someone found another person who was of the same temperament and of similar intelligence. Perhaps this was the something he'd known he didn't have. But this was also his secretary, a woman whom he paid, who was not in his social circle at all. He would never have met her if he hadn't hired her. If he weren't paying her to be here.

Maybe this was yet another thing he could look at from the outside without understanding. He'd need to harden his nonexistent heart so he wouldn't allow for the possibility of getting damaged in some way.

She was opening her mouth to speak when he interrupted. "I'm going out tonight. You won't be needed." He didn't have to try to use a clipped, impersonal tone. It was the tone he used most often, except when he spoke to his dog, who didn't seem to like being told what to do.

Similar to his master.

"Of course," she replied in a demure tone, the stain on her cheeks indicating her emotion, but nothing else about her betrayed any kind of reaction. Good. That was how it should be; he couldn't have her come to care for him in any way other than as an employer. It was too dangerous for feelings to get involved. "I did not realize you had an engagement, I did not see it on the calendar."

He wanted to snap at her, to tell her he wasn't constantly at home, by himself. Only he usually was, and he wanted to snap less than he wanted to lie. He'd only decided that day to accept the invitation since it had been too long since he'd put in an appearance in Society.

Why did people find the need to just . . . talk about things nobody cared about? Incessantly? If he hadn't come to realize that his peers wouldn't support his endeavors in the House of Lords without having seen him at a social function every so often, he would gladly refuse to leave his house except to do things he wanted to do.

But he had come to realize that, and even though it made him frustrated with people's stupidity—as most things did—he forced himself to do it. For the betterment of the world, if not for his own personal happiness.

"Your Grace, we are delighted to see you this evening."

Michael returned the comment with a tight smile. First of all, the wife of the man who'd spoken didn't look delighted at all. If anything, she looked nervous, as though he was going to pronounce judgment on her party-giving skills and the guests she'd persuaded to join her this evening.

Well, she wasn't wrong, he was going to, but he certainly wasn't going to share his thoughts with her. He'd found that people seldom wanted his thoughts, even though they said they did. He'd learned to temper his comments over the years.

Second, he'd heard his host say the very same thing to the couple who'd been announced before him, which meant that the man was lying—he couldn't possibly be delighted with each and every guest who'd shown up at his house. Surely there were a few—perhaps even Michael—that the lord didn't particularly care for. Why would he say he was delighted if he wasn't?

Michael shook his head without replying, merely offering a bow and the remnants of that smile, glancing over the heads of his hosts to see the rest of the crowd.

It appeared he'd arrived early, since thankfully there wasn't the crush of bodies he'd come to dread when he made his few appearances. A row of chairs was placed against the back wall, mostly filled with older women whose lorgnettes and feathers waved in symmetrical disapproval. The dance floor had a few couples, while a trio of musicians played something that grated on Michael's ears. The dancers appeared not to notice, however.

He took a glass of wine from a passing footman's tray and sipped, enjoying the slide of the cold liquid down his throat. He took a larger sip and closed his eyes, savoring the brief moment of pleasure. The moments were always brief; someone or something usually came along to disturb him. It was only in small moments like these that he was able to find what he supposed most people called happiness.

"Your Grace, do tell me how you like the flowers."

The small moment was made even smaller with the intrusion of his hostess, who seemed to have recovered herself enough to address him.

He arched an eyebrow, wishing it didn't bring him pleasure to see her visibly quail, and glanced to where she was pointing. Flowers. Yes, they were flowers.

"They are flowers." He spoke in his usual flat tone.

"Uh," the woman replied, her expression faltering. "Yes, they are. What do you think of them? Aren't they glorious?"

Why didn't people just come out and say what they wanted him to say instead of making him work for it? Just once, he wanted someone to say, *Your Grace, I want to hear you say my flowers are glorious. Go ahead, say it.*

"I suppose they are." In her eyes, at least. In his they were just—flowers. The result of a plant's need to draw attention to itself in order to procreate.

Rather like some of the ladies and their brightly colored gowns.

Flowers were much easier to understand than people.

"Thank you." She sounded as though she believed he'd thought the flowers glorious. Why was she so determined to lie to herself? To have him lie to her as well?

He shifted awkwardly, taking another sip from his glass, wishing he were anywhere but here. At home, with Chester snoozing on the rug, reviewing something that made sense.

Not here where people wanted him to say things that weren't the truth, where he was stared at as though he were something to be regarded, not interacted with—not that he wanted interaction with any of these people. Not if it meant he had to lie, and feel uncomfortable. Why would anyone search that kind of thing out? And yet these people did, people of his world, who yet weren't at all of his world. The world he inhabited, at least. One where people said what was on their minds, not for anything but to speak the truth. People who thought things out. People, in fact, who were like him.

Not that he'd yet to meet anyone like him, which was likely why his best friend was his dog, who only spoke when he had something to say, usually involving a visitor to the door or a need for food. And why he spoke to his family so seldom.

When could he leave? He shifted again, glancing up at the ceiling, not wanting to make eye contact with anyone. Eye contact inevitably meant conversation. Conversation meant feigning interest in things he couldn't see anyone should be interested in. Flowers, or the room, or the weather. Things just were, and discussing them didn't help anybody.

"Your Grace, if I—" It was his floral hostess again, and all of a sudden Michael couldn't stand it any longer.

"Excuse me, I must be going," he said, feeling as though he were propelled across the room and out of the door, a palpable relief flooding him as he spied one of the footmen holding the door open for him.

Wishing he didn't feel like such an anomaly.

WHY DO DUKES FALL IN LOVE?

39. Because they can only talk to their dog for so long before getting frustrated at the lack of response.

Chapter 4

"Cheltam, I think that is enough." Michael rubbed his eyes as he glanced out the window, noting the sky had gone dark and the streetlamps were lit. He didn't have an engagement this evening, thank goodness. Last night had been agony enough. "Is it seven o'clock already?" he asked, frowning at the clock in the corner as though it were its fault it was so late.

She turned to look at the clock also. "It appears so, Your—Hadlow." She turned back to him, her face showing concern. "I should find my daughter; I don't want your staff to have to take care of her all the time."

"Why not?" Michael shrugged. "There are plenty of people here; they could surely watch out for a young girl. What is her name, anyway?"

She straightened in her chair, a soft light coming into her eyes. "Gertrude. She is six years old, and very smart. At least I think so."

The pride and love she felt for her daughter seeped through her voice, and Michael felt a pang of longing. Odd, since he wasn't aware he'd been lacking in the parental love area until she spoke. He didn't think he'd ever heard either of his parents speak of him in such warm tones. Usually, they were congratulating him on some success or another, or reminding him of his duty to his title and family. The only memory he had of warmth in his family had been his brother, who'd had the temerity to die when Michael was four. He presumed that his brother had loved him, but since it had been thirty years since he'd felt any sort of affection at all, he wasn't entirely sure. Just that the way she spoke about her daughter held an unfamiliar emotion that certainly seemed as though it was love.

He wanted to know more about it. More about her.

"We shall all dine together tonight."

Her eyes went wide. No wonder, since it was unusual for an employer to invite his secretary to dinner, much less a duke invite a widow and her offspring to partake in a meal. "That wouldn't be—that is, thank you," she said, no doubt noticing that he was about to remind her who he was in relation to her.

Michael nodded. If he had to resort to ordering his paid employee to keep him company—well, he would do that. "Half an hour. That should give you sufficient time to prepare." He watched as she rose, smoothing her skirts, tucking a few strands of hair behind her ear. His fingers itching with the urge to push those strands behind her ears himself.

"Thank you for the invitation, Hadlow." She lifted her chin. "It might be closer to forty-five minutes before we can get to the dining room. Gertrude needs to have her hair brushed and to change her clothes."

"I don't care what she looks like," Michael replied with a shrug.

Her chin went higher. "But I do, and that is what is important." She took a breath. "And if you will excuse me, I need to go locate her." She walked out without waiting for his reply.

Not that he had anything to reply; he was actually struck dumb, not having anyone ever saying their own opinion was more important than his.

He shook his head as though to clear it, pulling one of the papers from the stack on his desk closer. But his mind wasn't on what was written on it, but on her, and what she'd said, and how he felt now. Was he that much of a boor that he was discomfited by someone expressing their own opinion contrary to his?

He had to admit he was. And he did not like it one bit. He would have to reflect on how he replied to people, how he let them know what he thought without making it imperative that they agree. Something he had never done before.

"Gertrude?" Edwina walked down one of the hallways, peering into the corners, allowing a huff of frustration to escape her lips. Her daughter was an excellent hider, and she'd already been enthusing to her mother about all the excellent hiding places there were in the duke's town house. Not surprising, given that there were likely over a thousand rooms. Or so it felt to Edwina.

She hadn't been in this part of the house yet. Also not surprising since the duke had been keeping her occupied in the study, leaving no time for exploring.

"Surprise!" Gertrude popped out from behind a door, making Edwina shriek and Gertrude dissolve into giggles. She was accompanied by the duke's dog, Chester, who'd quickly learned that Gertrude left a trail of tasty crumbs since she was always on the go, and always hungry.

"You startled me, love," Edwina said, when she could catch her breath. Her daughter beamed.

"We waited for over half an hour, Mother," Gertrude said, her eyes round with pride for having endured such a wait. "Chester kept wanting to leave, but I gave him the biscuits Cook had given me for a snack."

"You were very patient. How did you know I would even find you?"

Gertrude shrugged. "I knew you wouldn't let me be lost for very long."

That assumed confidence, the assuredness that her mother would always come find her, made Edwina feel fiercely proud, as proud as Gertrude was for having scared her mother. That was why working for the duke was worth it—because she was continuing to give her daughter that confidence.

It was all worth it. Even adding in her discomfort at finding the duke just so remarkably attractive, so much so she felt almost squirmy in his presence.

She would just have to endure it, for her daughter.

What an incredible sacrifice, she thought. Having to tolerate being with one of the most charismatic, intriguing men she'd ever met for hours at a time. *Edwina, you deserve sainthood.*

She nearly laughed aloud at the thought, but knew Gertrude would want to know why her mother was laughing, and Edwina couldn't explain it.

"The duke has invited us to dine with him this evening. I came to find you so we could both dress for dinner."

Gertrude's eyes went even wider, if possible. She was so expressive, everything she ever felt showed on her face. Edwina hoped she never had to learn to temper her expressions as Edwina did—keeping herself guarded so as not to reveal what she was truly thinking.

"Can I wear the white gown with the ribbons? Please, Mother?"

Edwina smiled, taking Gertrude's hand. "That is just what I was going to suggest. Let's go get dressed."

They walked down the hall together, Chester following behind, Edwina's heart filled to bursting with love for her daughter and relief that she had kept them together, despite her late husband, Gertrude's father, having taken so little care that she even had to find employment.

* * *

"Your Grace?" Edwina walked into the dining room, holding Gertrude's hand. Chester had kept them company as well, Gertrude insisting on his being present while she dressed, even though Edwina worried he would mark up Gertrude's white gown with his paws. But he seemed content to be gently scratched on the ears, and then he flopped down on the rug in front of the fireplace, watching them as they scurried to garb themselves appropriately.

Gertrude's white dress had a bright yellow sash, and one of the maids who was helping them dress found a yellow rose, which she tucked behind Gertrude's ear, after stripping the thorns, of course.

Edwina was in one of the gowns George had bought her—dark purple, it was made of a lustrous silk that seemed to shift colors in the light. Its bodice was low but not immodest, and it had touches of black ribbon ornamenting it. He'd thought it was too somber for her after he'd purchased it, but she secretly loved it, and was delighted she could wear it without seeing his frown.

She had to be honest that she loved doing most anything now that he was gone. He hadn't been a bad husband, beyond his financial mismanagement; but he hadn't been interesting, or worthy of her love, or anything that made her want to be with him.

He'd treated her likewise, as an ornament to be admired by his peers, but it never seemed to

Edwina as though he actually knew her, knew what she liked, or even cared. She'd fulfilled the bargain of their marriage, always keeping herself as attractive as possible so he could preen in front of his friends, family, and business associates, but she had offered nothing more. And neither had he.

That she had gotten Gertrude out of it all made it worthwhile, but she didn't miss him. At all.

She hadn't lied to Carolyn when she'd said she didn't want another husband. But that was before she met someone like the duke—someone who was intelligent, and commanding, and respected her opinion. Someone she could respect and admire. He probably also wouldn't care what she liked, only—well, he did ask if she liked working for him. Expressing more interest in her with a few words than her husband had in their entire marriage.

"Over here, ladies." The duke's low voice sent a shiver through Edwina, one that reminded her of her great sacrifice. It wasn't fair that he had that commanding presence, that he also had a commanding voice, one that rumbled in a way that made Edwina wonder how he'd sound in the throes of passion.

Although that would imply he was passionate about anything, and thus far, Edwina had seen nothing to persuade her of that. That made it a bit easier to admire him—if she had thought he was likely to reciprocate at all, she would have been terrified at losing control, at allowing herself to fall into something more with him.

Because she knew full well that he would be

the first one to see that any more of an association with each other wouldn't be practical—he couldn't marry anyone of her station, and she couldn't afford to lose her living just because a handsome man decided to toss away all of his treasured logic to dally with her.

"Your Grace, this is my daughter, Gertrude. Gertrude, this is the duke, my employer." Gertrude kept close to Edwina's side, seeming as though she wanted to hide behind her skirts, but she held her hand out to be shaken, solemnly, by the duke, who bowed as he would to the grandest lady, as though Gertrude was the queen or something.

"It is delightful to meet you, Miss Gertrude," he said, keeping hold of her hand. "I was wondering who had so enchanted Chester that he saw fit to leave my side. You must be a special young lady."

Oh dear. He was being considerate toward her daughter, and she wasn't sure her heart could take that. This was not what she'd expected, having seen him and all his abrupt gruffness over the past few days.

Gertrude smiled shyly. "Chester told me you were grouchy, but you're not at all, are you?"

Edwina felt her face turn scarlet. "Gertrude, it is not pol—" only to be interrupted by the duke's laughter.

"Chester told you that, did he? He is not wrong, I am normally grouchy. Wouldn't you say so, Mrs. Cheltam?" And he turned his gaze to her, his mouth lifted in a smile, which she hadn't seen before.

"I could not say, Your Grace." Her stomach fluttered in an odd way.

"Or would not say," he replied. "You cannot, I understand." He was still smiling, and Edwina couldn't take her eyes off his mouth. She had noticed it before, of course, since she'd been taking a mental inventory of all his attractive features, but she hadn't realized just how attractive his mouth was—he had a full lower lip, even though his upper lip was rather thin. So when he smiled, and showed his strong, straight teeth, she felt a bit weaker in the knees than she had before.

"My mother is never grouchy," Gertrude continued, unaware that her mother was in the throes of massively admiring her employer. "Except if she does not have coffee in the morning." She frowned. "Right after Papa died we couldn't afford coffee, so Mother was grouchy all the time." The last three words she drew out to punctuate them, making it sound as though it had been a gruesome time.

It had been, but Edwina hadn't been ill-tempered because of a lack of coffee; her mood had been soured by realizing just how little her husband had left her. But she couldn't put that burden on her daughter, nor could she hide her emotions around her, so she'd blamed it on a lack of coffee.

"I will take care not to approach your mother without her coffee, then," the duke said, shooting Edwina an amused glance.

"Are we going to eat?" Gertrude said, looking at the table. It was huge, it could probably seat forty people, but there were place settings for three at one end, which made it look far more intimate than Edwina would have wished, given her state of mind regarding the duke.

"We are." The duke waved his hand to one of the footmen standing at attention in the corner without deigning to look at him. "Ask Hawkins to begin serving." The footman nodded and left the room, along with a few other of his compatriots.

"You should say please," Gertrude said in a tone of rebuke. "Mother says that only bad-mannered people don't say please."

Now Edwina wanted to sink into the floor. It was true, but she should have amended her words to Gertrude to say "bad-mannered people and dukes."

Thankfully, the duke didn't seem to take offense. "You are correct, Miss Gertrude. I am a bad-mannered person." He didn't sound as though he were doing anything but stating a fact.

"Let's sit, shall we?" Edwina spoke before her daughter could continue the conversation.

Gertrude opened her mouth as though to argue, but the lure of food overcame her desire to continue to debate the point. She allowed Edwina to guide her to one of the seats, the duke following them. Edwina sat Gertrude on one side of the table, taking the other side, leaving the head of the table for the duke.

"Do you care for wine, Mrs. Cheltam?" He gestured to one of the remaining footmen without waiting for her answer. The man, whom Gertrude likely already knew, approached the table, pouring a healthy serving of wine into Edwina's glass.

"Can I have some, too, William?" Gertrude asked the man. Yes, she knew him already. Of course she did. Edwina's daughter had the amazing ability to make friends wherever she went. It even seemed as though she might make friends with the duke.

William looked at the duke, his face showing concern. "Your Grace?"

The duke shook his head. "Don't ask me, it is up to the lady's mother."

"Please, Mother?" Gertrude looked at Edwina pleadingly.

She hesitated. If she said no, she'd be the mean mother. If she said yes, she'd be exposing her daughter to wine at a very early age. Then again, it was unlikely that Gertrude would actually like the taste, so perhaps it would be a good risk to allow her to sample some.

She did very much appreciate that the duke hadn't just answered for her. Another way he showed that he didn't seem to notice whether or not she was female. A fact she was supremely relieved about. "Just a small pour, please, William," she replied.

Gertrude beamed, watching as William poured a small amount into her glass. The duke picked his glass up, as did Edwina, and then Gertrude followed their lead, holding it in the air. "A toast to fine company," he said, touching his glass to Gertrude's, then to Edwina's.

"And food," Gertrude added.

"And food," the duke echoed with a grin on his face.

Edwina felt her heart swell as she watched them. It seemed as though things would be all right, that Gertrude had charmed the duke as she did most other people. They weren't in danger of starvation, they were housed well, and once she had her wages she would be able to afford to buy Gertrude some new clothing—her gowns still fit, but from the way she was eating, it was clear she was growing fast.

The door opened, and Hawkins entered, leading a line of footmen bearing serving platters. He indicated where they should be placed and watched as they were all put on the table. When everything was arranged to his satisfaction, he stepped forward and began to remove each lid from its platter, removing it with a flourish and handing each lid to a waiting footman.

It was very impressive. Another reminder, as though Edwina needed one, that she and Gertrude were living in a duke's household. That she was here only because he employed her. If he wanted her to leave, it would be as simple as terminating her employment.

"Will there be anything else, Your Grace?"

The duke shook his head in a decisive movement. Something habitual to him, Edwina had observed over the past few days. "Nothing else, Hawkins, thank you." He smiled at Gertrude as he spoke. "See? I can be polite when I wish to be."

Hawkins's mouth opened and closed a few times, but he didn't say anything, just bowed and left the room, taking the majority of the footman phalanx with him.

"Mrs. Cheltam, would you mind serving?"

"Certainly. Would you like some ham, Your Grace?"

He shook his head, glancing at Gertrude. "Go ahead and serve your daughter first. She has been waiting very patiently."

"I have!" Gertrude exclaimed.

Edwina couldn't help but smile at her daughter's enthusiastic support of herself. "You have, sweetheart." She rose to take Gertrude's plate and placed an assortment of the food on it—ham, stewed tomatoes, a bit of chicken pie, and potatoes. She placed it in front of Gertrude, then held her hand out for the duke's plate. "Your Grace?"

He handed it to her, his eyes glinting with amusement. She hadn't realized he possessed a sense of humor, much less one relating to food and six-year-olds and dinner.

"You can skip the tomatoes, Cheltam, I don't care for them," he said as she began to serve.

"Does that mean I don't have to eat them, either?"

Edwina shot a quick glance at the duke—*do you see what you've done?*—then looked at her daughter. "The duke does not have anyone he has to listen to."

"Thank God," he said in a low murmur. She wanted to giggle at how relieved he sounded, but knew that would only make Gertrude more recalcitrant.

"But you do, at least for a few more years yet. And I want you to eat your tomatoes."

She felt both pairs of eyes looking at her, and she resisted the urge to tell both of them to stop being so fussy, but then she would be the ill-mannered person at dinner this evening, not her daughter, as she'd feared.

So instead she went about making his plate— skipping the tomatoes—and handed it to him, not meeting his gaze, then set about making her own. Making sure to put plenty of tomatoes on her own plate.

Why Do Dukes Fall in Love?

82. So they can have someone remind them when it's time to eat.

Chapter 5

"I am so full," Mrs. Cheltam's daughter said, rubbing her stomach. Michael felt his mouth curl up at the corners, something he wasn't accustomed to. Nor was he accustomed to spending any time at all with children of any age. He didn't know if Mrs. Cheltam's daughter was indicative of the whole species, but he was surprised to find he actually liked her. She was guileless, clearly intelligent, and enthusiastic.

It was clear she had inherited her mother's looks and would be a beauty someday. She had dark eyes, like her mother, and hair just a few shades lighter. She did not have the beauty mark her mother did, but otherwise, she looked like a young version of Mrs. Cheltam.

Mrs. Cheltam, he'd noticed, hadn't tried to curb her daughter's enthusiasm for dinner, or conversation, or dessert, although she had kept her from having three desserts and had reminded her to say please and thank you a few times.

"Shall we go to the drawing room for tea?"

"I don't like tea," Gertrude said in a sulky voice.

He didn't mind that she had spoken rudely, if that was how she felt. He'd meant what he'd told her mother, that he preferred honesty to nicety. But it seemed her mother was not so sanguine; a blush was creeping up her cheekbones, and she had pursed her lips. "That is not polite. Please apologize to us."

Gertrude pouted as she spoke. "I am sorry."

"I don't like tea, either," Michael said, earning a quickly suppressed glare from Mrs. Cheltam.

"It is your bedtime. Excuse us, Your Grace."

Michael looked at one of the standing footmen. "You there. William, is it? Please find one of the maids to take Miss Gertrude up to bed. Her mother and I will take tea in the drawing room."

He could tell she didn't like it by the way her mouth opened, but she did not say anything, just met his gaze and tilted her head in a short nod.

Her daughter, on the other hand, apparently thought it was to be a great treat to have one of the maids put her to bed rather than her mother, judging by her smile. The novelty of it must have appealed to her.

He would far prefer to have Mrs. Cheltam put him to bed, but he didn't have a choice in the matter, did he?

He did not. He could not. Especially now that he'd met her daughter, and understood better why the woman was so fiercely determined to take employment, and to be a more than satisfactory employee.

What must it be like to be the only thing keeping a child away from utter poverty? Because that was what she had implied when he'd first met her, and besides, no lady would choose to work if she didn't have to. There would be too many disreputable men willing to take advantage of a lady in a precarious position, even if the lady in question had an honest desire to take and keep a position.

Thank goodness she hadn't ended up with one of those disreputable men. Even though he was noticing his own disreputability in his thoughts regarding her, he wouldn't act on any of his desires. She was too good a secretary and too worthy a woman to treat her so shabbily.

Even though he wished to. Not treat her shabbily, not that—but to see if her mouth tasted as good as it looked. To lick that beauty mark, to plunge his hands into her thick hair so he could hold her to him, to kiss the curve of her neck and the fullness of her breasts, which were more enticingly revealed in the gown she wore than he had seen thus far.

More than that, to be able to talk to her as an equal, a woman who could be his partner in conversation as well as in bed. Someone he could ask questions of without knowing he'd be totally bored by the answer. Someone who would ask questions of him that would make him think in a way he'd never had to before. Someone to challenge him.

The door opened, letting one of the maids in, making him snap back to attention. *Dear God, Michael*, he thought, *what are you doing?* He'd never wanted something he couldn't have before, and he wasn't quite certain how to handle that disappointment.

"Good night, Your Grace," Gertrude said with a curtsey.

"Good night, Miss Gertrude," he replied in a solemn voice.

"I will be up later, sweetheart," Mrs. Cheltam said, holding her arm out. "Give your mother a hug, all right?"

Gertrude flung herself into her mother's arms as Michael watched, feeling something in the area of his heart tighten. He couldn't be feeling a pang of jealousy, could he? That he had never gotten such a vigorous heartfelt hug from his parents? Or was it that he wished Mrs. Cheltam would open her arms to him in a similar manner?

"Off you go," Mrs. Cheltam said, finally releasing her daughter. "Thank you." She addressed the maid. "Only two nighttime stories, please. Even though she'll tell you I always read her seven."

Gertrude's face fell comically. "Mother," she said in a long, plaintive voice.

"Go on," Michael urged.

Gertrude rolled her eyes, but left the room, the maid following behind.

And then they were alone.

"Did you wish for tea, Your Grace?"

Michael shook his head. "No. Some brandy, perhaps." He stood, waiting as she rose also. "In the drawing room." He didn't wait for her reply—he never waited for anybody, did he, he was coming to realize—just strode to the door so quickly the footman couldn't open it for him. He held it for her as she followed, the skirts of her gown brushing his legs.

"Ask Hawkins to bring glasses to us."

He led the way to the drawing room, conscious of her following him. Of her scent, of how he seemed to always know where she was in the room.

He flung the door open and walked in, gesturing to the smallest of the three sofas in the room. "Sit there."

He thought he might have heard her muttering about orders and demanding dukes, but chose to ignore her. She was correct, after all. He was peremptory, given to issuing commands he expected to be followed.

She sat, rod-straight, her body not making contact with the back of the sofa.

"Is that comfortable?" he asked, nodding his head to where she sat.

"Is what comfortable?"

"Sitting like that. All straight up and down, not allowing your back to touch the sofa. All ladies do it, I've observed, but I've never really thought about it. It can't be comfortable, though."

She raised a dark eyebrow at him. And then lifted her chin. His chest tightened in delightful anticipation of what she'd say. He had to admit, he liked it when she was feisty, even though he deplored it in most other people. In all other people, in fact.

"It is not proper to comment on how a lady is seated, Your Grace."

He wanted to growl and laugh, simultaneously. Something about her made him want to needle her, to see just how improper he could get her to behave. That is, to speak. He didn't want her to do anything improper. Even though he absolutely did.

He should definitely change the conversation before he did or said something that would reveal just how intrigued he was by his new secretary.

He *should* change the conversation—but he didn't. "You do know I am not proper, at least not in the way you mean it."

She regarded him with her cool gaze. "And how do you think I mean it?" she asked in a deceptively soft tone of voice.

Something relaxed inside him. Something he didn't feel unless he was alone with Chester. Which wasn't alone, entirely, since he found he spoke to his dog a lot more than he did to most humans.

"Stuffy. Correct just because that is what one is supposed to do."

She arched an eyebrow. "But if we do what we are not supposed to do, then we have anarchy. Dukes do not do well in anarchy, or have you forgotten the French Revolution?"

He waved a hand in dismissal, knowing it would irk her. Delighted to see the spark of it kindle in her eyes. "Those aristocrats were fools, not able to see how things were changing. Change needs to happen in order for there to be progress."

Another brow arched, so both were raised up on her face, making her look entirely skeptical. And utterly fascinating.

"So you're saying that we should all unstuffy ourselves for there to be progress?" She shook her head in mock disapproval. "Your Grace, then we would have no need of people like you."

People like you. The words rang in his head, causing a buzzing in his head. "And people like me are . . . ?" he said, stretching the sentence out.

She frowned, as though annoyed. At herself? At him? "Not like you precisely, since you are you, but people in your position."

"You're saying I am different from my position? And yet I would imagine few people can distinguish the person from the position."

"I can," she announced, making that feeling in his chest blossom so it felt as though he'd taken an almost too full breath.

Now he definitely needed to change the course of the conversation. Before he said or more accurately did something he should not. It wouldn't be fair, to either of them. There was no possibility of anything more between them; she was his employee, not even remotely of his class. Even though he felt they were alike in the important ways.

He shoved those thoughts away entirely. Something he was very good at doing.

"Your daughter, should she have a governess?"

He was genuinely interested, he was surprised to find. Not that he would have asked if he weren't interested—he didn't waste time on questions when he didn't care to hear the answer. It resulted in a lot of silence between him and the people he encountered on a daily basis. Except for her.

"She should," Mrs. Cheltam replied, her expression slightly rueful. "We were about to hire one before my husband passed away."

Silence, again, as Michael didn't bother offering condolences. He had to admit that on the whole he was glad the man had died; without that, she wouldn't be here.

"You'll hire one for her. I'll pay the salary, of course." Michael was as startled as she seemed to be as the words left his mouth. What had he told himself about impetuous decisions? That they never worked out? And yet here he was deciding to bring yet another stranger into his household.

"That wouldn't be appropriate, Your Grace," she said, her mouth pressed into a prim line.

"Hadlow," he corrected. Which she knew damn well. "And I don't care if it's not appropriate. Have I given you the impression I care about any of that at all?"

He found he'd walked toward her in a nearly predatory way, as though he were going to pounce. The thought was immensely appealing.

Thankfully, the door opened to admit Hawkins before he could decide one way or the other. At which point he knew he couldn't do it, no matter how tempting it was to get her to unbend, to lean against the sofa back as he kissed her.

"I'll take those," Michael said instead, walking to Hawkins, who was bearing two brandy glasses on a tray. He picked them up, then nodded to his butler. "You can leave us."

Hawkins bowed and left the room.

Michael walked to the small round table where

the brandy was kept, placing the glasses down and lifting up one of the heavy decanters. He unstoppered it, poured a healthy amount in both glasses, and picked them up, the sharp smoky aroma of the brandy tickling his nostrils.

He returned to where she sat and handed her the glass. She looked skeptical, but took it from him. Their fingers touched, and he felt a pleasurable spark of something sizzle from the contact.

"To Gertrude's governess," he said, raising his glass. He waited until she brought the glass to her mouth to take a sip, then he drank.

The brandy burned going down, a painful pleasure that warmed him from the inside. He sat down on the sofa as well, making certain to keep to the farther side so she wouldn't get skittish about his intentions.

Not that he had intentions toward her—he certainly had desire, but no intention of acting on them. But she needed to know she was safe with him, even though they were alone in the evening drinking brandy.

"Will you need assistance hiring someone?" he asked, taking another sip. He was more prepared for the burn of the brandy on the second taste, and he rolled the fiery liquid on his tongue. He didn't care much about food, to his cook's chagrin, but he did enjoy excellent brandy.

"If you approve, I can find someone through the Quality Employment Agency. The ones who submitted me for your position."

Your position. He would have to start thinking about other things because he was finding he could discern the innuendo in nearly anything she said. Damn distracting.

"That will be fine. The governess will reside here as well."

"Thank you." She spoke in a low, honest tone, and he felt his chest swell at the sincerity of her words. No wonder people did nice things for other people, if this was how it felt when they got thanked. He'd never done anything out of the goodness of his heart, but perhaps he should think about it. Or maybe it was only her thanks that warmed him as thoroughly as the brandy did. He'd have to test it out, perhaps do something nice for someone who wasn't she.

Although he wouldn't want to be so hasty, would he?

"Can you answer a question for me?"

Michael shrugged. "If I want to, of course."

Did she roll her eyes at him? He thought so. He liked it.

"Why are you working so hard?" she gestured to the room. "You already have all this, you have more than sufficient funds, and you could just do the minimum of management to keep it all going. Why do you push yourself?"

He inhaled sharply, wondering why it felt as though she had gotten to the heart of him, somehow. Again. And with just a simple question. He took another sip of brandy, considering whether or not to answer, or to just shut her down with one of his usual rude comments.

And surprised himself when he did answer. Even more surprising was how it felt to have her ask one of those insightful questions he'd thought about. Like sharing something of himself, and he wanted to do more of it. But only with her, and because it was she. "I suppose it is because I wish to strive to be the best I can be, whether it is the best duke, or the best manager of my holdings, or the best representative in the House of Lords. Anybody can do what is necessary, and even perhaps do a little more, to congratulate themselves on making a bit more effort." His lip curled. "Those people don't know what it is to try, to run the risk of failure." He shrugged, meeting her gaze. "I do."

She regarded him with those dark liquid eyes, and it felt as though she were staring through into his soul. Fanciful though that sounded.

"I can understand that," she replied slowly. She looked away, toward the shelf filled with books, then out the window. Not that there was anything to see out there, nothing but darkness and a few trees brushing the window. "There aren't many men in your position who would continue to strive, to value the importance of trying to be something more."

"I am not most men." He stated it plainly, aware it was absolutely true and also that it could be seen as arrogant. Which he definitely was.

She looked back at him, a wry smile on her lips. "I admitted that before. Are you asking for a compliment?" It sounded as though she was . . . teasing him? He'd never been teased before. That he knew of. "You are definitely not most men," she repeated, this time in a voice that sounded as though it were redolent with meaning more than the few words she'd said. It made something quicken inside him, but also made him feel the stab of poignant emotion he hadn't had in thirty years. Of the potential for loss, but the equal potential for gain.

Edwina knew she couldn't blame her shaky feeling on the brandy. She wished it were as simple as that. But she'd had only a few sips, and she had to admit that she'd been all fluttery inside for nearly the entire evening, as soon as it was clear he was going out of his way to be pleasant to Gertrude. That surprised her, given how abrupt he was normally, and how he seemed almost proud of his brusqueness.

"Why were you so nice to my daughter?" She might as well ask him; it wasn't as though he were bound to take offense. He hadn't taken offense at anything she'd said thus far, from when she thought his plans were too ambitious, or that he had dealt with a tradesman poorly, or when she'd been short with him in the morning, before she'd had her coffee. In fact, at times it had seemed he had pondered what she had said, as though he were sifting the information through his hardworking brain. As though her opinion mattered.

"Why wouldn't I be? It seemed as though it would be a better expenditure of energy to be nice and have her relatively appeased through dinner than to antagonize her and have to deal with that." His mouth curved into a smile. "Besides which, I do like her. That was surprising to me, I don't have much experience with children. None, actually." He looked thoughtful. "I'd always heard they were beastly creatures, always wanting things and attention. Your daughter is not like that."

Edwina uttered a snort. "She can be, if there is something she wants. She found it expedient to be on her best behavior this evening. She likes living here very much, she doesn't want to leave, and so she understands in order to stay, she has to make sure I retain my position. Which means she will do what she has to." She tilted her head and looked at him. "Very similar to you, it seems."

He looked discomfited at being compared to a six-year-old girl, and Edwina wanted to laugh, only that would be entirely inappropriate. Not that he minded inappropriate things, of course, but if she had to guess she would imagine he would get a little tetchy about her amusement.

"What was your husband like?"

Oh. Of course he would ask. And ask so abruptly, without a hint of sympathy. That made it easier to respond, actually.

"He was—he was not particularly intelligent. He was stubborn, and loud. He adored Gertrude, even though he didn't understand her."

"Or you." He said it as though it were a fact, not a question.

She smiled in acknowledgment. He was so logical, so reasoned, and yet he could also see past the facts to discern the woman within. To see her. That was unexpected. That he could be so insightful while also being so seemingly emotionless. But he wasn't; it was just that his emotion was an expression of his honesty. "True. He did not understand me, either. I suppose I didn't understand him as well." She shrugged, as though it didn't matter. It did; she couldn't lie to herself. Or to him. "We married when I was only seventeen. He was twice my age, and set in his ways. We never really settled well together."

"And then he died, leaving you with nothing." Again, not an iota of sympathy or commiseration. Why did that make her feel better about talking to him about it?

"No, barely a penny." She spread her hands wide. "Which is how I come to be in your employ, Your Grace."

"Hadlow," he corrected in a near growl. She truly did wish she could laugh then; she'd only said the honorific to nettle him. And it had worked.

She looked at the clock in the corner of the room. She'd noticed she tended to lose track of time when she was with him—she was too busy assessing him, and the work he wanted done, to worry about seconds and minutes. It had been nearly half an hour since they'd come into this room. She placed the brandy glass down on the table beside her. "I should retire for the evening. I want to check on Gertrude, and my employer is quite adamant that I appear at my desk on time and ready to work." She smiled as she spoke, to let him know she was joking. Even though she was also partially serious—he was a hard worker, which meant that he expected his employees to work hard as well.

He didn't stand when she got up, and as usual, that both startled and piqued her. She didn't want him to consider her as a woman, he couldn't or he wouldn't have hired her, but she did wish she could discern any kind of appreciation for who she was and what she was doing. And that she was a woman doing a job that only men usually did.

But she couldn't have it both ways, could she? And she would far prefer that he think of her as a steady, hardworking employee than as a female.

"Good evening, Hadlow," she said as she walked out of the room. Sighing as she realized it would be another ten hours before she was in his company again.

"Good evening, Cheltam," he replied.

WHY DO DUKES FALL IN LOVE?

7. Because falling in hate is so much less pleasant.

Chapter 6

"Good morning, Mrs. Cheltam." The girl looked anxious, but Edwina didn't blame her—she was inside a duke's home after having been in a small school out in the country. It had to be a significant change.

"Good morning, Miss Clark. Thank you for coming to speak with me." Edwina had contacted Carolyn as soon as the duke had given her the authority to hire a governess, and it had been a few days before Carolyn had located a suitable candidate. Gertrude had initially been averse to the idea of having a governess, but had taken to it once Edwina had told her about some of the books she was currently unable to read.

"Can you tell me why you believe you would be a good fit for this position?" Edwina smiled at Miss Clark, who offered a tentative smile back. "That is, I have reviewed your qualifications, but I would like to hear them in your own words." Just as the duke had done to her—it was a good tactic to ask the applicant to speak for herself and not just rely on what was on the paper.

"I spent ten years at the Woodson School, the first six as a student, the rest of the time as an instructor. I taught composition, drawing, and French."

"That is a wide array of subjects," Edwina replied. "Which is your favorite?"

The girl's expression eased. "It is difficult to choose just one. The students—or most of them—were all so eager to learn, and it made teaching a joy. I found myself the happiest while teaching French, I think, since it was introducing the students to a whole other world of language." She looked embarrassed. "Although that sounds rather presumptuous, doesn't it."

Edwina chuckled softly. "Not at all. You sound enthusiastic, and that is the kind of person I wish to teach my daughter."

"Are you the lady of the house then?" Miss Clark looked confused, as she should—Edwina's gown, a simple but flattering dress in dark blue, was suitable to her position as a secretary, and not nearly as grand as a duchess would wear.

"No, I am not. I am the Duke of Hadlow's secretary, and my daughter resides here with me."

"His . . . secretary?" The girl looked askance, and Edwina felt herself bristle in response.

"Yes, his secretary. And only his secretary," she added sharply, and then felt terrible when the girl's expression fell.

"I didn't mean—that is, I apologize," Miss Clark said, looking down at the floor.

Edwina sighed. "I suppose it is an inevitable

thought, given how unusual it is for a woman to be employed thusly." And even more reason she absolutely should not be thinking about the duke in any way other than as her employer—not how tall he was, or how his presence made her stomach get all fluttery, or how his voice seemed to resonate through her entire body. Or how she found herself just looking at his face, noting the strong features, the long, sharp nose, the wickedly intelligent eyes.

None of that, Edwina, she reminded herself.

"If I were to be your daughter's instructor, I would provide instruction both in and outside the classroom." It seemed Miss Clark was determined to continue, not obsessing about her possible rudeness. Edwina liked that. "We would go for walks in the park to identify insect species, we would take on some of the shopping to practice her maths skills, and I would ask her to find our way home, so to practice her navigational skills. This in addition to the usual schoolroom activities."

"That sounds quite progressive. And exactly the type of thing Gertrude would find interesting." Her daughter, Edwina knew, liked to be challenged, to try new things just because they were new. Not unlike Edwina's employer. "I want to thank you for your time, and I would be pleased to offer you the position."

Miss Clark gasped aloud, and then a wide smile crossed her face. "Thank you so much, Mrs. Cheltam. I promise you will not regret the decision."

"We will set up your room, so if it isn't too soon, perhaps you could join us and start work on the day after next?" She wouldn't follow her employer's lead and just give the poor girl two hours to return.

"That would be wonderful, thank you. I have to tell Miss Carolyn about it."

"Yes, please thank Miss Carolyn for sending you over." Edwina held her hand and Miss Clark took it, shaking it vigorously. "I look forward to seeing you on Thursday, and I will speak with Gertrude and tell her of some of your plans for your time together. I am certain she will be as enthusiastic as I am."

"Excellent," Miss Clark replied. "Good day, Mrs. Cheltam."

"Good day." Edwina watched as the girl left the room, nearly bouncing in excitement. She couldn't be much more than eighteen—had Edwina ever been that young? By the time she was eighteen, she'd been married for nearly a year, and had come to realize just how wrong she and George were for each other. And that they were stuck together until death.

She stood in the room a few moments longer, thinking about how her life had changed so dramatically. And knowing she had only one chance, *this* chance, to make things right for her and Gertrude for the rest of her life. Or until Gertrude married, hopefully someone who loved her and understood her, not just someone who wished to possess her.

"You've hired someone then?"

She walked to her chair and sat, reaching for

her notebook and trying to avoid rolling her eyes.

How did he know already? Oh, of course, he probably had the keenest of hearing to accompany his height, good looks, wealth, and intelligence.

About the only thing he seemed to lack was any kind of charm and finesse. Although that bluntness was, in its own way, quite charming.

So scratch that. The man was irritatingly perfect.

"Yes, I have. She comes with excellent recommendations, she taught at the—"

He waved his hand dismissively. "Did I somehow give you the impression I cared about the person? If she meets your qualifications, it is nothing to me. As long as it means that your daughter will be properly cared for while under my roof, I don't care if her governess walks on four legs and breaks into song every evening."

That was so unexpected, and unexpectedly funny, she had no choice but to laugh, bringing her hand up to her mouth to try to contain her giggles.

He did not join her, however. He merely looked annoyed, as though he hadn't realized just how ludicrous his words sounded.

When she was able to stop laughing, which was long after his expression had gone from annoyed to exasperated, she spoke. "I cannot thank you enough, Hadlow. For taking such an interest in my daughter."

He frowned, as though embarrassed. "I don't take an interest, I merely want to ensure my secretary—the only somewhat efficient one I've had in years—is going to stay in my employ." He spoke gruffly, and she had to suppress yet another smile.

Did he really not know he was at all goodhearted? She shrugged as she realized it didn't matter what he knew or didn't know about himself—she had that knowledge, and it made her feel more relaxed around him, somehow. Knowing he had a bit of kindness tucked within himself, so hidden he didn't recognize it.

It would be her little secret.

"What are we working on today?" She made her voice overly lively, just to see if he'd get that irritated look on his face again.

Who knew she was so mischievous? She certainly didn't—it wasn't as though there had been the opportunity, being married to George and all.

But she was learning all sorts of new things about herself since she'd arrived at the duke's house, just a little over a week ago. She knew she enjoyed looking at him, definitely enjoyed teasing him, liked how he assumed she was intelligent and capable enough to handle what work he was throwing at her, and even liked how exhausted and spent she felt each night as she headed to bed—as though she had done something worthwhile that day, rather than just being an idle ornament or something. The way George had always made her feel.

"We're reviewing the proposal from another railway company. The Victorian Rails, I believe. As though the name is going to give them any kind of advantage with the Queen," he said in a derisive tone.

"How many railways are there?" Edwina asked as she stood to look for the documents.

"I have no idea. Far more than there should be, I know that much." The duke just sat and watched as she shuffled through the mass of papers on his desk. She reminded herself he was her employer, he didn't have to help, although it would have been the polite thing to do.

Oh right. He was definitely not polite.

She found them, then straightened the papers she'd disarranged and returned to her seat. "Do you want me to summarize?"

He nodded, leaning back in his chair and closing his eyes. That was his normal listening posture, which Edwina didn't mind; she was better able to look at him without his noticing.

"The Victorian Rails is the best and most economic way to travel our great country," she began.

He gave an impatient wave, his eyes still closed. "Don't read all the hyperbole, all of them basically say the same thing. 'We will do the best with the smallest investment, and we have the best equipment and people.' " He opened his eyes, and she started guiltily. Had he caught her staring?

"They can't all be the best, Cheltam." He sounded angry, as though the inanity of the facile words irritated him. Again, of course they did. He seemed to find most of the world annoying, she was just grateful he hadn't put her into the annoying side of his ledger by now.

Perhaps in a few months he would, if he tired of her poking at him like a grumpy bear.

"I don't understand why they can't just tell the truth," he continued. "It's so much easier than prevaricating just to make something look better than it actually is. Don't people see through that kind of obfuscation?"

She raised an eyebrow at him. "I don't think people even know what obfuscation is, to be honest." She shook her head. "You don't seem to recognize how different you are from most people."

He uttered an exasperated sigh. "Of course I do, Cheltam, I'm a duke. One of the most privileged people in the country, if not the world."

"I don't mean that," she replied. "You are very aware of who you are, and what your position is in this world."

Now his expression looked genuinely puzzled. "What do you mean, then?"

"You are so intelligent." He blinked. Had no one ever said that to him before? Maybe they never attempted it, he was too rude. In addition to being so intelligent. "And you have this—this analytical mind that is quite different from the way most people think."

His expression remained puzzled. As though he'd heard her words, but didn't understand them. "Most people don't think the way I do?"

"You must know they don't. That's why you're always so, so irked at people in general, isn't it?"

His expression turned thoughtful. "I thought it was just because they were all irksome. People in general, that is."

She uttered a snort. "Well, that is true as well. People *are* irksome. But not to the extent you likely think."

He leaned forward, his green gaze locked on her face. She felt a shiver at that intense focus put on her. "You're different though, Cheltam, aren't you? You're like me." His tone was almost pleading, as though he were desperate for it to be so.

What made him feel so separate, so apart from people? Besides his natural intelligence. She had known a few intelligent people in the past, but none of them seemed to be as lonely as he did. Or, more precisely, as alone.

She opened her mouth to reply, then realized she didn't know what to say—*Yes, I am like you, only I'm not a duke, so I'm not nearly as arrogant? No, I'm not nearly as intelligent, although I can find my way through a sheet of financials? You and I are precisely the same, so now I have to go practice being humble?*

Not that any of those were the right responses.

"I suppose I am, in some ways," she said slowly. It hadn't occurred to her that they were similar— she'd been so focused on the differences. That he was wealthy, and male, and confident, and abrupt. That she was poor, and female, and diffident, and had thought of herself as overly polite, at least until she came into contact with him.

He leaned back, sighing in what sounded like relief. That there was someone out there like him? That she'd finally agreed with him?

"That is what is different with you, Cheltam," he said gruffly. "You don't irk me."

"High praise indeed," she shot back, trying to ease her discomfort at this moment of connection with humor.

He shook his head, as though to clear it, and waved his hand at her in his usual commanding way. "Return to the work. We have wasted enough time. Skip the parts where they say they are the best without proving anything."

Edwina chuckled as she looked down at the papers in her hand, wishing she had the strength to probe further into him, but unwilling to open up herself, which she knew he would demand, in all his logic. "That should take all of about five minutes, then."

He resumed his listening position—eyes closed, hands folded—and the moment passed, but Edwina's interest in him had only just begun.

WHY DO DUKES FALL IN LOVE?

4. Because dukes get lonely, too.

Chapter 7

"Chester! Blast it, where is that damn dog?" Michael looked under his desk, although he knew perfectly well his rather large dog would be noticeable if he were under there.

He glared around his study, as though it was the furniture's fault his dog had gone missing. Mrs. Cheltam wasn't there, either, but that was his fault; he'd sent her to deal with someone he did not wish to deal with himself, one of the many benefits of having a secretary in the first place. But he had to admit he missed her presence. And he wanted his damn dog.

He knew where his dog probably was. The traitor.

"Miss Gertrude!" he called as he strode out of the study into the hallway. Several of his footmen jumped, but he didn't waste time glaring at them, as he might have done under normal circumstances. He took the stairs two at a time, up two flights to where he'd instructed the schoolroom be set up.

"Miss Gertrude!" he called again as he nearly ran down the hallway. Not that it was imperative he find his dog; Chester was a slow, good-natured creature who wouldn't venture too far from his food source. But he did have to admit to feeling . . . jealous, perhaps, that his dog had decided that spending all of his waking hours and many of his nonwaking hours with the youngest and newest inhabitant of the house was his preference.

"We are in here, Your Grace." It was the governess speaking, her tone tremulous and nearly fearful. As it should be.

He walked into the room, his eyes narrowing as he saw Chester slumped on the floor right next to Gertrude's chair. Gertrude herself looked up at him with a bright smile on her face. Which made him feel something unfamiliar. Some sort of guilt?

"I need to take Chester for a walk," he said abruptly. As though Chester's life was hanging in the balance unless he went outside to relieve himself in the next few minutes, when actually the dog in question was sleeping. Likely drooling as well.

Gertrude's eyes—so like her mother's—lit up, and she jumped out of her seat. "Can I walk with Chester and the duke?" She directed her question to the governess, Miss Something-or-Another, who just looked flustered, sending a look of apologetic misery toward Michael.

"That isn't—that is, I don't—" the governess began.

"Fine, walk with us. Get your things, and you can meet us downstairs in five minutes." Michael leaned down to take hold of Chester's collar. His dog made a whine of unhappiness, but stood up willingly enough, wagging his tail against Michael's trousers.

That was one of the reasons he had a valet after all, wasn't it? To remove yellow dog hair from his clothing?

Gertrude uttered a shriek of delight so loud it made Michael wince, then bounded out of the room, presumably to get her coat. Perhaps her mother's permission as well, but Michael doubted his secretary, stalwart though she was, could withstand the pleadings of a six-year-old determined to take a dog out on a walk.

"Your Grace, I hope—that is, I hope this isn't too much of an imposition." The governess had gone scarlet, and was hesitating between each word. She was so awkward, in fact, that Michael almost felt sorry for her. Almost.

"It is not your fault, Miss—"

"Miss Clark," she supplied. Cheltam must have told him her name, but of course he hadn't retained it, since it hadn't been important. Now that seemed as though it were as rude as Cheltam was always implying he was. Was it? He wished she was here so he could ask her.

"Miss Clark. Gertrude has made a friend of my dog, and it is only natural to expect she would prefer to go outside with the dog—and me, of course—than stay here and do whatever lesson you are doing." He picked up one of the papers on Gertrude's table. "You are learning the countries of the world?"

Miss Clark's tone grew more assured. "Yes, Your Grace, I am teaching Miss Gertrude where all the countries of Europe are, and what languages they speak. In addition, we are learning a few phrases in each of those languages." She finished with a smile that revealed how pleased she was to be instructing the girl thusly.

Normally Michael would have cut her off mid-sentence, but he somehow didn't want to do something so—so abrupt, as Cheltam would say.

Was he going soft? He couldn't think about that now. He had a dog, not to mention a young girl, to walk.

"That sounds excellent." He must have sounded convincing, since she beamed in return, bobbing a small curtsey. He nodded in response, then tugged on Chester's collar. "Come on, you troublemaker," he said, walking out of the study. Feeling as though he'd somehow betrayed himself, his character, but not certain how. And not certain if he felt bad about that.

"My father never let us have a dog." Somehow, Gertrude had managed to wrest control of Chester's leash. Michael wasn't sure how that had happened, just that he'd handed it to her when he had remembered to tip his hat to a lady he thought he knew. The lady herself had looked startled; not only, probably, because he was with a young girl who was not related to him, but also because he'd tipped his hat in the first place.

He should have just ignored her, as he usually did most people he saw when in public.

But Gertrude had mentioned her father, Mr. Cheltam. Apparently not very lamented by his widow. He wasn't normally curious about people, especially dead people, but he had to admit—if only to himself—to being curious about this gentleman.

"What was your father like?" he asked.

She looked up at him as though he were an idiot. "He was *old*," she said.

He waited. He was very good at staying silent so as to make other people talk.

And waited. Gertrude just walked alongside him, seeming to think the conversation was at an end. Michael wished he could just demand she answer all his questions, but that would be to admit he had questions in the first place, and in the second place, to expect to get any kind of reasonable answer from a six-year-old. Or any sort of child. As he'd told Cheltam, he had no experience with children. He had been a child himself when his brother was alive, but then he had died, and since then his parents had spoken to him as though he were an adult. He'd felt like an adult, hewn into adulthood at the age of four because of his brother's death.

And now he felt like an adult who had no idea how to speak to a child.

"Why is Chester named Chester?" She looked

up at him, screwing her face up in a faintly dis-
approving look. "Because he doesn't look like a
Chester."

It was on the tip of his tongue to argue with
her, to tell her that Chester absolutely looked like
a Chester, but that felt ridiculous, even in his head.
So he told her the truth.

"When I was little, I had a book I liked to read."
He felt . . . awkward. He hadn't ever spoken of
this to anybody. Not that they would have cared.
"It had a family"—a family with a normal set of
parents and three normal children, no dukes or
any titles at all, actually. "They had a dog, and the
dog's name was Chester. So when I got Chester
here, I named him after the dog."

She kept looking at him, apparently processing
the information, until her expression eased. "Do
you still have the book?"

He shook his head, wondering why he felt
so—so relieved that she seemed to accept his
explanation about Chester's name.

"That's too bad. I like books."

"I do as well," he replied, to his own surprise.
Not surprised that he liked books; he knew that,
or he wouldn't have said it. Just that he felt as
though he wanted to share something with her,
this small creature who was so different from
him, and yet liked Chester and books, as he did,
and apparently didn't have patience for small
talk, like him also.

It was disconcerting to think he had so much in
common with a being who could be distracted by
the promise of a sweet, but there it was.

That he could be distracted by the promise of another type of sweet was something he did not even wish to contemplate.

"My father wasn't as tall as you are." She spoke as though it was the natural next thing to say. He had to admire that aplomb. "And he didn't like to read, like you do." He felt a sense of pride, already, that he had more in common with her than her father did. A dead man. Honestly, he was ridiculous.

"What did he like to do?" he asked, wondering if she would report his interest in Mr. Cheltam to her mother. What would she think about that?

A shrug. "Mostly talk about boring things." Michael resolved never to speak about anything she might find boring in her hearing.

Sadly, that meant he could likely never speak about anything, since the only things that interested him were new technologies, certain political issues, and—

And *her*. And he definitely couldn't speak about that.

"The duke took Gertrude out?" That was unexpected. And somewhat worrisome. She knew he hadn't the faintest idea of what to do with a child, what if he decided to bring her to a pub and give her ale? Or if he forgot he was with her, and stopped to talk to someone he knew and she wandered off?

But that would assume he would deign to drink in a pub in the first place or actually want to speak to anyone he might encounter.

She felt a tinge of relief.

She had spent the morning in a meeting with someone who had heard of the duke's business interests and wanted to persuade him to invest in their new venture, something involving playing cards, bird-watching, and vast amounts of the duke's money.

The duke would have just denied the meeting entirely, but the person behind the company was related to one of the members of the House of Lords, one who could influence votes the duke wished to pass.

So she had to take the meeting. And then she had spent an hour trying to make sense of the presentation, so she hadn't seen him all morning.

And now he wasn't in his study, and it seemed he was out with Gertrude somewhere.

"And the dog," Miss Clark added in a worried tone of voice.

Out with Gertrude and the dog, that is.

"Should I not have let them? I would have, only—only . . ." she said, her hands fluttering.

"I know," Edwina replied. "The duke is not someone you would say no to. Not to dukes in general, and definitely not this duke."

Miss Clark's expression relaxed. "Yes, that is just what I thought. And Gertrude begged as well; she is so hard to resist."

Especially when she gave one of her winsome smiles. But that didn't explain why the duke let her accompany him—she didn't think he would succumb to the blandishments of a six-year-old girl. Not when he seemed to have successfully resisted all the eligible young ladies in his world, what with not being married and all.

And then that thought hit her in the gut, causing an unpleasant ripple to course through her. Why hadn't he married? He must be either on the verge of it, or was perhaps betrothed already, although she would have heard the gossip about it belowstairs, if that were true. Or maybe not, since he seemed to be very good at not talking about things he did not wish to discuss. But it would make logical sense for him to marry, to have a hostess who could throw parties and dinners in order to ensure the people he wished to persuade to vote certain ways in the House of Lords were, indeed, persuaded.

Would his new wife be comfortable with him having a female for a secretary? If Edwina were married to him, she would not.

Oh. If she were married to him. *Oh.* She couldn't help but shiver as she thought about it—waking up beside him in the morning. Asking him if she looked presentable for a party, and him answering truthfully. She winced as she thought about that.

Being able to touch him, to find out what his shoulders felt like under her hands, if his legs were as long as they looked when he was wearing trousers during those times he was not wearing trousers.

That might be worth a few frank comments about how she didn't look her absolute best.

And while that might be a tantalizing daydream, it wasn't at all possible. When he married, he would choose someone who made logical sense. Someone who would be of his class, with all the proper bloodlines and ladylike behavior he needed in a wife. He would never choose a woman whose very existence in his life was a scandal, one that would reverberate through the House of Lords and all his plans.

But meanwhile, she had to return to reality, which was helping her figure out where her daughter, her employer, and her employer's dog had gotten to.

"Hopefully they will have just gone to the park. To allow Chester to, er, to allow him to . . ." She made a general hand-waving gesture in the air and hoped Miss Clark understood her.

Miss Clark's face turned pink. An indication she had, indeed, understood.

"But while we are waiting," Edwina continued, "perhaps you can give me an update on Gertrude's progress." Miss Clark had been here for close to a week, but Edwina had been too busy, and then too exhausted at the end of each day, to meet with her daughter's governess, trusting that Gertrude would tell her if anything was amiss.

Because Gertrude told her everything. She knew Miss Clark preferred apples to cherries, that she was raised in York, that she drew cats better than dogs, and that she smelled good.

Which meant she would hear everything about what Gertrude and the duke had spoken about today. If they had spoken, that is. She wouldn't put it past either of them just to walk together without speaking.

Miss Clark beamed at her. She was so very, very young. "She is such a lovely child; she is so inquisitive and smart, and she is just a joy to teach."

Edwina smiled. She couldn't doubt the sincerity in the younger woman's voice, which just meant Gertrude hadn't unveiled her I-am-determined-to-have-a-sweet-and-nothing-you-can-say-will-deter-me persona.

"Thank you for saying that." She patted Miss Clark's arm. "You do know you can tell me if there is ever anything you have concern about in regard to Gertrude." She uttered a little chuckle. "I hope I am not one of those parents who believes her child is perfect in every way." Because she most definitely did not.

Just as she had no illusions about the duke; he was entirely imperfect, his blunt, abrupt way of speaking, his no-nonsense attitude, his determination to keep moving forward.

And yet she couldn't help but find him intriguing. That was all of it, she assured herself. Nothing more than natural curiosity about an attractive, forceful, intelligent man she was in constant contact with.

Oh, Edwina, she told herself, *you are in so much trouble*.

"I will be certain to, should that ever happen, Mrs. Cheltam." From Miss Clark's tone, it sounded as though she thought it would never happen.

Edwina smiled in response. "Thank you, Miss Clark."

She left the schoolroom and walked the two flights down to the main floor, about to return to the study, where she'd left her notes, when she heard the door open, and Gertrude's voice chiding Chester—hopefully Chester, that is; hopefully she wasn't chiding the duke—about something or another.

"We're home, Mama," Gertrude said when she saw her. She clutched the dog's leash in one hand, and had her other—surprisingly—tucked in the duke's hand.

Edwina felt her eyes widen, then saw the duke's expression and wanted to laugh.

He looked almost embarrassed, as though he didn't want anyone to see him in such a situation. Holding a child's hand, of all things.

"Did you have a good walk?" Her look encompassed all of them, even Chester, but it was the duke who replied.

"Yes, it was fine." His words were spoken in a nearly wondering tone of voice, and she wanted to roll her eyes at him—seriously, did he think walking with a young girl and a dog was going to be the worst thing that had ever happened to him? From his tone, that was what it sounded like. And yet he had survived. She wished she could congratulate him on his miraculous return, but that would be far too rude. He would do it, if he thought of it, but not her. She had her limits, it seemed, after all.

"The duke likes books, too." Gertrude looked up at him, her hand still in his, a look of approval on her face. "And we both like Chester." She looked back at her mother. "We have many things in common, Mama."

Edwina's throat tightened. Her daughter had spent all of her life prior to now likely believing that adult men had nothing to speak with her about—Gertrude's father hadn't been interested in doing more than pinching her cheek and mentioning how she would one day look as beautiful as her mother.

"That is wonderful, Gertrude." She glanced up at the duke, who was looking at her with that intense gaze that still made her start when she saw it. "Thank you, Your Grace," she murmured. He nodded in reply, almost brusquely.

Of course. He was embarrassed to have done something that wasn't entirely practical. She wished she could tell him it was, in fact, entirely practical, since the alternative—telling Gertrude no—would have resulted in an uproar in the household.

"Miss Gertrude, you should return to your governess."

"Miss Clark," Gertrude corrected.

Edwina held her breath, hoping he wouldn't shut Gertrude down as effectively as he shut most people down.

"Miss Clark, of course." His eyes flickered to hers, the corners lifting up as though he nearly smiled. And she let out a breath, smiling in return.

"I will see you at dinner," he continued, releasing Gertrude's hand. "Both of you," he added, once again looking at Edwina. It felt as though he were able to say so much in just a look, and the worrisome thought crossed her mind that he could read her as well, which meant he might suspect just how . . . intriguing she found him.

Handsome. Engaging. Intelligent. Commanding.

But even if he did, she thought with a mental shrug, it wasn't as though he would care. No doubt plenty of ladies had found him the same way for years, and yet here he was, not entangled with anyone, at least as far as she knew. She would have to ask—discreetly, of course—about whether the duke had plans to marry anytime soon. She hoped not. For the future of her position, she reminded herself, nothing more.

"Thank you, Your Grace." She saw him open his mouth to correct her, but glance around at all the attending servants. He must have surmised—correctly—that there would be more talk than she could withstand if it was known she addressed him so informally in private. Thank goodness he didn't just insist, and damn the consequences. She could see him doing that, as well.

Damn the consequences. She wished she could do that, too. Although she didn't. Because if she could, she knew just what she wanted to do, and that would lead to far more trouble than just imagining what his shoulders felt like.

WHY DO DUKES FALL IN LOVE?

67. For the warmth and companionship of a lovely woman.

Chapter 8

Damn it, he'd done it again. Thought of something, and then *whoosh!* it had emerged from his mouth before he'd had a chance to think about it completely.

Why had he invited them to dine with him? It wasn't as though he didn't have a stack of invitations for dinner, which his secretary had reminded him just the previous day. He'd even told her to sort out which ones seemed the most promising, knowing that any hostess would welcome a duke to her table, even if he hadn't told her he was coming.

He still could. He could just change for dinner and leave, letting them know he wouldn't be having them to dine with him after all. It wasn't as though it was at all expected. It was entirely unexpected, in fact. He knew that, not just because he knew about the world—even if he didn't do what the world expected of him—but of how she looked when he'd said it, entirely surprised and, he thought, also pleased.

That was what made him want to do it, wasn't it? Knowing she would be happy, that the child would be happy, that he wouldn't have to endure conversation with anybody who didn't interest him.

Both of the Cheltam ladies interested him, although for very different reasons.

He shook his head at his own foolishness as he returned to his study. Already grumpy because dinner wouldn't be for an hour, which meant he had to wait. He didn't like to wait.

As it turned out, perhaps he should have waited longer. Or canceled it entirely.

"I want Chester to eat with us, too." Gertrude's bottom lip was pushed so far out of her mouth it looked odd. She stamped her feet, crossed her arms over her chest, and looked at him, glowering.

Cheltam glanced at him as well, obviously embarrassed by her daughter's behavior. He thought he probably shouldn't laugh.

"Chester cannot be in the dining room while we eat." He spoke in the tone that brooked no argument. "He is quite happy to spend the hour or so in my study."

Gertrude didn't seem to have understood his brook-no-argument tone. Because she did, in fact, argue. "But he doesn't like to be on his own, he said so," she replied, her voice sharp and plaintive.

"That's enough, Gertrude." He'd never heard Cheltam speak so sternly. "We will take our dinner in our rooms, Your Grace."

Well, that was punishing him as well as her, wasn't it?

He raised an eyebrow. "Miss Gertrude may take her dinner in her room with Miss Clark"— he'd remembered her name—"but you will dine with me." Because he'd be damned if he'd forgone going out this evening because he wanted to eat with her, only to eat by himself.

"But," she began, then shut her mouth as she seemed to realize he had used his brook-no-argument tone again. Thank goodness one of the Cheltam ladies understood it. "That will be acceptable, Your Grace." She lifted her chin as she spoke, then turned to regard her daughter. "You will have your dinner, and then you will write a letter of apology to the duke."

Gertrude glared at him, and he was surprised to find himself piqued. He'd thought she liked him, and here she was clearly annoyed at him. Which wasn't at all his fault.

All the times previous that people had been annoyed at him it had been his fault. This was an entirely new experience.

"I don't want to," Gertrude said belligerently.

"I don't care what you want," her mother replied. "You cannot be so rude to people, it is not how people wish to be treated, and you wish to be treated politely yourself, so you have to understand what you are doing when you are behaving rudely."

Hm. He hadn't thought of it precisely that way before. He had behaved in the most expedient manner, to get what he wanted, but he'd never thought about how someone else would wish to be treated. That was an interesting idea, and one he'd have to think about later on.

When he wasn't so hungry. Or, more precisely, when he wasn't so interested in spending time alone with this woman when they weren't working.

"Ask Miss Clark to come down here and collect her charge." He spoke over his shoulder to one of the footmen; it didn't matter which one. He heard the rustle of movement, a "Yes, Your Grace," and then silence.

"Do I have to?" Gertrude spoke in a much softer voice now, as though she'd figured out just what she was losing by her actions.

He didn't wait for her mother to reply. "You do. Your mother has reminded you that people do not like to be treated rudely, and if you wish to dine with us again, you will apologize properly and we will consider inviting you another time."

She lifted her chin in nearly a mirror to the way her mother did, and he did have to smother a smile. Only, it seemed, she didn't do so to argue with him. "Fine. I will. I am sorry." And she did sound it, and he glanced to Cheltam, to ask if she would change her mind, and her daughter could stay, but his secretary just looked at him and gave a quick shake of her head, so he didn't say anything.

"Miss Gertrude, I am here to take you back upstairs." Miss Clark looked flustered. As it seemed she normally did. Or perhaps that was only in his presence. He wouldn't doubt that. "Mrs. Cheltam, I am sorry for this." She took Gertrude's hand. "We'll go upstairs and you can eat your dinner, then work on your letter of apology." The footman must have filled her in on what had happened. "Say good night to your mother and His Grace."

Gertrude now seemed thoroughly abashed, and he felt something—was it sympathy?—for her as she blinked away tears and her lower lip trembled. "Good night, Your Grace. Good night, Mother."

They both watched as the girl walked out with her governess, Michael feeling a pang as she left. Only to be replaced, naturally, with a delight that now he could be with Cheltam, and her alone.

What was it about her? He had plenty of opportunity while they were working to look at her, to admire her beauty, so it wasn't just that. That was pleasant, of course; it was far more enjoyable to look at a beautiful thing than an ugly one. That just made sense.

Only she wasn't a thing, she was a person. A person of definite opinions, and ideas, and who was as close to him in intelligence as anyone he'd ever met before. He wouldn't go so far as to say she was as intelligent as he was—nobody could be, in his own, admittedly biased opinion—but she was sharp enough to follow when he spoke, to ask the right questions, to understand the salient point of what he was saying.

To make him feel not quite as alone.

"I am so sorry for Gertrude's behavior." She sounded apologetic as well, and he could tell by her expression she was nearly mortified.

"Isn't that what children do? Decide they want something and then act on it?" He shrugged. "It is nothing, do not concern yourself with it. She is a good child, but she is a child."

She gave him a wry smile. "And here you said

you had no experience with children. It sounds very much as though you understand them entirely."

He held his arm out for her, not that she needed guidance to reach the dining table, but he found he wanted her to touch him. To be assisted by him, even though she would say she needed no assistance.

"I do not understand them entirely, but it is only logical that their minds would be less tied to propriety than older people."

"It sounds as though you are describing yourself, Hadlow," she said in a low tone of voice as he settled her in her chair.

He paused, feeling a spark of anger at her words. She was calling him a child—again. Only, on reflection, she wasn't wrong, was she? He saw things he wanted, he asked for them, or he figured out how to get them.

Well, that concept led to some very interesting thoughts, didn't it? He wondered what she would say if he asked her: *Cheltam, I would like to engage in sexual relations with you. Just because I am curious, and I want you, and I think it would be more pleasant than not doing it.*

He chuckled at the thought, and she looked up at him. "What is it?"

He shook his head as he took his own seat and beckoned to the footmen to begin serving. "Nothing, just a passing fancy."

Although the thought occurred to him that this fancy was not passing. Which meant he absolutely should not say anything to her about any kind of relations that weren't of the professional, working sort. He wasn't bound to propriety, certainly, but there was bound to be awkwardness, no matter what happened, and he didn't think the benefit of sexual relations with her—if she even said yes—would outweigh the negative aspects of it all.

He didn't think so. Did he?

Dear God, he did. He did think it would be worth it.

He was in so much trouble.

Hadlow—and when had she started thinking of him as Hadlow, anyway?—was remarkably quiet during dinner. Edwina glanced at him worriedly a few times, thinking he was upset about Gertrude's behavior, until she realized that if he were upset, he would say so. And she didn't think he was upset in the first place.

So what was bothering him?

They'd finished the meal, with her scarcely knowing what she ate, only that it was food, and now she was full, and they had barely spoken to each other. He could have just eaten by himself if he didn't feel like company. She felt—well, piqued that he hadn't seen fit to engage her in conversation.

"Shall we go to the drawing room?"

She opened her mouth to respond, only to realize the footmen were all still there. She knew he wouldn't balk at saying something that would cause talk, but he was a male, and a duke, and whatever he said would be fine, because of who he was.

She couldn't very well do the same thing, not being male or a duke. And he was her employer, although she knew he wouldn't consider that, either, unless she did something stupid in his employ. Then, she knew, he would have no compunction about letting her go as soon as he discovered the error.

So she nodded, and rose, waiting until he came to her side, putting her hand on his arm, allowing him to walk her to the drawing room, aware that the footmen and Hawkins all stood in attendance in the hallway between the two rooms.

He opened the door and let her precede him, then closed the door behind them.

It was just them now.

She should say something, only what was there to say? *You haven't spoken to me at all, and I am irritated by that, only I shouldn't be, it is just that I have come to think we are friends as well as employer and employee, and that you liked talking with me.* That was part of what she was feeling, but not all. *You haven't spoken to me, and I am fascinated by you, and if I can't find out what your shoulders feel like, I should at least get to converse with you.* That was closer.

"You didn't talk to me at all during dinner." Well, that wasn't precisely how she meant to put it, but there it was. She'd said it.

He walked toward her, still not speaking, and her breath caught. There was something determinedly predatory about his movements. Something that made her heart start to beat a little faster, and she felt a warm flush creeping up her face. She had to be imagining it, though, hadn't she? He had never given her any kind of indication he had even noticed she was female. For goodness' sake, he never even stood when she entered the room unless it was to take her somewhere he wanted her to be, like seated in her chair at dinner.

Nonetheless. She felt something in the air between them, and she waited, lifting her chin as he approached.

"I didn't speak to you," he said in a low growl, "because if I did, it would be to ask you something entirely inappropriate."

Oh. Suddenly her whole body felt warm, and her breasts pressed against her corset as she took a deep breath.

"Wh-what is that?" Her voice was strained.

He stopped directly in front of her, so close she could see the faint lines bracketing his mouth, so close that if he wanted to he could—he could—

"I want to kiss you. Will you allow me to kiss you?" His eyes, his intensely dark green eyes, stared at her, his whole body immobile as he waited.

If he wanted to he could kiss her.

And this was up to her, wasn't it? He wasn't the type, she knew that, to leverage his title and strength and sheer Hadlow-ness of him to get what he wanted. But all of that was alluring, surprising that she would find it so, having loathed when her late husband had attempted to dominate her in any way.

But with him? She would welcome it. She wished he hadn't asked, wished he had just taken her, claimed her mouth with his.

But that wouldn't be honest, or fair, and he might be the most abrupt and rude man she had ever met, but he was also the most honest.

And he was still waiting for an answer, his eyes not leaving her face, his hands clenching and un-clenching into fists at his sides.

That was what decided her. That clear, ex-pressed need, that want epitomized by the move-ment of his hands.

"I will let you kiss me," she said in a soft voice. "Only if you let me kiss you as well."

He smiled then, slowly, the smile of someone who is very, very pleased.

He'd decided to just say it, to let his want be known between them. The worst that happened would be that she'd slap his face and say no, and leave his employ.

And then he'd have thrown away a damn good secretary, which would sting nearly as much as her telling him no in the first place.

But somehow he didn't think she would. She kept looking at him during dinner, worrying her bottom lip—the lip he wanted in his own teeth—and he knew that it wasn't just because the con-versation was minimal. He'd caught her glancing at his hands as he ate, an expression of something, something very intriguing, on her face.

So he decided to just say it. If he didn't, he'd always wonder what would have happened if he did, and he was nothing if not decisive.

And she'd said yes, and in the most Cheltam

way possible—*Only if you let me kiss you as well.* And he would let her, but only after he'd gotten to plunder her mouth as he wished to. As his whole body was telling him to.

He clasped her elbows in his hands and drew her closer. Her breasts touched his chest, and he felt the skirts of her gown swirling around his legs. Capturing him. Not that he wanted to be let go.

He looked down at her face, her gorgeous, vibrant, lovely face. "I've wanted to do this ever since I met you," he murmured, lowering his mouth to kiss the beauty mark on the right side of her lips. "And this," he continued, moving his mouth to hover over hers before closing the distance between them, feeling the soft warmth of her lips under his.

Her lips were so sweet. He could taste the wine they'd had at dinner, and he just kept his mouth on hers, not doing anything more, just touching her lips with his, savoring the intensity of the moment. Until she put her hands on his waist and drew him in even closer, opening her mouth as she did so.

And then his tongue dove into her mouth, licking and sucking, their tongues tangling as they kissed. She slid her hands around his waist to his back, holding him tightly to her. His erection pushed against his trousers, she must feel it, his cock throbbed with wanting to be buried inside her. Maybe to bend her over his desk— their desk—and thrust inside, her naked breasts pressed against the leather of the desk.

But right now this was more than enough. This

kiss, with her passion and desire coming through with every movement of her mouth, her lips nibbling on his, her tongue boldly pushing inside his mouth, keeping to her promise of kissing him.

God, this was the best kiss he'd ever had. He knew that already, and it wasn't nearly done. At least he hoped not.

He put his hands to her waist as well, spanning her rib cage, his fingers splayed out just under her breasts. She wriggled so his fingers were on her breast, and he smiled, still kissing her, letting her know that this was entirely what he wanted.

She had her hands under his dinner jacket, kneading his back, her fingers dropping lower until they hit the upper part of his arse. And then she smiled as well as she clutched him, rubbing his buttocks with her fingers, her mouth open, and hot, and wet, and passionate. As firm and impatient in her desire as she was when she wanted him to answer a question.

If she asked now, he would have to say yes. To whatever it was she wanted, if it meant she wouldn't stop kissing him, wouldn't stop touching his body.

He palmed her breast, feeling the sharp stab of her nipple, even underneath all the layers of clothing she must be wearing. He wanted to feast on her, to take that nipple in his mouth, to suck and lick her breast as thoroughly as he was her mouth.

He pinched her nipple, not hard, but just a little pinch, and she gasped into his mouth. And grabbed his arse even tighter, moving in so closely to his body she was touching him at nearly every point.

This—this was too fast, too soon, too much. He couldn't stand it, because if things continued he would have her over the desk, and he needed to be certain that this eventuality was something that was eventual and inevitable for her, too.

So even though he thought he might die from not continuing to kiss her, he withdrew, gasping, leaning his forehead on hers, his hands still on her breasts, his cock still huge and throbbing inside his trousers.

"Oh," she said in a disappointed tone of voice.

"Oh," he repeated, smiling against her skin. "Thank you." He drew back and looked at her, noting her flushed face, her mouth wet and reddened from their kiss. Her eyes sparkling and yet also sultry.

She was beautiful before, but now she was absolutely intoxicating. And he wanted to drink her up, to take her until he was drunk on her, to forget everything that was sensible and logical and anything that wasn't she.

He heard her swallow. She released her hold—reluctantly, it felt like—on his arse, but kept her hands on his waist.

"What now?"

He shrugged, knowing he was likely going to say the wrong thing, the type of thing a less honest, more polished man would never say during such an encounter, but unable to find what it was he should say rather than would say.

"We now know what it is like to kiss one another." He wanted to do it again, right now, but didn't want to pretend that this was anything but what it was—an interlude in their working relationship. A very pleasant interlude, but an interlude nonetheless. "I would like to do it again at some point. If our work is completed, and there is nothing else requiring our attention."

She stiffened and withdrew. His body felt the lack of her warmth, of how she felt pressed against him. And he felt the lack of something else, but he didn't know what that thing might be.

He was experiencing all sorts of new things since she'd arrived. He thought he liked it, but he wasn't entirely certain.

"That sounds pleasant." Her tone was nearly flat, and he had the urge to take her mouth again, to show her what passion felt like so he could render her as flustered as he felt himself. But she'd replied just as he'd wanted her to, hadn't she, and so he couldn't be angry at the result of his words.

Even though, inexplicably, he was.

"Excellent."

And then they just stood there, looking at each other, him feeling as awkward as he'd ever felt in his entire life. Which wasn't difficult, since he had never felt awkward before.

"If you will excuse me, I should go check on Gertrude. Good night." She ducked her head and walked out of the room without waiting for him to reply. He admired that, even though he wished she had said more. Although what would she say? *That was the best kiss of my life?* That was what he wanted to say. But what if she'd had better?

She couldn't have had better. He knew that.

I am glad you said what was on your mind, and my goodness, I would like to touch your body all over?

Again, probably not something she would say.

So saying good night was probably as close as he was going to come to an acceptable set of words from her.

Leaving him alone in his study with a raging erection, plenty of . . . feelings, and confusion about what to do next.

All entirely unexpected.

And again, he wasn't certain he liked it. But he did appreciate that it was different. And he didn't feel quite as alone.

WHY DO DUKES FALL IN LOVE?

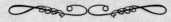

17. Because they can't help themselves, no matter how
hard they try.

Chapter 9

*O*nce again, she was shaking as she left his study, only it wasn't as simple a reaction as having obtained a position that would allow her and Gertrude to survive.

This was far more complicated than simple life and death.

This was—what was it, anyway? First she'd been upset that he hadn't spoken to her, and then she'd been startled that he had asked her for a kiss. Not so startled, of course, that she couldn't answer.

She winced as she recalled what she'd said— only if she could kiss him as well. That was so, so *forward*. Although it was on her mind, and he wanted honesty at all times, didn't he? He'd just proven that with his comment about doing it again if they had time and their work was done.

With him, it seemed the work was never done, so she had likely just had the first and last kiss she would ever have with the duke. *Her employer.*

She began to ascend the stairs to the floor where

her and Gertrude's bedrooms were. Her mind not thinking about anything but that kiss. That one kiss.

Which was one kiss more than she should have ever had, despite how she'd come to look forward to their working together, to seeing his impressive mind work at an incredible speed.

Not to mention seeing his impressive form. She suppressed a groan as she thought about what she'd done, not just the kissing, but the fondling.

She had definitely put her hands all over his backside. And now she knew firsthand, so to speak, that it felt even better than it looked.

How was she going to face him the next day? What with having touched him, and kissed him, and accidentally but entirely deliberately moved his hands so they rested on her breasts?

She began to ascend the second flight of stairs, trying to push all that away so she could concentrate on being a good mother to her child—not a wanton who wanted her employer to touch her everywhere, not just the places he had touched her.

It would be fine. He would treat her as he usually did, it would be an odd interval in their working relationship, and hopefully in time she would be able to forget it ever happened.

Probably by the time Gertrude was a grandmother, if Edwina hadn't died of embarrassment and longing first.

"Good morning." That sounded perfectly normal, didn't it? Not as though she'd spent half the night reliving the kiss, and the other half feeling mortified.

Gertrude had greeted her at her bedroom door with a blotchy face and an apology letter. Edwina told her daughter a bedtime story—one definitely not involving commanding dukes and stolen kisses—and headed to bed herself.

He didn't even look up from his papers, damn him. Didn't he even think that this would be odd? No, of course he didn't. Edwina couldn't repress the snort as she thought about it, which did draw his attention.

"Is something wrong? You're not getting ill, are you?" He raised an eyebrow. "I can't have you getting ill, not when we've got so much work to do."

She lifted her chin. "I am not getting ill."

He didn't reply, just gave her one long appraising glance—perhaps he was searching for signs of illness, she thought sourly—and returned to looking down at whatever it was that was more interesting than she was.

And now she sounded like a scorned lover, or someone far more dramatic than she knew she was. If she was going to keep working here, and not cause some sort of unpleasant scene, she would need to learn to keep control of her emotions. Whether her emotions were wanting to kiss him senseless or slap him in the face.

Sadly, she knew what she would prefer. And it wasn't to hit him.

"What are we working on today?" She was delighted to discover she had kept her tone calm and even.

He pushed some papers toward her, again without even glancing up. Did he regret kissing her so much he didn't even want to look at her?

That would be awful, even worse than his thinking there would be a time for kissing, and it would be after work.

"More railway proposals." He sounded annoyed. Well, so was she. "I can't find any substance in any of them, I want you to take a look to see what they're actually saying."

"Of course." She reached forward, and he clamped his hand on her wrist. He did look at her then, his eyes dark and intense. She nearly forgot to breathe. "And this afternoon we'll be attending a demonstration of one of the engines. I'll need you to take notes on the process."

"An engine demonstration?" She couldn't help but sound skeptical. And potentially very bored, but mostly skeptical.

"Yes, it's the most amazing thing, Cheltam." He spoke in a tone of voice she'd never heard from him before—wondering, and happy, and excited. "They didn't know about any of this when I was a little boy, and now this, this miracle." He seemed to recall just who he was, and how he should be speaking, because he cleared his throat and spoke in his normal tone. "That is, I wish to review the mechanics of it."

"Of course."

He darted a quick look at her face, as though daring her to comment on his unexpected enthusiasm, but she just gave him a sweet, and sweetly

false, smile, knowing that would irritate him far
more than her being amused by his tone of voice.

He'd done it again. Spoken before thinking. It was
getting to be a habit, one he hadn't had before she
entered his employ. And she sat on the opposite
side of the desk—that very desk he'd had some
vivid thoughts about the day before, thoughts
which had haunted him well into the night—and
looked as though nothing untoward had happened between them.

As though she hadn't sucked his tongue into
her mouth, hadn't let him touch her breasts,
hadn't pressed up against him so thoroughly he
could still feel the imprint of her on his body.

His brain was already processing what he
could accomplish in the carriage ride to the engine
demonstration. And wasn't that pathetic? He was a
duke, a young, unmarried duke, a man of fortune
and, he could say without prejudice, not unattractive. He could have nearly any woman he wanted,
and yet he didn't want any of them.

Except for this one. Whom he wanted very
much.

Even though he knew full well he shouldn't
want her, that he couldn't have her in the way
she deserved to be had—he'd seen mésalliances
before, wondered at how a person could so forgo
logic as to make himself a pariah in the eyes of
Society. He would never do anything so foolish.
But he did want her.

And he had never wanted anything without eventually getting it. This was going to be another new experience for him.

The knock came just as Michael was about to suggest they go to the demonstration. "Enter," he said, not bothering to look up.

Chester barked, and he heard the pell-mell of little feet, and then the child herself popped up in front of his face, all smiles and eagerness. "Miss Clark said you were going out to see an exhibit, and I asked if I could go, too, and she said it was up to you." She widened her dark eyes, so like her mother's. "Can I go? Please?"

"Gertrude, the duke has not invited you to go, and it is certain to be quite dull."

She sounded as though she actually thought that, and he felt a pang of disappointment—disappointment at what, he wasn't certain. Nor was he certain he wanted to find out.

Something, that thing inside him that appeared to make decisions entirely without him, supplied his next words. "It will not be dull, Cheltam." He nodded at Gertrude. "You may attend with us, but you must listen to your mother, and we will bring Miss Clark, because your mother will be working."

"Oh, thank you, thank you," Gertrude replied, bouncing up and down in her glee.

"You're welcome, just stop that, you're making me dizzy."

Gertrude turned to address her governess, who

was standing just inside the door. "Did you hear? We can go, too!"

"That is wonderful. You must thank His Grace."

"I did already," Gertrude pointed out, not incorrectly.

"Of course, well, we will go get ready."

"We will be leaving in seven minutes," Michael added. "If you're not there, we will go without you."

"Oh!" Gertrude left the room with a shriek, Chester trotting along behind her, leaving them alone. Again.

"That is very kind of you," she said in a soft voice. "I know it is not what you would have preferred."

Not at all, since I was scheming how to continue what we began the night before, Michael thought grumpily. But didn't say it, of course, since he still had work to do, and now he had a demonstration to attend with a six-year-old, an easily startled governess, and the woman who was driving him mad.

That was all. A simple matter, really, for someone with his brainpower. Even though he wasn't thinking with his brain at the moment.

"Tickets," the guard standing at the entrance to the exhibit hall said in a bored tone of voice. He took the tickets Michael handed him without even bothering to look at them.

Edwina smothered a snort at the thought that this might be the only time someone was not impressed with the duke's very presence.

"Over here," the duke said, using that enthusiastic voice she'd heard only for the first time earlier that day. Gertrude trotted along behind him, her hand reaching up to take his. He took it, and Edwina felt her heart begin to get a little soft.

Awkward-sounding, but that was the truth of it.

"How do you stand it?" Miss Clark said in a whisper.

Edwina turned to look at the younger woman. Her eyes were darting around the room, her face lit up with excitement. Of course, she probably had never been to something like this before. And didn't seem to be anticipating the massive amount of boredom Edwina was.

"Stand what?" Because there were a lot of things she couldn't stand—how Gertrude pouted when she didn't get her way, how her late husband had been such an idiot about women, about how she was unable to stop thinking about the duke, and how he'd kissed her—but she didn't think Miss Clark would be asking about any of that.

"Working for him."

Because I've kissed him? Because I seem to be unduly obsessed with him?

She feigned ignorance, mostly because she *was* ignorant. For all she knew, Miss Clark could be talking about the fact that he was so very tall, it would be difficult for someone as short as Miss Clark to look him in the eye.

Although that did seem rather unlikely.

"I don't understand." Edwina tried to keep her demeanor casual. As though it didn't matter at all that she was working for a remarkably attractive man who happened to seem to find her attractive as well. Not anything to concern herself with.

"He is so—so scary," Miss Clark replied, lowering her voice even more. Given how noisy it was in the exhibition hall, it wasn't necessary, but Edwina appreciated the girl's discretion.

"Not to me." And she knew she was telling the truth—she found him attractive, almost excruciatingly so, but he didn't frighten her. If anything, she found she looked forward to the challenge each morning. It felt . . . invigorating to work with him, to ask him the kind of questions that would result in one of his very rare nods of approval, to present him with what he needed even before he realized he needed it. To tease out his kindness that lurked under all his logic. To watch as he revealed tiny fragments of who he really was, but only to her. "He is a bit"—*rude*—"abrupt, but that just means he is direct in what he wants."

Miss Clark's eyes narrowed in thought. As did the rest of her face—it looked compressed, as though someone were screwing it up tightly.

"I suppose that is better than having to work for someone when you don't know what they mean. With him, at least, he says what he means."

"Yes, he does." She shivered as she recalled it—*I want to kiss you. Will you allow me to kiss you?*—and had to shake herself when Miss Clark continued to speak.

"Are you getting ill?" she said in a concerned tone.

Edwina opened her mouth to reply as rudely as

the duke ever had—*No, I'm not, and I wish people would stop asking me that*—only that was rude, and she wasn't quite at Hadlow-level rudeness yet.

Maybe if she spent more time in his company she'd have that to look forward to.

She grinned as she walked up to where Gertrude and the duke were examining some sort of mechanical equipment.

"That piece there," he said, pointing, "that is the reach rod." Gertrude nodded. The duke glanced at her before returning to his perusal of the engine. Which looked, to Edwina's eyes, like a bunch of odd-fitting metal parts put together. Apparently—at least judging by the two of their faces—fascinating odd-fitting metal parts put together.

"And that one?" Gertrude pointed to another piece of metal.

"The radius rod."

"And that part?"

Edwina held her breath, hoping he wouldn't lose patience with Gertrude's eternal questions.

"The cylinder. It's circular, see?"

And let her breath go.

"What is that one?" Gertrude pointed again.

The duke shot a quick glance at Edwina, looking pained. Maybe he was annoyed? She was just beginning to step forward when he spoke. "The eccentric crank."

The eccentric crank.

She stopped dead in her tracks as she started to laugh. Laugh so hard, in fact, she snorted, a very unladylike sound that made his eyebrows raise and a few people nearby look at her.

She waved her hand at him apologetically, unable to speak in the throes of her giggles.

Gertrude turned and glowered at her, as though peeved at her mother for interrupting her time with the duke and the engine.

The duke cleared his throat, his jaw clamped shut, his lips pressed into a firm line. But Edwina knew his expressions well enough to know he wasn't upset—a faint flush had stolen over his cheekbones, and he was staring determinedly at the engine, so she could tell he was just embarrassed.

At least he had enough awareness to recognize he, too, could be called an eccentric crank.

The thought just made her giggle some more, and then he did look at her, rolling his eyes in exasperation.

"Can we go look over there?" Gertrude said, taking his hand as though it were entirely natural for her to do so. He nodded, but not before narrowing his eyes at Edwina, as though promising she'd hear about his ire later.

She hoped so. She definitely hoped so.

WHY DO DUKES FALL IN LOVE?

66. Because even a duke is powerless when it comes to the heart.

Chapter 10

Michael had never had anyone laugh at him. As far as he knew, at least. It felt—odd. Not entirely unpleasant. Rather as though she was sharing a joke with him, one he was the butt of, but still sharing something.

He walked with Gertrude, her hand in his, toward another one of the exhibits. This was a first as well—sharing something he loved so much with someone who seemed as interested in it as he was.

"Gertrude?" A man's voice called her name, and the girl turned her head to look in the voice's direction.

Michael did as well, unconsciously tightening his hold on her hand.

"It is you," the man said, a wide smile splitting his face. He was of average height, and larger than average width, and dressed in the clothing of a merchant or a banker or someone. He wore a large black hat on his head, which he removed as he approached them, revealing thinning black hair and rather large ears.

Michael did not like him instinctively, but since Michael tended not to like most people instinctively, that didn't seem worth mentioning.

"Uncle Robert," Gertrude replied, but not letting go of Michael's hand, he noticed.

"And your mother is—oh, there she is," the man said, his eyes going past Gertrude to alight on Cheltam, Michael presumed.

"Good day, Robert." She spoke in a more subdued tone than Michael was used to. Of course he'd figured out this was the younger brother who had mismanaged her late husband's affairs—he could see where she wouldn't want to greet him heartily.

The man looked at Michael pointedly.

"Yes, of course," she murmured. "Your Grace, this is my brother-in-law, Robert Cheltam. Robert, this is the Duke of Hadlow."

Michael was strangely reluctant to let go of Gertrude's hand, but had to, since the man was holding his out for a handshake.

"A duke, Edwina," the man said in a knowing tone of voice, a tone that made Michael bristle. Thankfully he didn't say whatever he was going to continue with saying, hopefully because of the glare Michael knew he had on his face.

"I work for the duke, Robert." She spoke forcefully, if quietly.

"Of course you do," the man replied, still speaking in that same smug tone. Michael resisted the urge to punch him in the face.

Really, everyone should be grateful that Michael

was learning not to do things he wanted to—things like tell people they were idiots, or tell people they were being even bigger idiots, or kiss his beautiful secreta—

Right. Never mind. Maybe he would punch the man after all.

She must have sensed what he was thinking, since she put a hand on his arm. "It was nice to see you, Robert. Tell Ellen that Gertrude and I send our greetings to her, and hope that you are all doing well."

"Yes, thank you, Edwina," the man replied. He glanced at the duke, then at Cheltam—Edwina, that is—then back at the duke. "I will be on my way, then." He stepped forward to chuck Gertrude under the chin, as she tried to duck her head to avoid the touch. "You behave for your mother, now." He looked up at Edwina, his expression hardening. "Since you don't have your father anymore."

Michael was now seriously considering not just punching him, but knocking him down and stomping on his ridiculous hat.

Thankfully, Mr. Cheltam turned and walked quickly away, leaving him with a tingling in his hands, which had curled up into fists, and a fierce urge to take both ladies home immediately, for no other reason than that they'd be in his house, under his protection.

Only that wouldn't be what either one wanted, would it? Gertrude was, as he'd already gratefully noticed, pleased to be there in the first place, whereas Cheltam would raise her chin and make some pointed remarks about her being able to take care of herself.

He took a deep breath, trying to calm himself. This whole finding-people-one-might-possibly-have-an-interest-in thing was complicated. He hadn't expected that. Which made it all the more interesting, adding layers of interest to his . . . interest.

Now he would have to admonish himself not to be an idiot.

If only he could avoid being idiotic—again—with her. He wasn't entirely certain he could, however.

Interesting.

For a moment there, Edwina thought she might have to extricate Robert's face from Hadlow's fist. Thankfully, he hadn't done anything, but she still felt herself wary, as though he might go off at any moment.

Not that she thought he was impulsive—his proper-time-and-place-for-inappropriate-indulgences-with-his-secretary remark would indicate that—but she did know he did not like people who—

Well, she could just stop there.

But to finish her thought, she knew he did not like people who presumed, or insinuated, or did anything but flat-out say what they meant. He'd told her that during one of their first times working together.

It was unpleasant seeing Robert again, but its

unpleasantness was assuaged because she didn't have to worry about him, or what he might say, or do. George had stipulated that his brother had guardianship of Gertrude, along with Edwina, but Robert had made it clear he wanted nothing to do with any of that, beyond a perfunctory offer for Gertrude to live there.

"I'm not going to live with Uncle Robert, am I?" Gertrude's question made her throat tighten, even as she tried to keep her expression calm.

"No, you're not." The duke spoke before she could, and she wanted to snap at him, to tell him she could answer her daughter on her own, but she also felt grateful that he had replied so quickly and so assuredly.

Even more after she saw Gertrude's face, which broke out into a smile. "Good. Because he smells funny, and there are no treats, and he doesn't even have a *dog*." The last part was spoken in outrage, as though not having a dog was the worst thing imaginable.

Edwina was grateful that in her daughter's world that might very well be the worst thing imaginable. And it was up to her to keep it that way.

"Miss Gertrude," the duke said, taking her hand again, "can we go over there? I want to look at those other engines." He looked over his shoulder at her, his eyebrows narrowing as though to ask, *Are you all right?*

She nodded, and allowed herself to breathe a little more deeply. It was just a chance encounter, it didn't mean anything.

What did mean something was that she was communicating nonverbally with him. She hoped he couldn't read her entirely, or else he would know about all the times she'd watched him from under her eyelashes, when she was supposed to be examining boring documents or transcribing notes or doing anything that was less interesting than looking at him.

"Mrs. Cheltam," Miss Clark said as the duke and Gertrude walked away, "I hope you did not think it rude of me to discuss our employer as I did." As usual, the woman—or girl, really— sounded worried.

Edwina turned to her and patted her arm. "No, of course not." Even though it actually was rude, wasn't it? But like him, she thought she preferred people being honest and open rather than hiding things away. It made things much easier.

I want to kiss you.

Yes, like that.

"Should we go find a place to sit?" Edwina nodded in the direction the duke and Gertrude had headed in. "I am guessing they will be some time."

"That sounds lovely," Miss Clark said. "I am not accustomed to all these crowds, I have to admit to being a bit nervous around so many people."

Again, Miss Clark probably could have stopped at "being a bit nervous," since it seemed nearly everything made her nervous—the intimidating duke, the people gathering together to view engines—far more than Edwina would have expected, given her own lack of interest in them. But it made sense that Miss Clark would be skittish; from what she'd offered during their initial meeting, she had spent many years at a small school, the last few of them as a teacher after her parents had died unexpectedly. Leaving her with nothing. Rather like Edwina herself, only Edwina also had a child to care for. And she felt decades, not just years, older than Miss Clark, who somehow managed to retain an air of innocence, despite having been forced to encounter the hard truths of her life such a short time ago.

The two of them walked to the side of the room, where there were fewer people, and Edwina thought she saw a few benches. They found an unoccupied one and sat, Edwina allowing herself to lean back, smiling to herself as she thought about the duke commenting on her posture.

"Have you worked for the duke long?" Miss Clark asked, wriggling her feet in a very girlish way. Edwina smiled, then shook her head.

"No, just a few days or so before you joined us."

The other woman looked surprised. "I would have thought you had been there for some time; you seem so comfortable with him."

She wished she could tell Miss Clark she was comfortable, entirely too comfortable, but that he also made her uncomfortable in a very pleasant way. But of course she couldn't. She didn't think she should even share that kind of information with Carolyn—it would be just as her friend had feared, her getting entangled with her employer.

Thankfully, Miss Clark changed the topic before Edwina had to figure out anything to say. "I was wondering about taking Gertrude out for longer walks. Would that be acceptable to you?"

"Of course, you don't have to ask. As long as you don't mind having a third accompany you," she said with a grin, thinking of Chester.

Miss Clark laughed. "Not at all. It wouldn't shock me if he suddenly started to recite his alphabet, he is with Miss Gertrude most of the day. I like dogs. We had one when I was small." She gave a wan smile. "Before everything happened."

There was a story there, Edwina could tell. "Do you want to talk about it?" she asked softly.

Miss Clark shook her head, her eyes suspiciously bright. "No, not here. Thank you, though. It is comforting to know I could, if I wished to. I am so glad Miss Carolyn recommended me for the position, I am very happy, even if the duke does frighten me a little." She laughed. "A lot."

Edwina found the duke and Gertrude in the crowd, a contented sigh emitting from her mouth as she thought about how much had changed in the past month. Not only was she handling the bare necessities of life for herself and her daughter, but she felt as though she had, perhaps, found a home, a place where she belonged, where she was valued for something other than her appearance.

Although she didn't think the duke would wish

to kiss her if she was the male secretary he might have wanted to hire, so perhaps her appearance did play somewhat of a part in her current mood. But she didn't mind that, since she had agency over what she did with her appearance—she knew she could tell him she did not wish to continue kissing him after all, and he would be fine with that.

She wouldn't, she knew that, but he would.

WHY DO DUKES FALL IN LOVE?

5. Because they can.

Chapter 11

"That was your brother-in-law. The one to whom your husband entrusted his business dealings?"

It was the day after the engine exhibition, and she was settled into her seat opposite his, her cup of coffee half drunk already. He hadn't been able to fall asleep until long into the night, his mind blurring with ideas and images of the day—the particulars of the engines, the way Gertrude had asked him questions, how Cheltam had looked when she saw her brother-in-law, how he felt when he thought there might be a threat. It was all entirely disconcerting, and he wasn't certain he was comfortable with it all.

Not to mention, there had been no opportunity for more kissing, and he had found himself thinking more about that than he reasonably should have. In the past, when he had been pursuing a lady, he had spent only as much time as the pursuit seemed to warrant. Now, he found himself thinking about her at the most inopportune times—when his valet was shaving him, when he was supposed to be reviewing documents, when he was lying awake instead of sleeping.

"The very same," she said, her tone flat.

He glanced up at her. She wasn't looking in his direction, but was staring down into her cup, as though it were far more interesting than he was. Given what her daughter had said about her mother's need for coffee, perhaps it was. But he didn't like it, even if it was true.

"He cannot do anything to you, can he?" And why did he ask, anyway? Maybe he just wanted to hear her say she felt safe here. That she knew he would do whatever was necessary to keep her and her daughter protected against any potential danger.

Although that would imply a far closer relationship than he should be having with his secretary.

Although to be honest—as he always was—the relationship seemed to have progressed far beyond what he would have expected of the usual employer/secretary relationship.

He did not generally think about kissing his employees as a rule, for example.

Nor did he want to immediately pummel anyone who might seem to threaten anyone in his employ.

No, never mind, he did. It just hadn't happened all that often.

But still. It was different.

"He did offer to take Gertrude, after George died. George appointed both of us her guardians.

But he did not offer a place for me, so I declined. And that was the end of it."

She didn't sound concerned at all about her brother-in-law's potential interference. "Ah, so that is why you were willing to let the position go rather than be separated from her."

She nodded, biting her lip. The lip he still wished to bite himself. "I suppose that was foolish of me, to possibly decline, but—"

"It wasn't foolish," he interrupted, sounding fierce even to himself. "It was what you should have done. It isn't right that a person in your circumstances would have to even consider making that kind of a choice. Children belong with their parents."

When had he ever thought about what it would be like for people in her circumstances? He'd have to admit never. He'd never thought about what it would be like to have to confront such a possibility. His parents had of course been wealthy, he'd been sent to school, but those were the only times he had been away from them. He had taken that for granted, he supposed, since he'd never thought about what it would have been like to be on his own, without any kind of parental support. Plus as the heir to a dukedom, he was secure, knowing his place in the future.

To think of Gertrude, all the tiny willfulness of her, having to live with that unpleasant toad of a man—granted, Michael didn't know him, but he had to assume he was an unpleasant toad—instead of with her mother, who loved and cared for her.

It made something in his chest area hurt. That was unexpected. He hadn't felt that kind of pain since—well, since many years ago.

"I have you to thank for us being able to stay together without starving." She spoke in a low, resonant tone. A tone that cut through the hurt in his chest and made it ease. "Thank you. For hiring Miss Clark, and ensuring that your staff is kind to Gertrude, and—"

"Well, I haven't done that, precisely." Should he have? He hadn't even thought of it.

She laughed. "No, perhaps not directly, but the way your staff behaves is the way you wish them to behave—not judging anyone without knowing them first, not being all fussed up about propriety and the honor due your title."

"That would be just silly," he said, almost without thinking.

"Mr. Hawkins did take a few moments to come around," she added, "but now it is just comfortable." She looked at him, raising her chin. "And uncomfortable, because of, of this," she said, gesturing in the air between them.

It wasn't the time he'd deemed appropriate to discuss or engage in the activity, and yet he found he was more than eager to. Mostly because he hadn't been able to stop thinking about it.

"This," he repeated. He steepled his fingers in front of his face and regarded her. Damn, she was so lovely, she made his chest hurt in an entirely different way. A pleasant, anticipatory way. "What are you thinking about 'this'?" he asked, making the same sort of gesture she just had.

She swallowed, and lifted her chin. *Please don't let her say "this" was a mistake that should not be repeated.*

"I think that we are both intelligent adults. And that what we do is our business, and our business alone." She shrugged, but he could tell she wasn't casual about her words, not at all. She licked her lips before continuing. "So if we choose to do more of 'this,' we should." She took a deep breath. "Do you wish to?"

"The question isn't if I wish to, but if you do." He leaned back in his chair, keeping his gaze riveted on her face. "There is no possibility of this being anything more than what it is, you understand."

"I wouldn't want it to be so," she snapped back. Somehow, even though that was the answer he wanted, he felt disappointed. Odd.

"Then what do you say, Cheltam?" His breath hitched in his chest as he looked at her, as she returned his stare, as he felt the impact of a new event, something to which he would look forward—God, but he'd look forward to it—and anticipate, and savor, and get to have. Her. Her with all her beauty, but more than that, with her wit, and intelligence, and how she challenged him.

He would bet she would challenge him in bed, too, or on desk, or on sofa, or wherever they engaged in "this." His cock rose in his trousers, and he felt the shock of lust traveling through his whole body.

He'd rarely, if ever, had such a visceral reaction to a woman before. It should make him nervous—

hell, it *did* make him nervous—but it also made him feel somehow more alive than he had a few weeks ago.

"I say we should, Hadlow," she replied, a wry twist on her lips. She dropped her gaze to her coffee cup, that siren's smile playing on her mouth. The mouth he was going to be able to kiss, when their work was done, of course.

Except—"Damn it," he muttered, getting up and striding over to her side of the desk. He clamped his hand on her arm and drew her up out of her chair, his other hand going to her waist to pull her into him.

And then he lowered his mouth to hers, claiming it, branding it with as clear an agreement to their bargain as if he had signed a legal document.

Oh, he was kissing her again. How had she gone so many days without this? She was awkwardly twisted, standing in front of her chair, him to the right of her, devouring her mouth with a ferocity she fully reciprocated. She broke the kiss for a moment, and he looked at her as though he was devastated she had stopped it, but she just pushed at his chest, pushing him backward toward the sofa behind him. His expression eased, and he walked backward, his hands on her elbows drawing her with him.

He sat down and reached up to draw her onto his lap. She felt his hardness underneath her bottom and it made her ache, deep inside, lower down where the activity generally took place.

George had rarely kissed her, and she had been fine with that, since he tended to slobber and maul at her mouth in an entirely unpleasant manner.

If the duke didn't kiss her, however, she thought she might cry. Thankfully, she was able to spare her handkerchief since he resumed kissing her, his hands touching her as though he couldn't feel enough of her, his tongue inside her mouth, exploring, licking, sucking.

Owning. She grasped his shoulders—those broad, strong shoulders she'd been admiring, along with the rest of him—and wriggled closer, making him groan low and deep in his throat.

She had made him like this, made him needy, and wanting, and groaning, for goodness' sake. Not the precise, logical duke she worked for, but the man she was kissing, the man whose mouth was ravishing hers, whose hands were sliding their way to the top of her gown, his long, elegant fingers working at the neckline of her bodice. She pushed up into his hands, wanting, nearly desperate to have his hands on her body, on her breasts, bare, without any kind of fabric between them.

She wanted to feel his naked skin on hers, also. She yanked on his cravat, untying it with impatient hands, sliding it off his neck and dropping it to the floor. She slid her fingers under the collar of his shirt, touching his collarbones, the strong slide of his shoulder. Her fingers undid the first few buttons of his shirt, and then her palm was on his chest, rubbing the hard planes, feeling the soft prickle of his chest hair on her skin.

He wasn't able to reach her nipples, not with her gown laced as it was—at least, she assumed that was what he was working toward—but he'd slid his fingers as low as he could and was rubbing her skin, making her achy and hot and needy as well.

His erection was a hard throb against her, and she shifted so it was resting against the part of her that seemed to practically be clamoring for it—she'd never felt like this before, that was for certain. No wonder some married women looked so thoroughly smug all the time, if this was what they got to feel every evening.

With George, she'd gotten to feel pressed down into the mattress and then somewhat messy. That was about the sum of her marital experience.

But this—this was already way, way better than anything she had done or experienced before, and they were both still fully dressed.

He withdrew his mouth, his breathing loud and ragged in the still room. "I have never," he began, only to shake his head as though he couldn't even find the words.

"Me neither," she said in a murmur. She looked at where she'd bared his skin, wanting to rake her teeth on his neck, nip at his collarbones, run her hands all over his naked chest.

But this was—this was too fast, too much, and she was acutely aware that just beyond this room was his staff, and her daughter, and her daughter's governess, and even his dog. None of whom would understand what was happening here, not if they discovered it.

"We should go slowly," she said, unable to keep her fingers from stroking his neck.

He looked as though he were about to argue, and she couldn't blame him—she didn't entirely agree with herself, either, but it seemed as though it was the best way—but then he nodded his head. "I do not wish to push you into anything you are not comfortable with," he said at last, his words coming out slowly, roughly, as though it hurt to speak.

"You will not," she said. She knew that, just as she also knew she felt as though she were on the verge of losing control, of losing herself in finding him. She couldn't allow that, and what was more, her priorities—or priority, since Gertrude was everything on that list—demanded it. She needed to treat "this" as it was—something that was enjoyable, but not all-encompassing.

Which meant, unfortunately, she should remove herself from his lap and they should continue to work together.

She couldn't resist kissing him one last time, just a soft, gentle kiss as she redid his shirt buttons.

He could find his own cravat; there was only so much that was required of a secretary, she thought wryly.

She let out a deep breath and rose, feeling how shaky her legs had gotten and how it felt as if she'd been running for an hour—all breathless, and hot, and trembling.

He kept his gaze on her, stretching his arms out along the length of the sofa. Looking every inch the aristocrat he was, each indolent, comfortable inch of him.

And, she couldn't help but notice, quite large in that area as well. And not at all seeming to be embarrassed by it.

Of course he wouldn't be. She doubted he was ever embarrassed, except she had seen him that way, hadn't she? When he was with Gertrude, holding her hand, of all things.

If she bet on such odd things, she would bet that was the first time he'd actually been embarrassed. The thought made her smile.

"I suppose you are about to tell me we should get back to work, since we won't be doing this for a while." He frowned, as though the thought that it would be a while bothered him.

Or maybe that was just her.

"Yes, we have to make the final decisions on which company, if any, to invest in. Isn't that what you said a few days ago?" Not that she had much of an idea of what she was saying—honestly, she was still thinking about his *that*, and wondering when would be the next not as entirely inappropriate time to investigate things—but she was trying, at least.

"About that," he said, and she gasped, wondering if he was talking about the same "that," only of course he wasn't. "I think we should take a tour of some of the factories that are manufacturing the engines. To see for ourselves rather than relying on papers that anybody could write anything on." He stood and returned to his desk, moving as unself-consciously as ever, as though it was habitual for him to be doing these kinds of things during the day.

Maybe it was. What did she know about him, anyway?

Although she doubted he had ever done this sort of thing with anyone in his employ, she imagined he found his pleasure elsewhere, outside his home.

It was just her luck that the man with whom she most wished to be intimate was also her employer. She had to keep that in mind as she continued the "this" they were doing.

Although he had just mentioned a trip. A trip away from the house, from his servants, from Hawkins, from Gertrude—Miss Clark could watch over her, Edwina knew that—not to mention the dog.

Just them and the no doubt dozens of servants necessary to see to the duke's comfort. Well, they wouldn't be precisely alone, but they'd be more alone than they were presently.

That conjured up many terrifying, intriguing, exciting, and altogether dangerous ideas. Not all of which she had the temerity to think the duke had thought of when he'd suggested— no, not suggested, ordered—it. He probably thought it was the most efficient way to make his decision.

As well as the most efficient way for her to get her naked skin closer to his. Not that she should be thinking about that, but to deny she was would be lying to herself. And as she had told Gertrude repeatedly, a lady does not lie.

Unless it is down with a duke, her treacherous mind added, making her turn pink all over and utter some sort of strangled snort, at which point the duke looked at her with one eyebrow raised as though to ask what in heaven's name she was doing.

Well, she couldn't answer that, so that made two of them.

WHY DO DUKES FALL IN LOVE?

84. *We prefer to say we step deliberately and with honor, with no falling.*

Chapter 12

Why hadn't he thought of it before? It was the most practical solution to his various and respective problems—he could go see things for himself rather than relying on literature and salesmen, and he could be alone with her without being encumbered by anything but his valet, his coachman, a few footmen, and the unpleasantness of travel.

Which, since he was a duke, was as close to pleasant as possible, but was still not being at home with his own things and his own comforts.

Except he'd be bringing the comfort he most wanted with him—her. Although he was not comfortable when she was around. He was aroused, intrigued, fascinated, and piqued, but not comfortable.

That feeling of comfort would likely come in time, probably close to the end of their—whatever this was—their relationship, right before he devolved from being comfortable to being bored. That was inevitable, he'd found, no matter how interested he'd been at the outset. There was only so much sexual relations could compensate for, things like a lack of intelligence, a greedy nature or, in one case, a grating laugh. He hadn't yet discovered what Cheltam would do that would annoy him, and eventually bore him, but he had no doubt it was coming.

That was why he had never married. Even though it did make some sense to do so. He knew that people who were filled with more propriety than he was would say it was his duty to produce heirs to his title. And he would say if he could find a person to spend the rest of his life with who would then produce more persons he had to spend the rest of his life with, he would. But he hadn't, and he wouldn't sacrifice his own comfort just because it seemed somehow more proper to leave his holdings and title to a son rather than to the cousin who currently stood to inherit.

His cousin was a genial man, not slavering to become the duke, but not skittish about it, either. He and Michael saw each other approximately once a year at Michael's country estate when he went there for the annual holiday party that had been a tradition several dukes earlier. He saw most of his family, few though they were, at the event. He could tolerate them all only every twelve months.

That was one task he wouldn't stop doing, even though it did add to this discomfort; he recognized the greater good in presenting himself to his family, tenants, and staff at least once a year to achieve the goodwill he knew was essential to keeping his estate working as well as possible. And his family from thinking he was a completely arrogant ass.

Although they probably thought he was nearly a completely arrogant ass. Which he was; he knew that about himself.

Meanwhile, however, he had a trip to set in motion. He wouldn't have to do any of the planning, of course; that was what his staff, including his secretary, was for. But he had to be present, to ensure that the servants planning the trip knew he was observing things so would be unhappy if the plans were not perfect.

So why was he so frustrated?

Because the moment he'd thought of it he hadn't been able to step outside into his carriage and head to his destination. That delay in order to guarantee a flawless journey had never bothered him before, but now? When he was anticipating the chance to be with her, alone?

Now that irked him, nearly as much as stupid people did. Which he was finding, to his annoyance, were most of the people on his staff.

Because how could they not know he wished to be on his way now, if not sooner? That he had things, terribly important things, on his mind that required that he—and she—leave the house?

Even she was irking him because she insisted on making the proper preparations, not just dashing off with him, hopefully leaving most of her clothing behind.

Not that that was practical, of course. And

he did have to grudgingly admire her ability to plan while also maintaining his correspondence, her daughter's frequent whining that she wasn't going, too, and Hawkins double-checking every minute detail of what would be needed.

"Hadlow." It was clear, from her tone, that this was not the first time she'd spoken his name.

He glared at her from across the desk. The thought crossed his mind that if he were hoping to embark on more than a few kisses with her, perhaps he should be pleasant, but then he realized that she already knew what he was like, and she wouldn't be fooled. What's more, perhaps she wouldn't like the pleasant him. Because she would know it wasn't the truth about him, and she'd know why he had changed, and she'd mistrust him.

He didn't blame her. So he resolved to be just as unpleasant and abrupt as he normally was, not that he really knew how to act any differently. And it felt oddly right and comfortable to make that choice when he knew full well he could choose to do something else. It was as though he wanted to really be himself, as opposed to just being irritated, around her. And he had noticed, surprisingly, that he had the ability to be polite when he wanted to. He had just never wanted to before. It was all due to her.

"What do you want, Cheltam?" He waved his hand at the massive amount of papers currently lying haphazardly on his desk. "Isn't it enough that you have brought a lumberyard's worth of paper into the house? Do you need my advice for what to do with it?" He gave a long, sweeping look at the surface of his desk. "I'd say burn it."

She rolled her eyes and huffed out a breath, but she looked amused more than annoyed. Not that he was relieved, of course, that she hadn't taken offense at his words; he was just grateful he wouldn't have to deal with a prickly secretary, especially on the verge of embarking on this type of journey.

"If you recall, those are not my papers." She leaned forward and squinted at the pile, then plucked one sheet from the stack. "This one is. I apologize that it had the temerity to get in your way."

And then she looked at him, one eyebrow raised as though daring him to say something to get her back up even more.

He wanted to. His throat itched with it, the urge to snap at her, knowing that she could handle it, unlike all the other people he usually resisted the urge to snap at. But more than that, he discovered to his surprise, he wanted her to actually like being with him, not just swept away with the skill of his kissing or whatever made her so unbend when they were alone together.

So he laughed, an odd sound coming from him, he knew himself. He rarely laughed. He couldn't remember the last time he'd done more than emit a mild chuckle.

But this—this was a full laugh, a laughter born not only out of what she had said to him, but what he was anticipating doing, and soon, and his general enjoyment of her company.

And after a moment, she joined in, leaning back

in her chair, letting her head fall back, her mouth open, her eyes closed.

He had never seen anything quite so joyous and delicious in his entire life.

Dear God, when were they leaving on the journey, anyway?

Hadlow had been as grumpy as Edwina had ever seen him today. Since that night, the second kiss night, she'd felt as though they were altering their treatment of each other—not just in that way, although that way was quite pleasant—but in their burgeoning . . . was it friendship? She'd heard him laugh, which she didn't think she had heard before, and he seemed to welcome her teasing.

But not today.

"I said I do not require more than two footmen," he said in a growl.

Thankfully he was speaking to Hawkins, not her, but that just meant she felt sympathetic, and yet could do or say nothing; she knew the duke would not welcome her interference, and Hawkins himself would be horrified.

"But Your Grace, what if one of the footmen becomes ill?"

Edwina straightened in her chair, lowering her gaze down to the top of the desk by instinct. She didn't know if the duke was capable of shouting Hawkins out of the door with just his voice, but she didn't want to be borne away as well because she hadn't taken precautions.

He truly was an imperious man, wasn't he? But that was just he, she knew enough by now.

"If one of the men becomes ill," the duke said slowly, drawing out each word through gritted teeth, "then we will make do with one healthy footman and one who perhaps needs to rest. We are taking two coaches, are we not?" he said, turning to Edwina.

She nodded and consulted her notebook. "One for you to travel in, and the other for the luggage and me."

"You may go, Hawkins," he said after a moment. Hawkins bowed and left, not without shooting a concerned glance at Edwina.

She wished she could tell him she, at least, wasn't afraid of the duke, even when he was as irascible as this. She had to admit she found it rather amusing, although she knew well enough not to smile or laugh or anything. But to see him being so—so autocratic and petulant, just like Gertrude when she wanted something terribly badly—well, it made her want to grin. Knowing that he might be a duke, and wealthy beyond all measure, and handsome and commanding as well, but he was still a human, with human emotions, and some of his emotions were less admirable than others—she had to say she found it almost endearing.

That she would never share with him.

"You'll be traveling in the carriage with me," he said in a low tone.

Now she did feel something, but it wasn't fear; it was a frisson of interest, of excitement.

"And why would I do that?" she replied. Who knew she would like poking the bear—in this case, the bearish duke—as much as she did?

"Because we can work while we travel." He'd stood as he spoke, and he began to make his way over to her side of the desk, a distinct gleam in his eye.

Uh-oh.

"But it isn't entirely respectable for us to share a carriage. Alone," she said, swallowing as she thought about it, although she wasn't entirely sure how comfortable any of that would be in a carriage, not to mention what if a horse threw a shoe or that suddenly ill footman got suddenly ill, and they had to disembark all of a sudden, only she wasn't precisely gowned properly, and he was even grumpier because he'd been interrupted in the middle, and everyone would know, and—

"It is entirely respectable." He walked closer so he was looming over her chair. "You are my secretary, I am your employer, and I require that you stay in my presence so that when I need you to take notes I need not stop the carriage and transfer you just to listen to me."

Put that way, it sounded entirely reaso—No, no it didn't, but it did sound like him.

"Perhaps you might have some thoughts on that part of the engine," she said, lowering her gaze to the floor and holding her breath.

"What part is that, Cheltam?" He was still standing over her; she could see his shoes right there, closely followed by his legs, and then all those other parts of him.

She lifted her head quickly and stared him in the face. "The eccentric crank," she said in a soft voice, her lips curving into a smile as she spoke.

And then she froze as she saw how his expression flattened, how his eyes narrowed and he suddenly looked almost . . . mean. But in an odd way—or maybe not so odd, since she knew precisely why she felt that way—it made her breathe a little faster, and her whole body feel as though it was shooting fireworks or something equally dramatic, even though she knew perfectly well she was still just sitting in her chair, looking up at him.

"You are saying I am an eccentric crank, then, Cheltam?" he said in a misleadingly soft voice.

His tone made her shiver. In a good way.

The knock at the door came just as she was wondering just how she could prolong this delicious torture of both of them, of their words sparking in the air like two swords in a duel.

The duke nearly snarled. "Enter," he said, then strode to stand in front of his bookcase, his back to the door.

Abrupt as usual. And yet she couldn't blame him for his reaction; she rather felt like snarling herself.

Hawkins opened the door and glanced at the duke's back, then looked at Edwina. "Mrs. Cheltam, there is someone here to see you."

She saw the duke twist around, as though to

ask who dared to visit his employee, but didn't say anything.

"If you will excuse me, Your Grace," she said, dipping the briefest of curtseys, just enough not to horrify Hawkins, and walked out of the room.

"I've put the gentleman into the second salon, Mrs. Cheltam." Hawkins cleared his throat. "He said his name was Mr. Cheltam, he is not—" and he let the words hang in the air, as though saying "your husband" was something he couldn't possibly commit to saying.

"No, Mr. Hawkins, he is not." Thankfully. "I believe it is my brother-in-law; we encountered him the other day when the duke went to the exhibit."

What was he doing here, though? It wasn't as though there was any pretense of closeness between them. She didn't think she'd ever have to see him again, not until she'd run into him.

She knew she didn't like him, and that the feeling was mutual. He had belittled her work on George's financial affairs, and then had been even more belligerent toward her when it was apparent his efforts were not producing the same results as hers had.

She had to say, she much preferred the duke's method of dealing with a female. Or a male, for that matter. He simply didn't care, he didn't judge anyone in advance based on their gender. He seemed to consider people idiots until they proved themselves otherwise, but he didn't discriminate— anybody could be an idiot in his eyes, neither more nor less.

It was egalitarian if also incredibly arrogant and condescending.

So it was with some trepidation she stepped inside the room after Hawkins opened the door for her.

He stood when she entered, an expression she was unaccustomed to on his face. Of course—it was nearly friendly. She didn't think she'd ever really seen him smile before, at least not directed her way. It was disconcerting, and made her even more anxious about why he was here. It couldn't be about Gertrude, could it?

"Good afternoon, Edwina," he said.

"Good afternoon." She didn't sit; she didn't want him to convince himself this was a social call. It wasn't as though this was her house, anyway.

"Yes, well, it was a pleasure to see you the other day. I know George would want me to make certain you were doing well, and it seems"—and at this he spread his arms out to indicate the room—"that you are."

She decided not to remind him they were in the duke's home, not hers. That she did not have a home, not after he'd mismanaged all of George's money so she was forced to vacate her home.

If she were the duke, she would remind him of all those things. But then again, if she were the duke, she'd have wealth and houses to spare, so she wouldn't have had to endure marriage at all.

Perhaps that was why he wasn't married yet? Although why she was concerning herself with that question when her unpleasant brother-in-law was standing right in front of her was also concerning. Two concerns heaped on top of each other.

"Gertrude and I are doing well, yes." She hoped that would satisfy whatever odd impulse he'd had in paying a visit in the first place.

"Yes, I am glad of that, and that is—you see, Edwina, I have an opportunity," he began, and her chest began to tighten, hoping his words weren't leading where she clearly knew they were, "and if it were known that the Duke of Hadlow was an investor, and thought highly of the project, it would be a marvelous boost for the endeavor."

It would, wouldn't it? Too bad she had no intention of furthering any of Robert's schemes.

"I wish you every success with it, Robert," she said, and she saw his face tighten, his smile diminish, as he appeared to anticipate what she was about to say—but really, why would he possibly think she'd agree anyway, given their history?—he was more of an idiot than she had thought, "but the duke is my employer, and it would not be appropriate for me to suggest he invest in your venture."

"You never could see a good thing when it was right in front of your face," he said, his tone low and vindictive.

Keep yourself calm, Edwina, she told herself. It would be altogether satisfying to tell him just what she thought of him, and how his brother had left her, and what she thought of him sniffing around now, but it wouldn't serve anything.

And—"see a good thing"? Could he possibly be referring to his brother, her late husband? Or, more likely, the work he'd done to ruin their finances. The rage surged inside her, and she wished she could just be honest. The thought crossed her mind that perhaps the duke was correct about being honest—it would definitely produce immediate results, in this case at least.

But she couldn't afford to. She wasn't a duke, she wasn't a man, and he wouldn't listen anyway. "Thank you for visiting." She walked to one of the small tables, the one holding the bell. She picked it up with trembling hands and rang it.

The door opened a few moments later, only it wasn't Hawkins.

Now she really felt anxious.

The duke glanced from her face to Robert's, his keen gaze no doubt taking in every detail—her likely pale face, that she was standing, that Robert looked angry, that her hands were twisting together.

He closed the door and walked in, standing just in front and to the side of Edwina, as though to shield her. It made her feel comforted, even though the only thing Robert could threaten her with was removing Gertrude from her care, and she knew he couldn't be bothered to do that, no matter how many schemes he had.

"We met the other day." It wasn't a question. And it was delivered in a sharp, flat tone that made Robert visibly squirm.

Was it wrong that that made Edwina secretly pleased? Probably. But she didn't care, not when it meant that finally, *finally* Robert was being made to feel as inadequate as he'd tried to make her feel. But not succeeded. It was typical that only a man could accomplish that, since Robert wouldn't have paid attention to a woman.

"Yes, Your Grace, we did," Robert said, a slight stammer to his words. "And," he continued, and Edwina wanted to squeeze her eyes shut and beg him not to continue because she might dislike her brother-in-law, but she didn't want to see him verbally demolished, as she knew he would be, "I was telling Edwina, my poor brother's widow, about an opportunity I've been entrusted with finding investors for, and I understand you are a savvy businessman with an eye for a good chance to make money."

She wanted to wince even more when she heard his sycophantic words and tone.

"And what is this investment?" the duke replied.

He spoke in a mild tone of voice, which only made Edwina grow even more anxious. Although what would be the worst that happened? The duke would verbally flatten Robert, Robert would continue to dislike her, and he would go away, knowing she had the duke's support.

Sometimes it took facing your worst fears to recognize that they weren't so bad after all. Now she almost looked forward to the verbal flattening.

"If I may, Your Grace," Robert said, and he drew forward a satchel that had been strapped onto his back, presumably, since she hadn't seen it before. He rustled in the bag for a few moments, the silence growing increasingly deafening, until he withdrew a sheaf of papers and waved them in triumph.

Was her life to now be defined in pieces of paper?

"If you could take a look," he began, thrusting the papers toward the duke, who just looked down his nose at them.

"I think not. You can summarize, certainly," he said in his most supercilious tone.

That is, she suspected it might be his most supercilious. Although he might have even more within his ducal repertoire.

She never wanted to experience the entirety of his ducal repertoire.

"Well, there are opportunities in the Far East, places where they grow tea leaves, but they are not as dear as they are in China. These countries don't know what they have, and you can hire workers to pick the tea for pennies a day, and then export it here, and sell the tea at higher prices since it comes from more exotic places than does our usual tea."

Even to Edwina the scheme sounded ridiculous. Now she was definitely looking forward to hearing the duke's demolishment of it.

"So you and your fellow investors believe that English tea drinkers will want to drink tea from places other than China? And that they will pay more for the privilege?"

"Precisely," Robert replied, beaming at the duke with approval.

"No."

"Pardon?" Robert blinked at the duke, as though he couldn't believe what he'd said. Edwina could join him, having expected some sort of blistering set-down, not a simple word.

"No." Now he folded his arms over his chest and appeared, to Edwina at least, to exude an almost palpable menace.

Robert blanched and stuffed his papers back into his bag, throwing an anguished look toward Edwina.

Not going to help you, she thought.

"You may leave," the duke said in a stronger tone than he'd yet used. "And if I find you have been bothering my employee, Mrs. Cheltam, in any way, you can be certain I will discover it and take proper measures."

That was definitely a threat.

Robert glanced between the two of them a few more times, and then he bowed. "Thank you for your time, Your Grace." He rose and looked at Edwina. "Edwina, please give my regards to Gertrude and tell her her cousins miss her."

Thank goodness he wasn't going to press the point, given how the duke had spoken, and what he looked like now.

"Thank you, I will." She stood to the side to allow him to walk out of the room, then exhaled and looked at the duke, who remained in his Intimidating Aristocrat pose, his arms crossed, his expression fierce.

"Thank you," she said, at last. "Even though it was not necessary for you to—to—"

"Interfere?" he supplied, raising one eyebrow as he spoke.

She grimaced. "That is what I meant, although

now you say it, it sounds churlish. I will leave it at thank you." She bit her lip and looked at the grandfather clock in the corner. "If you will excuse me, I must finish the preparations for the journey. And Gertrude and Miss Clark are no doubt waiting for me as well."

She nodded at him and left the room, relieved nothing worse had happened, wondering why she trembled even though nothing worse *had* happened.

WHY DO DUKES FALL IN LOVE?

26. Because no one dares to tell them they shouldn't.

Chapter 13

When he saw her in the room, confronting that toad who dared to be related to her, he wished he could just tear the man's head off and toss it on the ground. And he did not mean figuratively.

Where did that protective anger come from, anyway? It wasn't as though he had claim on her, beyond the relationship of employer and employee. And kisser and . . . kissee? Although she had kissed him just as much.

There wasn't anything more to it than that, he assured himself. But he knew he was lying, and he loathed lying, even within the confines of his own mind. He stood in the second salon alone for at least five minutes, concentrating on slowing his breathing, his mind full of images of her face, pale and tight, and her brother-in-law's look of venom when Michael had first entered, only to be replaced with a look of supplication.

If asked, Michael would say he preferred the look of venom. It was more honest. The man didn't like Edwina, that was clear, just as much as she didn't like him. That was likely why Michael had felt such a strong reaction—knowing the man had those feelings, and yet had felt compelled to pay a visit, as though they were on friendly terms.

Now he could say with some certainty that they would be on no terms at all, or he would have something to say to Mr. Cheltam. He actually hated that she shared the name, that any part of her could be connected to him.

And yet—and yet he had met people like Mr. Cheltam before, and they hadn't bothered him. At least not to the same extent. Usually he assessed the type, found them wanting in intellect, honesty, or both, and dismissed them from his mind.

Not Mr. Cheltam though.

He didn't think anything would have happened if he hadn't come into the room—he knew Cheltam well enough to know she could handle herself, and besides, there was a houseful of servants who would have come running if they had heard anything. But he hadn't even considered not entering, not when Hawkins had told him who was visiting her.

It made him uncomfortable. Uncomfortable that he felt the need to watch over her, to guard her. As though he had taken a flag and planted it, proclaiming her as belonging to him.

She would likely scoff at the idea of belonging to him, of being owned by anybody, and he would join her in the scoffing. Nobody should be owned by another, even though the law said a husband could own a wife, and fathers could do what they liked to their children.

It wasn't right, it wasn't something with which he agreed, and yet he could see the appeal of it now. Being able to state, in action if not in words, that she was his property. His to protect, his to do with as he pleased.

Which only reminded him that they were not currently ensconced in his carriage together. Now he really wanted to hit something.

He shook his head, trying to clear it, but knowing it wouldn't be clear until he'd satisfied—well, so many things. His curiosity, his hunger, his desire.

"I've narrowed down the choices to five companies, as I see them, out of the original seventeen." Cheltam sat beside him in the carriage, her head bent over the mass of papers on her lap.

Finally. They were finally off on the trip, after more delays than Michael would have thought possible, all handled adroitly—if not as speedily as he would have wished, given he wished to be on his way immediately—by Cheltam with Hawkins's throat-clearing assistance.

Hawkins had only cleared his throat once when he discovered Cheltam would be sitting in the duke's carriage.

Their first stop would be in a few hours, to take refreshment at some inn that Cheltam had deemed suitable for someone of the duke's importance. The duke himself didn't care, just as long as he could have something to drink and stretch his legs.

Speaking of which—he straightened his legs and put his feet on the cushions opposite, folding his arms over his chest and wriggling until he was comfortable.

She glanced at him then, one eyebrow raised. She did not say anything, however, perhaps because he was returning the glance with his own eyebrow.

"As I was saying, I've narrowed the choices to five. Unless you would prefer to take a nap?" She spoke to him as though he were six years old, like her daughter.

He did not like it, not at all, and he wanted to just haul her over into his lap and kiss her senseless to show her just how much not like a six-year-old he was. Only that would be an impulsive and probably rash thing to do, much like a six-year-old.

He wished sometimes he weren't quite so able to discern the logic of things. If he weren't, he would currently have her on his lap, his mouth on hers, his hands roaming over her body.

He shifted as his body reacted to his thoughts.

"I will not be napping," he said in an imperious tone. "I do not nap."

He thought he might have heard her smother a snort, but he decided to act as though he hadn't heard that. Showing, at least to himself, that he was not a child prone to impulsivity.

"What five companies, and why did you choose them?" he continued.

She returned to looking down, flipping through

the sheets of paper. "The Victorian Rails, the Powers and Smith Corporation, the Right Way Railway, Cortwell Investments and Holdings, and the Better Engines Company."

Those were the same companies he would've selected himself. "And why did you choose them?"

He hadn't expected to be entertained when listening to her reasons for making the choices she did, but in this regard, unlike usual, he was surprised. She spoke well and intelligently about her findings, but she also included details that added life and a layer of depth to each company, many of which were amusing.

"So you're saying the Cortwell Investments representative refused to look you in the eye?"

"It was the oddest thing. You'd think I had some sort of growth sprouting from my head or something. I kept dabbing at my face with my handkerchief, in case there was something on it, but to no avail. The man spoke to my ear, the wall behind me, and at one point even my elbow, but he never did meet my gaze." She shook her head. "I suppose it was because I am female, but you would think, as your representative, that he would overcome his antipathy to my gender."

Michael chuckled. "I doubt he had antipathy toward you, Cheltam." He reached over and took her hand, which was resting on her lap. On top of all the correspondence she had just summarized. "You are a woman, yes, but on top of that you are a beautiful woman."

He felt her shift, as though uncomfortable, and squeezed her fingers. "I am only speaking the truth, honestly, as I do. Surely you know you are beautiful?"

When she spoke, her tone was subdued. "Thank you. Yes, I know I have a certain amount of beauty, I suppose. Else why would Mr. Cheltam have wanted to marry me? He had only ever seen me a few times before he offered marriage, and we'd never had any substantive conversation." A pause. "Either before or after we were wed."

She sounded rueful and sad, and he felt something in the area of his chest at hearing her words. Odd, that something she said would cause a physical reaction.

"At least you were spared his conversation. If your late husband was anything like his brother, he was an idiot."

A silence, and then she let out a sharp laugh, leaning her head back against the carriage cushion. "Of course you would say precisely the truth, even though I'd never really dared to think that to myself before." She laughed again, shaking her head. "There is something to be said about your way of communicating. I like that about you." He felt himself warm at her words. "Imagine how much easier life would be if we all just said what was on our minds." She tilted her head and looked at him, a mischievous gleam in her eye. "Not to mention how much more difficult, as we all learned what we thought of one another."

He met her gaze, noting how she looked at him, how the air suddenly felt heavy with everything they hadn't yet said.

"And what do you think of me?"

She bit her lip and then smiled. "Why, that you're an eccentric crank, of course."

Oh my goodness. Did she think him irresistible and compelling when he was just seated behind his desk, his long, elegant fingers leafing through his accounts or steepled in front of him as he listened to her?

That was nothing compared to how irresistible he looked when he was, judging by his expression now, both piqued and intrigued. Oh, and interested, she'd have to add.

Interested, presumably, in the same thing she was, which boded ill for her widowed virtue. But what was the point of being a widow, a widow who had no intention of ever marrying again, if one could not finally get to do for fun what one had to do within the confines of marriage?

Did that make her a woman of easy virtue? No, not unless you were speaking about her virtue in regard to this man. She didn't think she would ever meet anyone who compelled her as much as he did, the remarkable mix of intelligence, logic, humor, arrogance, and that overpowering handsomeness that made her breathless each and every morning she entered his presence.

"I suppose that is as good an epithet as any," he said, his gaze traveling down her body to where their hands were clasped. His gaze was so—so intense it felt as though he were actually touching her in other places, and her body tightened and felt as if it had gotten suddenly more sensitive, as though any touch would make her body feel as though it were vibrating.

Honesty. That was what was called for, was it not? "When we stop for the night, after we have retired, I am wondering if you—" and she licked her lips and took a deep breath. "That is, I would like it if you would want to come to my bedchamber."

There. She'd said it. Spoken aloud what they'd nearly almost discussed earlier, only this time, she'd spoken with complete honesty. Not prevaricated, by just asking him if he would want to come; she'd told him she would like it. Nothing ambiguous there about what she wanted. What she hoped he wanted.

He smiled at her, the look in his eye making her shiver, and raised her hand to his lips. "I would like it also," he replied before placing an open-mouthed kiss on the back of her hand.

Six hours later, Edwina was regretting her honesty. Well, not precisely *regretting*, but perhaps questioning her sanity. Much worse than regret. Regret was when you wore something not quite warm enough for the weather; questioning your sanity meant you wondered if there was an enormous monster made of ice currently breathing down your neck.

And soon he might be breathing down her neck. On her neck. And other places as well. She shivered thinking about it.

Which meant, perhaps, that she hadn't dressed warmly enough for the weather.

But that wasn't it, was it? It was her shivering with the thought of it, with the anticipation of feeling his hands on her body, his mouth on hers, seeing what he looked like when he was less than perfectly garbed.

She was shivering again when she heard a soft knock on the door. She bit her lip and stood, drawing her wrapper a little closer around herself. As though that would protect her when he came in. Protect her from herself, because she knew in the deepest part of her that this was going to happen. That she wanted this with an almost overpowering intensity, only increased when she thought about him, and his commanding air, and his intensity.

She took a deep breath and opened the door.

And felt her breath whoosh out of her as she looked at him, all the lean and powerful height of him.

"May I come in?" He spoke with a trace of humor in his voice, but also a hesitancy she hadn't heard from him before. As though this was important to him.

And then she knew it would be all right, this would happen, and it would be what it was— wonderful or not, she had no idea—but it would be all right. If it wasn't wonderful, it wouldn't be repeated, and she knew him well enough to know he wouldn't press her. If it was wonderful—well, then she would have a slew of other problems, all glorious, amazing ones; when to do it again, how to keep herself from thinking about it when she should be working, why she absolutely shouldn't feel guilty about it.

How it could never be permanent. Logic wouldn't allow for it.

But he was still standing at the door, his eyebrow raised in question, and she felt herself flush as she grabbed his wrist and pulled him inside, shutting the door behind him. Sliding the latch so they were entirely and completely alone.

She pushed him against the door and put her hands on either side of his arms, trapping him, even though she knew he was allowing her to do so.

She stared up into his eyes, her breath catching—again—when she saw the spark of desire, of passion, of hunger reflected in those green depths.

"Well?" he said, inclining his head. "You have me. What do you want to do to me?"

And she pushed herself up on her tiptoes, leaned into him, and placed her mouth on his.

Her mouth was so warm, and so soft. He resisted the urge to pull her in closer to his body, letting her take the lead. Knowing this wasn't something she was in the habit of doing, and he knew he would have to be prepared if she decided it wasn't something she wished to be doing after all.

But, oh Lord, he hoped she wouldn't. Her tongue licked at the seam of his lips, then pushed inside, her hands sliding over the wooden door to rest on his shoulders. He felt her rise up more, as though she were climbing him, and he allowed his knees to bend so he could lower himself a bit to meet her. To be her equal, as much as it was possible.

She growled in what sounded like frustration, and he smothered a chuckle. She removed her mouth from his and glowered at him. "Do you find this funny, Hadlow?"

"Absolutely not." He felt his mouth curl into a smile, and her glower intensified. "Well, a little."

She leaned back, keeping one hand on his shoulder while she punched his chest with the other. "You're not making this any easier."

He wrapped his arms around her, as he'd been longing to since he entered the room only a few minutes earlier, and drew her against him. Him leaning on the door, and her leaning against him, all the warmth and soft curves of her pressing into his body.

"Is this better?" he said in a whisper. Willing his cock to stand down, just for a moment, so he wouldn't scare her.

She nodded. "It is. I want this, I do. I'm"—and she laughed, but it was more of a rueful laugh than anything humorous—"just not very good at this. You're going to have to help."

And wasn't that something to make his cock pay attention all over again?

"I will, Cheltam. Leave it all up to me."

And with that he pushed her away, sliding his hand down her arm to take her hand, leading her to the bed and sitting her down on it, kneeling on the floor in front of her.

She gazed down at him, her eyes wide and dark, her tongue reaching out to lick her lips. Soon it would be him licking her lips. And other places. He couldn't wait.

Only he had to wait, didn't he, since he wanted this to be satisfying for both of them. To be everything he'd only just begun to realize he'd been thinking about from the first time he saw her.

He placed his hands on her ankles, feeling the delicate bones under his palm, rubbing his fingers on her instep, feeling her start to relax under his caress.

"I'm fairly certain I've never had a duke at my feet before," she mused after a few minutes.

"I'm fairly certain I've never knelt at any woman's feet before," he replied in a soft murmur. "But I seem to make an exception for you, Cheltam. From being my female secretary to letting your daughter talk me into bringing her to an exhibition to having you dine with me because the alternative is far less pleasant." He hadn't thought about it beyond the rudiments, but she'd changed his life the moment she'd entered it. There were so many things he hadn't realized before. That he was lonely, that he longed for the kind of connection it seemed he had with her.

And now things were about to change, irrevocably, between them. Or so he hoped.

He kept the pressure on her feet, then moved up to her ankles, rubbing them until he heard a soft moan. He felt his throat grow tight, and he swallowed before looking up at her.

She had her eyes on him as well, and now he could see the frank desire in her gaze, how her lids drooped over her eyes, how her mouth was parted, her lips still red and swollen from their kiss.

"Do you want me to go on?" he asked, sliding his hands up her calves to her knees. Pushing her dressing gown up so it rested on her thighs. And then his hands were on her thighs just above her knees, and he had to resist the urge to just push the dressing gown all the way up and taste her there, just under the dressing gown. Right where her thighs parted. Would she already be wet? He felt his jaw clamp as he held on to his admittedly hard-pressed self-control. Self-control he'd never had to question before, not until now.

She glanced down at his hands, her eyes widening as it appeared she'd figured out just what he meant. "Oh," she said, only it didn't seem to be as much a conscious statement as an involuntary utterance.

"Can I take that as a yes?" he asked, wanting to tighten his hold on her legs but knowing that he absolutely would not push her beyond where she was willing to go.

Unless she asked him to.

"Mm-hm," she said, that pink tongue licking her lips again.

"Excellent," he said, pushing his hands farther up her legs so her gown was now tangled at her waist.

Baring her to his gaze.

He felt her tremble, and he glanced up again. Keeping his eyes locked on her face, so he could say what he should before he absolutely couldn't. "You're certain?"

She blinked, and he could have sworn she rolled her eyes. "Am I not making myself clear, Hadlow?"

she asked in the tone he'd come to expect from his secretary. His very bossy secretary. "I want this. I want you," she clarified, and she reached her hand forward and touched his cheek, grazing her knuckles on the stubble that had come in since he'd gotten shaved that morning.

He turned his head and bit her index finger, then drew it into her mouth, sucking and licking the digit as he smoothed his hands over her thighs. Her smooth, soft thighs, so womanly under his hands.

So close to right there where he was longing to touch. He heard her gasp, and then she put her hand on his head, gripping his hair until he had no choice but to stand up and crawl onto the bed, careful not to crush her, but lying so his leg was between hers, his cock right at her hip.

Her fingers remained entwined in his hair, her gaze locked on his mouth. He put his hand on her shoulder, then slid it down to her elbow, pausing as he met her eyes. He moved his palm to her breast, and watched her eyes close and her body shudder as he caressed it. He could feel her hard nipple through the thin dressing gown, and he brushed against it, once, twice, until she gripped his wrist and pushed his hand so it was pressing against her breast. Hard.

She wriggled, throwing her leg over his. And then shuddered again as her mound made contact with his body. She let go of his hair only to reach around his waist, tucking her fingers into the waist of his trousers. "These should come off, Hadlow," she said in a husky voice. She ran her fingers around the waist until they reached the front of him. And then she slid her fingers down so they were splayed between them, her palm on his length, beginning to rub his cock with enthusiasm if not skill.

He could teach skill. He couldn't teach enthusiasm.

Lowering his mouth to her body, he sucked her nipple into his mouth and licked, drawing the hard peak deep into his mouth, squeezing her breast and shifting his leg so she had all of herself on him.

And then none of it was enough. He leaned up so he was on his knees on the bed and put his hands to the fall of his trousers, beginning to undo the placket as he watched her face. "Touch yourself for me, Cheltam," he commanded. He pushed his trousers down so his cock jutted out from his smallclothes. He was pleased, in a ludicrously masculine way, to see how her eyes widened as she took in the sight of him.

"And your shirt," she commanded, sliding her hand down her body. Her fingers hovered above herself for just a moment, and she bit her lip, looking unsure, until he placed his hand on top of hers and began to move both of their hands in rhythm. "I'll take my shirt off when you're touching yourself," he said.

"I—I never," she began.

"There's a lot you've likely never done, but that doesn't mean it isn't worth doing. Especially if it's with me," he said, nodding to their hands. She moved, just a bit, and let out a soft moan that went straight to his cock.

If she didn't know about that, then there was even more reason to despise the late Mr. Cheltam. That he had had this woman in his bed and didn't treat her with the kind of care that Michael was going to—well, he could tell she'd missed out a lot on her marriage, and he was going to remedy that lack in her education.

After all, it was mutually beneficial, which meant it was an overall good to the world, and that was something he'd decided on doing. Even though he had to admit that this particular over-all good benefited only the two of them.

But it would make the world a happier place, of that he was certain.

And he was just the man for the job.

92. Love is the grandest of emotions, and dukes are the grandest of men. It just makes logical sense.

Chapter 14

Edwina didn't think she had ever felt this intensely before. Yes, she had felt intense emotion, but this—this was intensity everywhere, from the tips of her fingers to her brain to places she knew she had but didn't know could react like that.

She never wanted it to stop. She wanted it to stop right now, because if it continued, then it would eventually stop, and she might spend the rest of her life mourning the cessation of it.

She lay on her back on her bed, the duke—Michael—half lying on her, his weight a welcome burden. He felt so strong and male on her, and she wished she could just strip him naked and admire him. Which he might like as well, only she never wanted him to move from this exact position. Unless it was to—well, perhaps she did want him to move.

He did move then, and she had the passing thought that he could read her mind, only if he could, he would see everything she was imagining. Not that he'd be shocked; her most forthright fantasy would no doubt be tame compared to what a handsome duke had done in his real life. But he would know her deepest desires, and if he knew them, then he might act on them, and then she really would yearn for a return to this for the rest of her life.

If it weren't for Gertrude, she might even suggest he just place her in a room somewhere where he could visit her and do this to her, and with her, all the time.

He ran his hand over her stomach, frowning as his palm reached the fabric of her dressing gown. "This has to come off," he said in his normal commanding tone. He didn't wait for her to reply, he just lifted her up into his arms and drew it off her shoulders, yanking it off the bed and flinging it to the floor.

"Much better," he said, his gaze traveling from her face down her body, lingering at her breasts, her waist, her hips, and then—then there. He muttered something as he slid down her body, his hands gripping her hips, then going to her thighs, pushing them apart as he lowered his mouth to—

Oh my God. He was not. *He was.* He absolutely was kissing her *there*, and her mind went blank for a moment, all sensation lost, until it returned with a vengeance, her whole body feeling warm and vibrant and nearly on fire. If being on fire meant feeling entirely sensual and lost to the moment, right now, with thoughts for nothing but this.

He groaned against her, and Edwina felt him lick her, there, causing her to shudder and sparks to travel over her skin. She didn't know if she could take it, the intensity, the feelings, all whirling inside her, making her squirm, making her gasp and shudder and beg him not to stop.

That was she, wasn't it? The one pleading with him, "Please, oh my, oh please, oh yes," until her words deteriorated into a series of noises, of meaningless sounds that were all she could manage.

And still he kept up his licking and sucking of her there, now thrusting a finger inside her, making the pressure build up, spiraling into some peak she had never experienced before.

And another finger, stretching her, the increased pressure only adding to the overall sensation, the only sound in the room her moans and the soft sounds of his tongue, his mouth, on her. She should have been embarrassed by those sounds, he had his *mouth on her*, she'd never known such a thing was possible, much less that it would feel so tremendous, but she couldn't be embarrassed, not when it felt so wonderful, not when it felt as though it were building, and she was floating upward on some blissful cloud, driven by his mouth on her.

"Oh God, oh," she said as she felt the journey reach a supremely satisfying end, her entire body shaking with the impact. He lifted his head to look at her, his mouth wet from her, his eyes the darkest green she'd ever seen, his lips curling up in satisfaction.

In a few minutes, or maybe it was an eternity, he spoke. "There is nothing lovelier than watching you climax," he said, his voice husky with desire.

Her voice was shaky. "Is that what it was?"

"You didn't know." It wasn't a question.

She shook her head. He crawled up her body, and she realized he was still partially dressed, his trousers open, his—his thing thrust straight out, enormous, and reminding her that he hadn't—what was the word?—climaxed yet.

And she wanted him to, wanted him to feel as glorious as she did at this moment, wanted him to lose himself for a moment in the passion of it all. If he could; could such a logical, measured man lose himself like that?

But she'd seen him after they'd kissed, heard how his voice shook. He could. And she could make him that way. She had that power, even she, a poor widow whose only goal was survival, could bring this man to his knees.

Literally.

Which benefited her, of course, now that she knew what his being on his knees could do to her.

"Come here," she said, surprised at how confident she sounded. Perhaps that was what climaxing did to her—she wouldn't know, never having done it before. Maybe she should just try to do it every day so she could conquer the world.

He smiled, a feral, sensuous smile that she felt all the way to her toes. "And what do you want, Cheltam?" he asked, his voice full of smoky promise. A promise he'd already kept. Was there more? There couldn't be more. Could there?

"I want you," she said, and she paused, taking a deep breath as she found herself saying the words. "I want you inside me." *And on me, and around me, and everywhere it is possible for you to be.*

I want to be subsumed in you, lost to your touch, and feel, and scent.

But she didn't say any of that. She didn't have to; within moments, he was on top of her, bracing himself on his elbows, his face mere inches from hers. So close she could see the lines fanning out from the corners of his eyes, the ones that showed he could, and did, smile on occasion.

And she felt him there, too, a hard, hot reminder that he hadn't yet finished. *Climaxed.*

He frowned, and she panicked; had she done something wrong? Was he about to leave? Should she not have insisted he—but no, she knew enough about men, although admittedly not that much, to know that any man would want to finish.

"I will be right back," he said, kissing her briefly on the mouth. "I need something." And he got off the bed, still not yet entirely naked, but it was enough, or nearly enough, to see his naked back, the muscles flexing as he bent down to pick up his jacket, pulling something out from the inner pocket.

He turned, and Edwina's mouth went dry at the sight of his chest. She knew he was broad and strong, but she hadn't anticipated how the sight of him would impact her. How his wide shoulders would narrow into a slim waist, the muscles of his chest well-defined but not bulky, a narrow line of hair leading down into—yes, well, and there was that, of course.

He was holding something, something she couldn't identify, and she panicked all over again, feeling completely out of her depth in this whole sexual encounter thing. He laughed at her expression.

"It's a condom. I presume you don't wish Gertrude to have a brother or sister." He tossed the item on the bed and began to remove the rest of her clothing, but even that wasn't enough to distract her.

"But—but," she sputtered, and he glanced up at her.

"You do know me well enough to know that I would plan for a logical event, don't you?" His voice held a note of humor, and she relaxed as she absorbed what he was saying. Of course he would be prepared. He was nothing if not logical, it wouldn't have made sense for him to be otherwise. No matter how odd it might seem for him to be striding around carrying condoms on his person.

Only what if it wasn't? What if this happened all the time?

"Cheltam, what is it? What's going on inside your head?" He was now entirely naked, still erect, and now climbing back onto the bed, drawing her into his arms, touching her with gentleness, not lust.

"Do you do this all the time?" she asked in a small voice. Not feeling at all confident, not at that moment.

He laughed against her hair. "Not all the time, no. I haven't—that is, I haven't done this at all since about a month before I hired you." He drew back and met her gaze. "Is that what is bothering you? That this might not be as important to me as I presume it is to you?" He didn't speak with anything approaching arrogance in his tone, just matter-of-factly. Of course he'd know it was important to her, no matter that it was a temporary thing by necessity. And of course he would confront it directly rather than just pretending it wasn't something.

"Let me tell you. I haven't had the desire for anyone else since I met you." He lowered his mouth to hers and kissed her softly. Softly, even though he was hard against her hip. "This is special to me, and I was hoping it would happen, which is why I made sure I had something in case it did happen. Neither of us wants any complications."

Of course not. No complications. Just this, this intensity, this meeting of mind and body, of shared pleasure. That is, shared once he—

"Well, then," Edwina said, letting a slow smile curl her mouth, "let us stop talking, then."

"Your wish is my command." As though she could tell him to do anything he didn't want to do, but she wasn't going to argue with him, not when his hand was running up her body, his fingers plucking at her nipples, his mouth finding hers.

And then he groaned, and pulled her closer, reaching down to take the condom and put it on, his fingers shaking. Then positioning himself at her entrance as she waited, biting her lip as she anticipated their joining.

How had she lived this long without this? And how would she live without it, when it was over?

WHY DO DUKES FALL IN LOVE?

49. How else are there to be more future dukes?

Chapter 15

She was more than he'd expected. Yes, she was a lovely, intriguing woman, but he found himself wanting more than just pure sexual satisfaction. He wanted to assuage her concerns.

He'd never had that impulse before; either his bed partner wanted what he did, or they just . . . stopped. He'd never spent the time to explain himself before, nor had he found himself caring.

But meanwhile, she did want what he wanted, and he'd given her more than it seemed she knew to expect. He couldn't help but feel stupidly proud of that, as though triumphing over her past husband and his obvious shortcomings was something he could crow over rather than take in due course.

He ran his hands over her body, relishing the curves and softness of her. His cock appreciated it as well. He didn't know if he'd ever been so hard before, nor had he wanted so desperately to enter a woman, and yet—and yet, he wanted to continue to make it good for her, not just thrust his way home and come to the inevitable conclusion.

It seemed as though she had different thoughts, however, since she reached her hand between them and clasped him, tightening her grip on his shaft and running her hand up and down, guiding him to her entrance.

He'd never been so grateful to be directed where to go in his life. He normally did not take direction well, nor was it something frequently offered, but this? Yes, he would gladly go where she wanted him to, if it meant he could enter her.

And when he did it was better than he'd imagined. She was tight, and wet, and he slid home so fully his balls touched her skin. She wrapped her arms around him and drew him even closer, wrapping her legs around his hips and beginning to move.

"Just like that," he said as she began to rock. He drew out halfway, then pushed himself back in, liking how he slammed his body onto hers, knowing—by her groan—that she liked it as well.

He raised himself up on his arms and looked down at her face, her gorgeous, expressive face. "Kiss me," she whispered, and he lowered his head to hers as he began to move, pushing in and pulling out in an intoxicating rhythm.

Then he couldn't kiss her anymore, he couldn't do anything but feel, and he lowered his mouth to her shoulder and buried his face into her neck, continuing to move, in and out, faster and faster, her hands grabbing his arse, her husky breathing in his ear.

Until—"Aah," he groaned as he came, thrusting in one final time, shuddering as the intensity of his climax seemed to reverberate through every fiber of his being.

He fell onto her, panting, unable to move, barely able to breathe. Certainly not able to think about anything but her, and this, and how amazing it felt.

Like nothing he'd ever experienced before. Which, when he thought about it later, would likely terrify him. But for now, he was content to let the bliss wash over him, to just be and not think, something he had little to no experience doing.

"That was . . ." and she paused, and he had the very unfamiliar feeling of uncertainty. It was terrible? Unexpected? Never to be repeated?

"Amazing."

He smiled into her neck and nodded in reply. For once, he was in complete agreement with someone.

Of course it wasn't enough to do it just once; he did it two more times in the course of the night. Because if there was something to be done, it was inevitable that the Duke of Hadlow would do it better and more often than anybody else.

Not that she was complaining. How could she complain when she could barely speak? And each time after he'd drawn her close, his arm held her, as though she was likely to go anywhere. His long limbs tangled with hers, seeming as though he was on alert even though he was naked and in her bed.

At long last she could tell he'd fallen asleep. She raised her head cautiously to look at him, to drink her fill of his beauty in the early hours of the dawn. He didn't look much less intimidating when he was sleeping, but it was easier to stare at him. This close she could see the scruff of his stubble, the strong planes of his face, the sharp angle of his nose.

If she were to think about it much more she'd realize she seemed almost . . . desperate staring at him like this. But he was in her bed, so wasn't it her right? If they were in his bed, he could stare his fill at her.

And wouldn't that be lovely.

She didn't pretend to be asleep when he stirred, opening his sleepy green eyes to look at her. "I should go back to my room," he said in a much more rumbling tone than he normally had. She felt secretly thrilled that she got to see him like this, less than entirely awake, his voice a bit scratchy. Surely only his valet ever got this treat, and she didn't think his valet enjoyed it nearly as much as she did.

Instead of getting up, however, he gathered her in his arms and lowered his mouth to her shoulder, kissing her softly as his hands roamed over her back, to her arse, onto her hip. As though he was assessing his possession, which normally would have made her balk, but with him—with him she wanted him to own her. If only for a short time. Mostly because she knew he wouldn't ever truly own her, not as her late husband had presumed to, nor any other man might if he found himself in her bed. The duke wasn't like that, she knew that, and she knew he was a rarity among men for it. And so she took it, craved it, the feeling that she belonged to him, that her body was his, and vice versa.

He ran his hand once more over her curves and kissed her mouth, then drew back, a look of desire on his face. Again, she thought? The man was a modern sexual miracle.

But it didn't seem as though he felt he could act on that desire, since he rolled away from her and leaned down to gather his clothes, flinging his shirt on over his head and stepping into his smallclothes and trousers.

All that lovely naked skin hidden away behind his clothing. His admittedly luxurious clothing, but nothing compared to the splendor of him.

He ran his hand over his face and glanced out the window, frowning. "You have kept me here too long, siren," he said with a sly grin.

In answer, she sat up and threw a pillow at his head. He ducked it easily, grinning wider. "I kept you here!" she exclaimed. "I'm not the one who wanted to—to—three times," she sputtered, feeling her face heat at talking about it.

He placed his hands on the bed and leaned toward her, an amused look on his face. "You're saying I'm the one who wanted to fuck?" His eyes drifted to her mouth when he spoke, and she felt her whole body tighten, as though he had kissed her. And he had used that word, a word she knew of, but had never heard anyone she knew say. It sounded so erotic the way he said it, the F so forceful, the final K sound so emphatic.

Just like he was—forceful and emphatic. And yes, she did want to fuck him.

Honesty. "No, I wanted to—to fuck as well," she replied, faltering as she spoke, but liking the way he reacted when she said that word, his eyes blazing, his hands reaching for her even before she finished the sentence.

"Damn it, siren, I have to go, or my valet will think I've been stolen in the night." He smiled and leaned closer to kiss her. "And then he would likely insist on sleeping in my bedroom to ensure my safety, when I am hoping that tonight you will come to me." Another kiss. "Will you come to me?" he asked in a longing tone of voice.

"Mm-hm," she murmured, swatting his hand away when it reached for her breast. "You have to go, or else we can't do this again," she said, biting her lip at the thought.

"Then I will. I'll see you at the breakfast table in a few hours."

He left quickly, only giving her one final glance as he left, a heated look that made her glance at the clock and calculate how long it would be before nighttime when she could do it all again. With him.

* * *

"Good morning, Cheltam." He just barely glanced up as she sat down on the bench opposite him. He gestured to the cup in front of her, blissfully full of coffee. "I ordered that for you, I don't want you falling asleep in the carriage when we're working."

Since I kept you up all night, she thought he would add if he could. Actually, he would say that if he'd thought it, so perhaps it was good that only she had thought it. There was only so much honesty the employer/employee relationship could handle, after all.

"We'll be heading out in half an hour," he continued. She picked up the cup and took a sip, feeling the heat of the coffee slide down her throat. It felt good, but not as good as that.

Well, nothing felt as good as that. Would tonight be a disappointment, then? Because there was no way the second (or, to be correct, the fourth) time with him would be as good as the first (three)?

Would she forever be comparing everything to that? *Well, this cake is scrumptious, but it's not as wonderful as when I had sexual relations with the Duke of Hadlow. That is a marvelous hat, but not nearly as beautiful as the Duke of Hadlow's backside.* She snorted to herself as she thought of it, and now he did look at her, one eyebrow raised as though he knew precisely what she was thinking.

Please don't let him know precisely what she was thinking, because that would be very bad. Or very good, because then he might just sweep everything off the table and pick her up and lay her on it and enter her with one heavy thrust, and then—

And then she would be the subject of so much scandal she would have no choice but to abandon Gertrude.

So no on the table thought.

"We'll be touring the Powers and Smith Corporation today," he continued, keeping his gaze on her. Did he know how it made her squirm? Judging by the amused glint in his eye it did, the scoundrel. "You will present your assessment of that company while we travel. It should be two hours before we get there, plenty of time for us to discuss." A pause as she just looked at him. Stared at him, to be honest. "Cheltam, are you there?"

She jumped in her seat, feeling her face flush. "Yes, Your Grace, I am. The Powers and Smith Corporation."

"Don't 'Your Grace' me, especially after last night," he muttered. His hand reached across the table, almost as if he were going to take hers, but he let it lie there, between them, an awkward reminder of what they had done and what they could never be to each other, all in one gesture.

She swallowed. That hand—that hand had been on her body, inside her, holding her legs apart as his mouth . . . She had to put what happened into a tidy box inside her mind or she wouldn't be able to do her job, and she had no illusions that he would keep her in his employ if she couldn't do her job properly, no matter what she had done with him the night before.

"What kind of information are you looking

for?" She picked up her cup again with a hand she willed not to tremble, or grab his, or do anything that indicated they were more than admittedly unorthodox employee and employer.

He shrugged. "You know what I require." As though she did, when she had no clue, having just asked him that very question. Not to mention, or God forbid even think about, what he might require elsewhere.

Oh, what else might he require? She could not think about that. Or else her already flushed face would explode, and wouldn't that be embarrassing? Humiliating immolation, that's what it would be.

She would just have to think about that later. When they were together not being employer and employee, but lover and . . . lover. Both of them equal. And she wanted to take as much as give, and wanted the same from him as well. Equals in bed, if nowhere else.

Which was why she had to keep her mind on what she needed to do now, not what she might possibly be looking forward to later.

"I will just run up to my room and collect my things, then," she said, draining the coffee. If she couldn't kiss him good morning as she secretly wished to, at least there was coffee.

Even though coffee was not nearly as satisfying. But much less shocking.

"Excellent," he replied, waving his hand as though in dismissal. Which shouldn't smart as much as it did—she was his employee, after all, and he had given her orders for the day. But still.

This was going to be difficult to navigate, wasn't it? But she had to, unless she wanted to be either unemployed or without a lover. And she wanted neither.

So she would have to figure it out.

WHY DO DUKES FALL IN LOVE?

10. Why not ask why the sun shines, or the rain falls?

Chapter 16

"Your Grace?"

Michael did not bite his valet's head off, but he did have to bite his tongue so he wouldn't. It wasn't Collins's fault that Michael had gotten very little sleep the night before, and now was chafing because he couldn't have her again, right now, right in this bed.

He was getting more reasonable, wasn't he?

"I need nothing else, just get yourself into the carriage as soon as you can. Cheltam will settle the bill."

Cheltam. He had to remember that during the day, she was Cheltam. Not Edwina. Not his lover. He was normally quite good—excellent, in fact—at compartmentalizing his feelings, ensuring that nothing bothered his emotional distance.

Mostly because he had never allowed anyone to bridge his emotional distance, save for Chester, and Chester was relatively easy to please.

But Edwina—he had thought of her even before he had seen her that morning, he'd asked for a cup of coffee so it would be waiting for her when she arrived downstairs. He was never ever thoughtful, he knew that, and yet—and yet he found himself wanting to do things for her, to bring that quick, pleased smile to her mouth.

And bring other things to her mouth as well; he wasn't that thoughtful. But he had never found himself thinking at all when he'd been involved with anyone. Mostly because he wasn't involved at all—his affairs were transactions, a simple matter of releasing sexual tension, nothing more.

This was entirely different, and it scared him. Terrified him, in fact. But that didn't mean he was going to put a stop to it. He wasn't that thoughtful.

It did mean he would have to work harder than usual to maintain his emotional distance to ensure that this was simply what it was, and that they both knew it would inevitably end.

It had to. There was no way he could see any way for it to continue forever without changing who he was.

Although he couldn't quite persuade himself not to take the stairs down to the carriage at less than a hurried pace, or feel a pang of disappointment when she wasn't already inside.

The door opened just as he was settling in, and she glanced around, as though there would be someone else waiting inside. He felt a pang of jealousy toward the unknown person, which was ridiculous since there was no person. And ridiculous because he was never jealous.

"There you are." He spoke without thinking

it through, then wanted to smack himself in the head for uttering something so nonsensical. *There you are?* Of course she was there, as though if he hadn't said it she'd have been somewhere else.

She did not comment on his inanity, thankfully, just tucked herself onto the seat opposite, the one where she'd be riding backward. And not next to him.

Before he even realized it, he'd reached out and grabbed her, hauling her over to his side before pulling her into his arms and kissing her with all the passion a few hours of separation required.

Which was, apparently, a lot.

Her mouth opened immediately, and her hands reached up to clasp his shoulders, then on up to plunge themselves into his hair. She made a little noise in the back of her throat, and he wanted to take her, here, in the carriage, rucking up her skirts and having her, even though intercourse in a carriage—particularly for a tall person— seemed highly impractical.

Not that he'd ever had intercourse in a carriage, but of course he'd considered the logistics before. Because he was he, and things needed to be thought through before acting on them.

Except for all of this, which he was thinking about hardly at all, just feeling, and doing, and—

She drew away from him, her eyes already dreamy and soft, her mouth redder than normal. "We're not moving."

No, because they weren't fucking.

"Oh, the carriage?" he said after a moment when he realized what she meant. He leaned up and rapped on the roof. The carriage lurched right away, sending them on their journey. Although not to where he ultimately wanted to be, which was—

Stop it, Michael, he chided himself. This was just a momentary feeling, it would pass.

Although since he'd never had this kind of "momentary feeling" before, he wasn't so certain it was momentary. Nor what he should do with all of it, what with the wanting, and the not being able to have, at least not right away. The perplexing need to discuss it, which he'd been burning to do since leaving her bed.

But not only could he not do that, he would not. He would not admit to anyone—much less himself—that this was more than what it appeared to be. It would end, she would be his extremely efficient secretary, and that would be it. There couldn't be anything else.

"Are you—are you ready to hear my report?" she asked, her voice shakier than he was accustomed to. *No doubt because you have just mauled her in the carriage, you idiot.*

But she seemed to like the mauling.

Never mind that now.

"Yes," he replied, settling back against the cushions of the carriage and folding his hands in his lap. Trying to will his erection to subside, since he did not wish to test the limits of the interior of his carriage. Even though he absolutely did.

"Excellent." She picked up a sheaf of papers she'd laid on the seat and rifled through them, making a little huff of exasperation as she reviewed each paper. "Here it is. The Powers and Smith Corporation. Founded just five years ago, now projecting to supply twenty percent of the country's engines. Mr. Powers is the engineer in the enterprise, whereas Mr. Smith is the businessman."

"We should require Mr. Powers to show us around then," Michael said. "The last thing I want to hear is more vagueness about how this company is more forward-thinking and efficient than that company, without hearing any actual facts mentioned."

"No, that would not please you at all, would it?" she replied in an amused voice. "It must be so frustrating to be you."

He folded his arms over his chest and glared at her. "And what do you mean by that?"

She looked as though she wanted to laugh at him, but thankfully kept herself to a slight smile. She put the paper back down on her lap and looked at him, tilting her head. "It is just—just that for you, things are so simple. They should be this way, everyone should know they should be this way, and people are idiots if they do not see it this way." She shook her head. "And yet not everyone—let me say hardly anyone—sees things the way you do. You must walk around being aggravated all day when people aren't what you expect them to be." She did laugh then. "It is a good thing you are a duke, because imagine how horrible your life would be if you had to answer to anyone? If you were, say, a banker who had to deal with stupid people worrying about their money, or a fruit seller and people would argue with you about the freshness of your peaches, or what have you," and then she just stopped, clamping a hand over her mouth as her eyes danced.

He'd never been laughed at before as much as he had with her, and yet he didn't mind it, even though he was already explaining to his mythical customers why the peaches weren't rotten, they just got bruised in the course of shipment, and they were still fresh, and he could throw in an extra peach for their trouble.

But he didn't say any of that, thank goodness, or she might very well explode in laughter, having just proven her point.

"I am very fortunate to be a duke, yes," he said in his most arrogant, aristocratic drawl. He raised an eyebrow for emphasis. "Because instead of having to discuss one family's business, I have to oversee all the business ventures of all my family's holdings. I have to tease out which person's reporting is suspect, where best to invest my money so as to provide proper return for future generations, and I have to pretend excitement at rubbing elbows with my peers, most of whom are useless drains on their own holdings and constituents." He hadn't realized just how resentful those responsibilities made him. But he wouldn't shirk them. He couldn't. It wasn't who he was as a person.

She'd narrowed her gaze on him as she spoke, no more humor in her expression, and she nodded after he'd finished, looking thoughtful. "I did not mean to be glib," she said, and he shook his head, wanting to let her know that no, she hadn't been, she'd figured him out entirely, and it was such a relief to have someone understand just how he felt, why he wanted to scream at everyone he encountered—save her and Chester, oh, and also Gertrude—and why he felt some days as though he swallowed more words than he spoke.

"It's just," she continued, and he could see by her expression that she thought she'd offended or hurt him, "it just must hurt to be you is all I was trying to say."

"It—it does." He was surprised at just how hard it was to say the words, even though they were what he thought. Them, and so much more. "I know I might seem like I am an unfeeling, arrogant . . ." and he paused as he tried to think of the right word.

"Syllogist?" she supplied.

"I was thinking more along the lines of 'caviller,' or perhaps just the more succinct 'prig,' " he said, smiling as he spoke. " 'Syllogist' is so much kinder."

"You should be kinder to yourself," she replied, surprising him. He hadn't realized he wasn't.

"How so?"

She shrugged. "I can tell, you think poorly of yourself for coming close to berating Hawkins when he dares to question you, or snapping at me when I've not done something you expected would be done. But that is you. You are not always a nice man"—and that hurt, oddly enough, even though he knew that about himself—"but you are an honest one, and that is valuable, and far rarer, I believe."

"So you think I should snap?"

She rolled her eyes. "No, that is not what I am

saying. I am saying you should give yourself more credit for not snapping, but for heaven's sake, don't take it up just because it is easier. You are the last person I would ever expect to do something because it is easier, anyway," she finished.

"True." It felt right, and oddly satisfying, to have her understand him so thoroughly. When had that ever happened before?

Oh right, *never*. His closest friend was canine, and his next-closest friend was probably—her. It was so lonely, being him, and so being with her, both in the daytime and now in whatever nighttime activities they were embarking on, felt so special.

But what if they weren't? What if this was how people who were normal, who weren't he, behaved all the time? How would he know that?

"You're thinking about something. Did you want me to continue with this report, or do you have enough information?" She frowned. "How long is the journey to the factory anyway? We should be there soon, if Smaxton is correct."

Michael felt a twinge—or more than a twinge—of jealousy at hearing her speak about someone else. "And who is Smaxton?" he said, trying to keep his tone neutral.

She rolled her eyes again. Apparently his tone wasn't neutral enough. "Smaxton is your coachman, the one with the wife and five children, who smells of tobacco."

"Oh." Sad, truly, that he didn't know his coachman's name. Perhaps if he did know it, his coachman would end up being his closest friend, supplanting his dog, and making her his third-best friend.

Although he highly doubted that.

"I have enough, thank you." Although he really didn't, but she wouldn't be able to provide what it was that he most needed to know when considering an investment—what the ultimate costs would be, if it felt as though it were the right decision, if he thought it would make the world a better place for his having done so.

Not unlike taking a lover, he thought, suppressing a grin. He did not think she would appreciate the comparison, so he did not mention it. Even though he dearly wished he could share the thought with her, as it seemed he wanted to share so much.

"Since we do have some time, tell me about yourself."

He blinked. Nobody had ever asked him to talk about himself, mostly because they knew all the relevant facts: He was a duke, he was thirty-four years old, he was so many inches tall, and he was brutal when he encountered stupidly curious people.

Probably the last item was the one that meant nobody asked him anything.

"What do you want to know?" He sounded stiff.

She shrugged. "I know who you are now, but tell me more about yourself in general." She smiled. "I can't imagine what you were like as a little boy."

"Younger," he replied quickly.

She looked at him and rolled her eyes. "Of course you would say that. That I would know, since I do understand how time works. What were you *like*?"

She stressed the last word, and he allowed his mind to travel back, to remember things he hadn't deliberately recalled in years.

"I had an older brother," he began, and he saw her expression change into one of concern, because of course he wouldn't be the duke if his older brother were still alive. "His name was William, and he was my hero. I followed him around as soon as I could walk, and he only got frustrated with me a few times, which is remarkable given how annoying I was."

"I am guessing you asked loads and loads of questions," she said in a fond tone.

He snorted. "Yes, my mother said it was a good thing I went to sleep, since otherwise she'd have to answer questions twenty-four hours a day."

"What happened to your brother?"

His chest tightened. "I didn't know then, but he had a weak constitution. We went fishing one day, I was only four, and he fell into the water. Not enough to drown him, but it was nearly winter, and the water was cold." A pause. "He died a few months later."

She reached forward and placed her hand on his arm. "I am so sorry."

Just those few words eased the feeling in his chest. He didn't doubt she was sorry. He could hear it in her tone of voice. He believed it, unlike when other people offered their apologies for something or another.

"Thank you," he replied, placing his hand on top of hers. "Thank you." This was by far the most . . . intense dalliance he'd ever had with a woman.

Even though he knew it was everything more than a dalliance. Even though it never could be.

She'd never thought that showing emotions was a particularly attractive quality—her late husband had shown plenty of emotion, namely jealousy, and pride, and misplaced arrogance. But with him, with Hadlow—Michael, she supposed she might call him now, though that felt odd even inside the confines of her own head—his emotions were appealing. Even the ones that were less attractive.

That was, of course, because he was he. On anybody else those emotions would be annoying. Needy. But he wore them like an unfamiliar set of clothes, strangely awkward and ungainly in a way that she didn't think he had ever felt before.

It shouldn't make him more attractive. But it absolutely did. And when he had opened up enough to speak to her about his brother—she just wanted to cry and wrap her arms around him and protect him, of all the ludicrous ideas. A duke, especially his type of duke, wouldn't need any protecting. But that reality didn't diminish her feelings.

"Do you think," he began, sounding almost nervous, "do you think Gertrude would want something from this trip? I wonder if any of the factories produce models of their engines or something like that. Only if you think she would like them," he added hurriedly.

Dear Lord. Had she thought him appealing when he was vulnerably emotional? That was nothing compared to when he was thinking of something thoughtful he could do for her child, a being who had no hold on him, to whom he owed no obligation.

"She would love it," Edwina replied. She clasped the hand he'd placed on hers and squeezed it. Here, alone in the carriage, they could acknowledge what they'd done. Who they were to each other, couldn't they?

She hoped so.

He looked down at their hands, his thumb moving in small circles on the back of her hand. Sending prickles up her spine, and a warmth flowing through other parts of her body.

"This is," he said, speaking in a low tone of voice, "this is special to me, you know."

She hadn't known. Not exactly. She'd suspected, but she hadn't known.

"Yes, to me as well." She blinked away the onset of tears. Why was she even tempted to cry? "It is not as though I do this kind of thing every day."

"Of course you don't. I am honored you have chosen to do so with me."

He kept rubbing the back of her hand, and she felt as though that was the only thing she could feel or know about, his thumb on her skin, the way the carriage jostled their shoulders together, the constant thrum of the wheels and the distant jangling of the horses' harnesses.

They stayed silent for the remainder of the trip, Edwina as comfortable as she could possibly be alone in a carriage with her employer, her lover, and—and her friend.

"We're slowing," he said after about an hour of travel. Edwina jerked upright, not having realized she'd been dozing, and looked out the window of the carriage. The factory was to the right of them, a large, square building with a few stray plumes of black smoke emerging from the top. The carriage drew to a stop directly in front of the black wrought-iron gates, the script in the gates proclaiming they had, indeed, reached Powers and Smith.

"Let's hope this is a useful visit," he muttered in his usual aggravated tone. She suppressed a smirk—of course he was already aggravated, since he was likely anticipating the potential stupidity of whomever he might meet inside—and picked up her papers, straightening them and patting her hair, just to ensure she was looking tidy.

Smaxton opened the carriage door, holding his hand out to help her down the steps. She thought she heard him growl behind her, and bit her lip. Perhaps now that he was allowing himself to show his emotions he should take care to hide them a bit more. If anyone knew—her whole body suddenly felt as though it were freezing, and she swallowed hard against the rising anxiety. If anyone knew what they were doing, it wouldn't reflect poorly on him—what with being a duke, and male, and basically above any kind of judgment—but it would on her.

And yet she couldn't seem to stop herself. So she just had to be very, very careful. As did he.

Which was why, when he held his arm out to her, she shook her head no. He narrowed his eyes at her, and then nodded in return, seeming to process what she was thinking.

"Come along, Cheltam," he said, starting to walk toward the gate in a brisk stride.

She hurried behind him, darting a few surreptitious glances at his height, the breadth of his shoulders, the back of his head.

She had to be discreet, not entirely oblivious, after all.

WHY DO DUKES FALL IN LOVE?

22. Because a heart is responsible to nothing but itself.

Chapter 17

There was a flurry of movement as they approached the gates, and then a man stepped through the running mass of bodies toward them, a smile suitable for greeting a duke—not too friendly, just hovering on the right side of obsequiousness—on his face. This was obviously either Powers or Smith, his clothing completely clean and more expensive than even a site manager could afford.

"Good morning, Your Grace," the man said in a cultured accent. He glanced at Edwina, frowning for a moment, then returned to looking at the duke.

"Good morning. You are?" the duke said in his usual brusque tone.

The man didn't seem to take it as amiss as Edwina would have if he had addressed her that way.

"Mr. Smith," he replied. "Mr. Powers is tending to some emergency in the production room"— and then his expression froze—"not that it is a true emergency, not that anything is wrong, just that—"

"Fine," the duke interrupted with a wave of his hand. "Lead on, Mr. Smith," and at that he shot Edwina a look as though to say, *See? We got the businessman; we won't get anything useful out of this*, and she wanted to laugh at his grumpiness.

"Er, would you wish your—your companion to wait for you while we conduct our business?"

Edwina stiffened as she realized what the man thought—that she was the duke's paramour brought along as entertainment, presumably, on the trip. Of course he'd know the duke wasn't married, nor was her clothing as fine as would belong on a duchess. So the only alternative would be that she was his mistress.

Which she was, she supposed, only she didn't belong to him. She was not a property to be disposed of in an office while he went around looking at admittedly boring things.

"You are mistaken," Hadlow replied, his tone sharp, "this is my secretary, Mrs. Cheltam. She will be accompanying us on the tour."

Mr. Smith immediately looked chagrined, and Edwina almost felt sorry for him. "Ah, yes, of course. Your secretary," and the way he said the last two words, as though they should be accompanied by a wink, took whatever sympathy she had for the man and shredded it. It made her angry and sad, also—because it just meant that no matter what, this was just temporary. Anger because there was no logical way they could be together forever, and sad for the very same reason.

If he hadn't been a duke. If she had been closer to his class. But this, this was just a fraction of what it would be like if people knew about them.

But she couldn't daydream away on "ifs"; she had work to do.

"This way, please," Mr. Smith said, holding his arm out toward the large building in front of them. The duke paused to let her go first, and she stopped short when she realized that was likely the first time he'd acknowledged her being a female while working as his secretary.

Obviously he acknowledged her as female when he was acting as her lover, but those two situations were entirely different.

She followed Mr. Smith as he opened the door to the building, the noises of production and men talking getting louder. She stepped over the threshold, and was immediately inside what was clearly the main production room. It was an enormous space, with ominous-looking contraptions hanging from the ceiling, and rectangular worktables placed in a pattern in the room, at least two men working at each one.

"If you will step into my office, I can go over what we will see," Mr. Smith said, having to raise his voice over the din. He gestured to the left corner of the room, where Edwina saw a discreet door with the word "OFFICE" painted on it.

The duke placed his hand at Edwina's back and guided her to the office. It wasn't untoward that her employer would do such a thing and touch her to ensure her safety, but she was fairly certain that it was untoward when his fingers slid onto her waist and squeezed. She would have to have a talk with him about discretion, and its importance, if they were to continue this—this careful dance of employer and employee, of man and woman, of bed partners. Lovers.

And she would also have to have a discussion with her body, because her body was all too delighted that he was touching her inappropriately. Her nipples had tightened, and she was keenly aware of him at her back, the solid, strong warmth of him an almost tangible touch, just like his fingers.

His clever, clever fingers.

"If you'll just step this way, Mrs. Cheltam," Mr. Smith said, interrupting her salacious musings. The duke dropped his hand from her body as she walked into the office, noting its general neatness, impressed despite her not feeling too kindly toward its proprietor. There were bookshelves all along one wall, and on another, a small window looked out on to the factory space. A large desk, its surface bare except for a few papers and a pen, was at the left, with two chairs placed opposite.

"If you'd care to have a seat?" Mr. Smith continued, gesturing to the chairs. She glanced at the duke, who nodded, and followed to sit in the other chair after she'd settled herself.

Mr. Smith closed the door and took the chair behind the desk. He beamed at both of them, settling his hands on the desk. "We very much appreciate your taking the time to visit our humble premises, Your Grace."

Edwina didn't even have to look at him to know

his gaze had narrowed and his jaw had set at the man's falsely modest words. She felt a pang of sympathy for him—he encountered this kind of sycophancy all the time, due to his position. And of course he had less patience for it than a man of average intelligence did.

No wonder he seemed so relieved to be able to share his thoughts with her.

"I do not invest funds in something if I cannot be persuaded as to its eventual results. Whether the results are financial, or beneficial to progress, or some other tangible measure of success." The duke leaned back in his chair, the very epitome of aristocratic indulgence. "So tell me why I should invest in Powers and Smith."

The next half hour was spent with Mr. Smith going over, with great alacrity, the forward progress of the company, the dedication of its workers—above all, Mr. Smith—and how all the other engine manufacturers had less commitment, more mistakes, and faultier engines.

Edwina took a few notes, but now that she was aware of what the duke wanted—facts, not hyperbole—there wasn't very much to write down for later discussion.

The duke broke in on Mr. Smith's monologue as he was describing the specific quality controls for the engines—mostly Mr. Smith going around and checking himself. "Right, well, I want to see the premises," he declared, getting up and holding his hand out to Edwina for her to rise as well.

She placed her fingers in his and stood, dropping them as soon as she was upright. He frowned and clasped his hands at his back, rocking on his heels.

Mr. Smith's mouth had dropped open, but he recovered relatively quickly, standing up and nodding in agreement. "Of course, of course, just this way," he said, beckoning to the door from which they'd entered.

At least now they were moving, Edwina thought, even if what Mr. Smith was saying about the machines was similar to what he'd said in his office—he spoke in generalities about quality, and persistence, and innovation, without offering many specifics.

It was interesting, Edwina had to admit, to watch how the engines were made. Each part in its precise place, the motion of the workers themselves almost mechanistic. She could understand a bit more why the process fascinated him; there was only the quality of the work and the resulting product to assess, with no sprinkling of beauty, or fatuous words, or anything but the thing itself.

That could be applied to him, as well—even if he weren't a duke, he would be impressive. Fiercely intelligent, creative, handsome, strong, and honest. It was remarkable, truly, that those qualities had survived his title. She didn't think many men would have all that power and still be committed to doing something more with it. Most would be content to settle, to do what they had to, or what they thought they had to, but nothing more.

But not him. It was as though there was a force inside him, propelling him forward, into action beyond what most men would do. That force—she had to wonder—did that apply to his romantic life also? Was she just the most current one in his forward trajectory? Although even if she weren't, it didn't matter. They'd agreed to what this was, and it was not permanent.

A man walked up to them as Mr. Smith was discussing the quality of the materials used in the engine. Apparently they were excellent, because why else would he talk about them?

"Ah, Powers, here you are," Mr. Smith said. "Your Grace, allow me to present my partner, Mr. Powers. Mr. Powers is the man with the vision, I am merely the facilitator," he said, chuckling as though it was absurd for him to be "merely" anything.

Mr. Powers was tall and lean where Mr. Smith was medium height and running to fat. He glanced at the duke and Edwina, his expression neutral.

"How do you do?" he said in what Edwina recognized as a Welsh accent. He nodded, but didn't shake hands. "Smith has been telling you all about the engines, then?" he said, squinting toward his partner.

"Yes, but now that you are here, you can give us all the details," Mr. Smith said in an enthusiastic, albeit nervous, tone.

"The duke isn't interested in all the details." Mr. Powers spoke in a matter-of-fact voice. Which made the duke snap his head toward Mr. Powers.

"How do you know that?" he asked.

Mr. Powers shrugged as Mr. Smith opened and closed his mouth. "Why would you be? Either you want to invest your funds with us, and see what we can do, or you don't. Us telling you all about our engines isn't going to affect that."

"Oh, but it is." Edwina couldn't believe she was speaking, but here she was, interjecting herself into the conversation. Between all these men, two of whom likely thought she was just the duke's amusement during the trip.

The third—the duke—knowing exactly what she was to him, and that might include being an amusement.

A lowering thought, but now she had started speaking, she couldn't seem to stop. "The duke isn't like most of the men you have likely met who are considering your company as a worthy investment. He wants to know the specifics of the process, of the intricacies of the engines, and how this engine compares against the competition. He is not here to hear how wonderful he is. Look at him," she said, gesturing toward the man, who was now regarding her with a puzzled look. "Does he seem to be the type of man who needs someone to pay him false compliments?"

"And you are?" Mr. Powers said, approaching her with his hand outstretched.

She took it, speaking as she did so. "I am Mrs. Cheltam, the duke's secretary. So you see I have very specific and detailed knowledge about what the duke wants to learn in the course of this tour. You do know," she said, turning to address

Mr. Smith, "that we are visiting other factories during this trip?"

"Yes, I assume so, only I can assure you—"

"Assure us of nothing, just prove by facts that your company's engines are the best," Edwina said, cutting him off, amazed at her own audacity as she did so. But also keenly aware that Hadlow was looking at her with a mixture of awe and surprise. As though nobody had ever spoken up for him before, which they probably hadn't. Why speak for someone whose voice was bound to be listened to, no matter what he said? It wasn't as though dukes were generally in need of advocates, but this one was, especially when it seemed someone believed he was just another aristocratic dilettante.

When Mr. Powers spoke again, it was with an engaged warmth that had been lacking in his initial conversation. "Then please step this way, Your Grace, and I will show you all you need to see."

The duke nodded to her. "Mrs. Cheltam, come along and take notes, since you are so vehement on my needing this particular information." He spoke dryly, but with a slight teasing tone that made her insides melt.

Although she should not be engaged in melting, not while she was working.

She followed along, calculating how long it would be before they were alone, and she could caution him to be more discreet and also resume their activities from the night before.

Hopefully in that order, although she wasn't sure she could resist him once they were alone.

WHY DO DUKES FALL IN LOVE?

~~~~~~~~~~~~~~~~~~~~~~~~~

89. How dare you even ask?

Chapter 18

"A roast, some bread, whatever vegetables you have that aren't cooked within an inch of their lives, and a bottle of your best wine."

"Excellent, Your Grace," the nervous innkeeper said. They'd left the Powers and Smith factory an hour before, traveling to the inn that Cheltam had plotted they should stay at.

The innkeeper nodded again, and then left, backing out of the private room Cheltam had booked.

It had been a surprisingly good day, Michael thought. First there was how he'd spent the night before, which was definitely pleasurable. And then there was the factory tour, and how she'd defended him against an inaccurate presumption. That shouldn't have touched him as it did—after all, she was his employee, and some measure of loyalty was expected in return for her salary—but he knew it was more than that. It was because she knew him, and understood him.

She sat opposite, not looking at him, but instead concentrating on the ever-present papers that seemed to be as much in his presence as she was. She was, she'd told him five minutes earlier, making sure the notes she'd taken were legible, and reorganizing them into a clear document.

He didn't particularly care about the information she'd present, he'd already decided what he thought, but it couldn't hurt to have more information to support his own reaction.

And he had to admit it was refreshing, even if it piqued him, that he was in a room with someone and they were not focusing all their attention on him. Except for Chester, who didn't seem to notice when he was in the room unless it was time to go for a walk, everyone was focused on him when they were in the same room together.

He really needed to get more friends, people who would ignore him if they were together. Although he wasn't quite sure that met the definition of "friends."

The innkeeper returned, holding a bottle of wine and two glasses. He set them down, darting nervous glances at Michael as he opened the wine and poured.

"Your food will arrive soon, Your Grace," the man said, bobbing his head as he spoke.

"Thank you," Cheltam said, after a moment of silence.

"Right, thank you," Michael echoed.

The man bobbed again, and left.

"Here's where you're going to tell me I should be polite," he said.

She tilted her head and regarded him. "No, you

know you should be polite. You just choose not to. You don't have to. In my position—whether it's as your employee or a female—I have to be polite." She shrugged. "Sometimes I wish it weren't so."

"Would you be as rude as me if you could?" He planted his elbows on the table, which he absolutely knew he should not do, and leaned forward. Would he ever get tired of looking at her face?

Well, sadly, he could answer that. Most likely. He always had before. But for now, it felt as though he could never get enough of looking at her.

She seemed to consider it, glancing away from his gaze. "I don't know. I don't think so, because it just doesn't feel considerate. I hope I am always considerate."

Thoughts of how she could be considerate to him shouldn't set him ablaze with desire, and yet they did.

"Where is that food anyway?" The sooner they ate, the sooner they would retire for the evening, and the sooner he could have her again.

"Patience, Hadlow," she said in an amused voice. "It's only been five minutes."

"Don't they know who I am?" he said in mock arrogance. "Food should cook faster when it's for a duke."

She laughed, reaching forward to take his hand. "Some things are worth the wait," she said, glancing at him from under her lashes.

That look sent a shock of lust straight to his cock. If it weren't for the fact that the innkeeper would likely return soon, he'd have had her on the table right now.

"You know what you do to me." He spoke in a low rumble. Her face got pink, and she lowered her gaze, biting her lip as she did so.

"As much as what you do to me, Michael," she replied in a soft voice.

The use of his given name—the first time she had called him anything but "Your Grace" or "Hadlow"—felt like they were inhabiting a secret place, one where it was only them.

He cleared his throat, uncomfortable for a moment at all the feelings that were roiling inside him. Feelings he'd never had before, not even at the onset of a new affair. He should squash them, make sure they couldn't interfere with his life, his work, his position.

He leaned back in his seat, taking his hand away from hers. "I cannot wait to fuck you again, Edwina," he said, deliberately crass in his language. She had to know, to understand just what they were doing, and what this was about. He couldn't afford entanglements, not with her, someone he would tire of, eventually, someone who was not of his class, who was nothing more than his lovely, desirable, eminently fuckable employee.

She swallowed, and looked away. "I do hope dinner comes soon," she said in a voice that crackled with desire.

He sighed, feeling a relief, but also a pang, that she was just as clear as he was on what they were doing. He was being entirely contrary in his emotions—given that he was having emotions in the first place, which was contrary to his nature—

wanting her to become invested in him, but not wanting her to so there would be no hurt after.

Goddamn it. This was getting to be far more complicated than he'd anticipated. Mostly because of him, and his pesky emotions.

But one thing was true: he couldn't wait to fuck her again.

She knew what he was doing. He was reminding her that this was nothing more than what it was, for which she was grateful. Even if she was also resentful that she did seem to need the reminder, since she could so easily see herself falling in love with him.

She probably was already in love with him, if she were honest with herself. But she wouldn't be that honest with *him*—she knew admitting her feelings would cause him to push her away, to ensure that this ended even sooner than it should have. And it would end. He would need to marry someone, someone who had the right breeding, and was younger than she was, and who could be counted on to be the perfect duchess.

Not that she had any illusions that he would find someone who would be perfect for him. But that was his problem, not hers. Unless he suddenly decided his secretary/lover should take on the responsibility of researching the likely candidates, just as she was doing with his potential investments.

Oh God. Please don't let him be *that* practical.

"Here we are, Your Grace." The innkeeper returned with another servant, the latter bearing a tray filled with their food. The innkeeper oversaw the placement of everything, then nodded approvingly. "Is there anything else I can get for you, Your Grace?"

"Nothing more, thank you," the duke said, shooting a knowing glance at Edwina, as though to say, *See? I can be polite when I want to be.*

The door closed behind the man, and Edwina reached out to pick up a slice of meat on the tray.

"Let me serve you." He stood as he spoke, walking to where she sat, lowering his mouth to her shoulder and placing an openmouthed kiss on it.

Her entire body reacted, her nipples tightening, her legs coming together to squeeze in that place that felt so good when he'd touched it. He chuckled, as though he knew what he was doing to her, and reached over her other shoulder to pick up a slice of the roast, placing it on her plate. And then his other hand went to the bowl of carrots, taking a spoonful of them and dropping them on her plate.

He plucked the napkin from the table and unfolded it, placing it on her lap, touching her thighs as he arranged it. So close to where she tingled, where she wanted him, that she realized she'd made an involuntary noise. A moan, if she were to be honest.

And then his fingers gripped her chin, and he twisted her head so their mouths could meet.

Ah. This was the sustenance she wanted, not any of the food on the table. His mouth, tasting of wine and redolent with warmth, his tongue licking, tangling with hers. Her fingers went up to clutch his hair, pulling him closer, twisting more in her seat so she could have access to more of him, to their bodies touching.

He clamped his hands on her shoulders and raised her to standing, still kissing her, now folding her against his body. His clearly excited body.

She pushed against that part of him, loving how he responded with a low, throaty growl. Aware that she was doing this to him, making him lustful, and passionate, and almost—almost caring.

It felt special, even though she knew it was something he'd done before. And would do again, with another woman at some point in the future. But right now he was hers, and this was theirs, and she was going to enjoy it as much as she could.

His mouth ravaged hers for a few long minutes, then he broke the kiss, gasping, resting his head on her forehead. "We should eat something very quickly, and then we should go up to bed. *My* bed," he added, as though he needed to make it absolutely clear where this was all going. As if she would be heading off to her own bed after that kiss.

She nodded, and slid down his body, settling herself back in her chair, taking a sip of wine, and picking up her knife and fork. He returned to his side of the table, his eyes on her face, his gaze almost seeming as though it was going to devour her.

He placed food on his own plate and ate efficiently, spearing his meat and eating in fast bursts. If she weren't so intent on finishing the meal as quickly as possible she'd be concerned he would choke, but she was, and so she refrained from mentioning the possibility.

Not to mention, he wasn't a child, even though he acted with the headstrong impudence of one at times. But now she couldn't fault that tendency in him; she wanted the same thing, so much so that they finished their meal within about ten minutes. She looked at him as he took his last bite, allowing a seductive smile to cross her lips. His gaze alit on her mouth, and her lips tingled, feeling as though he'd touched her there.

"I am finished," she said, getting up from her chair. She dropped the napkin on the table and walked to the door, opening it and waiting for him. He didn't waste any time following her; he was too close, in fact, for mere employee and employer.

She turned to speak to him over her shoulder. "I will go up now. Wait a few minutes, and go to your room. I'll be there in ten minutes."

He looked as though he were going to argue, then just pressed his lips together and nodded.

She walked out, closing the door behind her, her whole body anticipating reuniting with his.

Edwina poked her head out of her room and glanced both ways in the corridor. Nobody was there, thank goodness. She darted out into the hallway, still dressed, but carrying her dressing gown over her arm. He would just have to help her undress, which she didn't think he would mind.

She could explain away wandering the hallway in her gown, but not in her sleeping attire.

Hopefully the inn would be quiet when it was time for her to return.

It felt so scandalous, which of course it was, but also adventurous. And exciting. She'd never done anything like this before, had any kind of clandestine meeting. Even before she was married to Mr. Cheltam, she'd kept herself away from impudent suitors, knowing that her parents were depending on her to make a good marriage so she would be settled.

She walked swiftly down the hall, keeping one hand on the wall to guide herself in the dark. His room was at the end of the corridor, so there was no chance she would knock on the wrong door.

And also there was the fact that his door was slightly ajar, leaking a soft light that guided her. She pushed the door open and shut it behind her softly, her breath catching as she saw him.

He lay on the bed nearly unclothed, his chest bare, wearing only his smallclothes. His penis jutted up from the fabric and his hand was on himself, his eyes heavy-lidded as he watched her enter.

"You started without me," she said in a low voice.

"I did," he said, sliding his hand up and down himself through the fabric. "I can't stop thinking about the noise you make when you climax. Or how your pussy spasmed in my mouth as I licked you."

"Oh," she said, feelings of shock and titillation warring for dominance in her mind.

The titillation won.

"Come over here so I can undress you. Unless you'd care to undress for me?" he said, raising an eyebrow. Still, his hand moved slowly, rhythmically on himself, and she was transfixed at the sight. He was so strong, so powerful, and he was touching himself because of her. She had the power over him now.

"I can do that," she replied in a whisper, her hands going to the back of her gown. She'd long ago mastered undressing herself when her husband hadn't been able to pay for a lady's maid any longer. For the first time, she was thankful for her husband's careless finances, since it meant she had acquired the skill that it seemed this man wanted her to demonstrate.

She slid each button through the hole, wiggling as she did so. When she'd unbuttoned a few, she pushed her shoulders together and slid the fabric of her sleeves down her arms. His gaze was on her chest, his hand working his penis as he regarded her.

She undid a few more buttons, then pushed it down her hips, stepping out of it, standing only in her shift.

"I can see your nipples through the fabric." His voice was strained, and she felt her throat get thick. "Hard and pink. I can't wait to get my mouth on them," he said. "Get that off and come over here," he said in his most commanding voice.

She had to admit she liked it when he told her what to do, when he said those shocking, dirty words to her. Something in her felt as though it had been kindled when he spoke. She felt the words bubbling inside her brain—she wanted to talk about how watching his hands on himself made her wet, how she couldn't wait to have him inside her—but she wasn't sure she could.

Although it would likely excite him, so perhaps she could try.

She drew her shift up and over her head, dropping it to the floor. Standing only in her stockings before him, pulling the pins out from her hair and shaking it free to cascade over her back.

"Damn, but you're gorgeous," he said, reaching his hand out to her. She walked to the foot of the bed and climbed up, moving forward on her hands and knees on the bed to his body. She paused there, where his penis was, and ran her hand over the top of him, then tugged at the top of his smallclothes.

"Let me help get you out of these," she said, feeling hesitant about all of it, but wanting to try.

Judging by his hissed breath when she touched him, she was glad she was being so brave.

She reached inside to hold him, moving his penis out of the way as she drew his smallclothes down his strong legs. She had to let go of him to pull his smallclothes all the way off, dropping them on the floor and returning to wrap her hand around him.

"What," she began, barely able to think the words, but knowing she wanted to say them, that he would want her to say them, "what do you call this?"

His hand wrapped over hers and he showed

her how to touch him, stroking up and down in a faster rhythm than he had done to himself. He glanced down at where their hands touched, and groaned. "It's my cock. You've got your lovely hand on my cock."

"And it is a lovely cock," she replied, licking her lips as she looked. The head of it was large, a drop of moisture seeping out through the slit at the top. The skin there felt soft, but as though it were a swath of velvet covering an iron rod.

"Could I," she began, licking her lips again, wondering why they were so dry, "would you want me to kiss your cock?"

"Oh God, Edwina," he said, flinging his head back and closing his eyes. "Please."

She hesitated for a moment, then lowered her mouth to him, licking the spot right at the top. And then she took him inside her mouth, swirling her tongue around him, tasting the salty flavor, smelling the warm musk that was his scent.

He arched his back and groaned again, which encouraged her to be more aggressive in her exploration, sliding her tongue down his shaft, burying her nose in the hair at the base of his cock.

She had to say she liked the word. It was hard, and forceful, and direct. Like him. Like his cock, as well, which was even harder than before, it seemed, thanks to her ministrations.

There was something so powerful about doing this to him, having him prone on the bed, his eyes closed, his cheeks flushed, his hands fisting at his sides as she slid her mouth up and down.

"I want to be inside you," he said, moving upright as he spoke, positioning her on the bed and lying between her thighs. He pushed a stray hair away from her face, his gaze seeming as though it were devouring her, moving restlessly from her eyes, to her nose, to her mouth.

And still he didn't enter her, and she felt so ready for him, so wet and wanting, she squirmed under him, shifting impatiently. "Now, Michael," she said, placing her hands on his back. "I want you inside now. Don't make me wait," she said in a near plea, hearing the catch in her voice as she begged.

He nodded, looking intent and serious, and put his condom on with one quick motion. Thank goodness one of them was sensible and remembered, because she certainly had been about to forget.

"Edwina," he said, sliding into her in one quick thrust. Oh. That. She felt stretched, wide open to him, feeling the throb of his cock inside her, how his body flattened hers, his chest hair tickling her skin, her hands on his strong back. Now moving down to his tight buttocks, pulling him in closer, even though it felt as though he was as far as he could go.

"Fuck me," she said, moving her hips softly.

His eyes blazed green, and he pushed up on his elbows, starting to thrust in and out, faster and harder than he had any of the previous times the night before. As though he knew she could take it, and what was more, that she wanted it this way. Hard, and fast, and rough.

"I love how it feels when my cock is inside you," he said in a ragged pant in her ear.

If she could speak, she'd tell him she loved it when he talked to her like that. There was something so primal about his language, spoken in his aristocratic accent, that turned her inside out, made her want to hear more of what he might be thinking spoken in that sex-roughened growl.

Just thinking about it made things swirl around inside, all focused on that one spot, the one that he was hitting regularly with his movements. It felt incredible, and the tension of it made her concentrate, made her grip her hold on his arse even harder, making her close her eyes and fling her head back, biting her lip.

"Dear God, Edwina, you're so tight," he said, pushing even harder. She didn't know until now that it was a good thing to be tight, but she was certainly glad she was, if it made him sound like that.

He kept thrusting, his breathing hard and labored. And then she felt it, the moment when it seemed as though she'd spiraled somewhere off into the stars, and she pulsed, and felt herself grip him, and then he groaned and shouted, collapsing on her as he climaxed.

He shook his head slowly, and his hair tickled her nose, since his face was buried in her shoulder. "You might be the death of me, woman," he said in a rough voice.

"I hope not," she said. "Then I would be out of a job and a lover. And that would be most disappointing." She kept her tone light, even though she wanted to tell him how she was feeling—that she had never felt like this before, that he was the most intelligent, intriguing, and handsome man she'd ever met. The fact that he was also the wealthiest and most titled didn't even enter into it, even though that meant that they could have no future together. Which was why she didn't speak in the first place. And so it did enter into it.

What would it be like if he were a regular— albeit still remarkably intelligent and impatient— person? Would they have a future?

She couldn't even dare to think about that, not when that was so far from what was possible.

He withdrew from her and she felt empty, missing him already. Even though he was right there, having pulled her into his arms and placing her head on his shoulder. She draped her arm over his chest and touched his skin, loving how the muscular ridges felt under her hand.

"How do you keep so fit, anyway?" she asked suddenly. Because she rather thought that most aristocrats tended to fat, but not him—he was lean all over, with all sorts of muscles where she hadn't expected them.

Another element of his appeal, although she was honest enough to admit it was a sensual element. She liked touching him, quite a lot. Would she like him as much if he were short and round? And still intelligent and arrogant?

She might not like her own answer. Thankfully, he wasn't either of those things, so she didn't have to wonder about it. The opposite problem of wondering what it would be like if he weren't a duke.

Thank goodness she'd evened out the impossible suppositions for the night, she thought ruefully.

"If I have been given a body to do work with, it just makes sense to keep the body as fit as possible." He was nothing if not practical. She should have figured that out for herself. "I ride, I box, I fence, I walk when it is a short enough journey not to bother taking out the horses."

"Ah, of course," she replied, running her fingers through the hair on his chest. "Of course you would be entirely logical about maintaining your body. I don't know why I even bothered asking, I should know you by now."

He raised her chin and kissed her softly on the mouth. "You do know me," he said in a low voice, and it seemed as though he was saying a lot more than just simply agreeing with her last statement. Her heart fluttered, and she had to clamp her lips together so she wouldn't burst out with what she was thinking—*I am fairly certain I am in love with you* wasn't what he would want to hear; she knew him well enough to know that. This was what it was, nothing more.

And nothing less.

So she just nodded, tightening her grip as she drifted off to sleep.

WHY DO DUKES FALL IN LOVE?

60. Because if they didn't, they would be very grouchy. And grouchy dukes are even more impossible than regular ones.

Chapter 19

"I have to go." Edwina's voice roused him from his dream, ones where he had somewhere to be and no way of getting there. It was an even worse iteration of the frustration he felt while he was awake, so he was grateful she woke him, but not grateful he couldn't continue to sleep with her.

He held her tighter, rolling her body up against his hip. "I don't want you to go," he murmured, finding her breast in the dark and caressing its fullness.

"It doesn't matter what you want, hard though you may find that to believe," she said in a cross tone. He released her immediately, feeling unexpectedly contrite that he was making it more difficult for her to leave. Because he knew she didn't want to as much as he didn't want her to, and yet her reputation was far more in jeopardy if anything untoward was noticed. So she should go, yes.

"You're right. I am sorry."

There was a silence, as though she was processing his words. "Did you just apologize?" she asked in an incredulous voice.

For some reason, that nettled him. Even though he knew her comment had basis in his behavior. "I can apologize."

She laughed and drew away from him. "Perhaps during the carriage ride tomorrow you can list all the times you've apologized. Maybe there will even be enough times so you don't finish before the horses move."

"Oh, now you're asking for it," he said, reaching for her and dragging her back onto the bed, her laughing as he did. He pinned her with his body, his legs on either side of her, sitting up and looking down into her face. It was just beginning to be dawn, so the light was faint, but he could still see her, see her bright eyes, and the hair she'd undone flowing all over his pillow.

He leaned forward as though to kiss her, but tickled her instead. "See what happens when you taunt me?" he said, easily leveraging his strength to keep her still. She was laughing, and begging, and flailing under him, and eventually he relented, moving his tickling fingers to her breasts, finding her nipples hard and peaked.

"I really have to go, Michael," she said in a low voice.

"I know you do." He caressed her one last time, then rolled off onto the edge of the bed, pushing her hip. "Get going, I've heard your employer is a dreadfully demanding man who needs you to be well rested."

She snorted as she picked up her clothing. "Do

you suppose I can just wear my dressing gown back? It seems silly to get all dressed just for a short walk down the hall."

He considered it, then got out of bed himself, reaching for his own dressing gown. "I'll keep watch for you. Better that than you enlist me as your lady's maid," he continued in mock horror.

"Thank you." She wrapped the dressing gown around herself, pulling her hair out from the collar to hang down her back. She looked rumpled, and delicious, and entirely sensual.

He really wished she didn't have to go. Just as much as he knew she did have to.

She gathered up her clothing, wrapping it up in a bundle and tucking it under her arm. "I'll see you in the common room in three hours," she said in a soft voice.

Three hours felt too long, but he knew enough than to argue with her.

He went to the door and opened it, poking his head out to scan the hallway. Nobody was there, and he gestured behind him for her to come through, watching as she scurried down the hall to her own room.

Only when he'd heard her door close and lock with a soft snick did he close his own door, getting back onto the suddenly too large–feeling bed.

Telling himself that it was actually smaller than his usual bed; he was probably just reacting to the difference.

Knowing he was lying to himself. Wondering what it would be like to have her in his own bed, his bed back at his town house.

* * *

"Good morning, Your Grace." Edwina settled herself in the seat opposite him, keeping her gaze on the table until she knew her face wouldn't reveal how she felt. What they had done. Anything that might indicate that their relationship was more than just a working one.

Of course there would be people who would chatter about the duke taking a female secretary anyway, and assume the worst. Or the best, from Edwina's viewpoint. But she had confidence he would be able to quell any talk with one raised eyebrow and a disdainful, dismissive comment.

She hoped so. She wouldn't be able to endure it if people were actually gossiping about them. Taking what they had and making it into something sordid.

"Morning, Cheltam." His tone was businesslike as well, and she felt a pang at knowing she wouldn't be able to hear his loverlike tones until that evening. And then? The trip would be over in a few days, and then they would be back in his mansion. With her daughter, and his staff, and all of London, likely, watching to see what the reclusive, difficult duke was going to do next.

So this might be it, the beginning and the end of it. She would not agree to leaving his employ to become his mistress, and it wouldn't be right to engage with him under the same roof as her daughter. Not to mention the servants, whose sharp eyes and ears were bound to be scrutinizing them.

Oh, it hurt.

"Are you quite all right, Cheltam?" he asked.

She started, feeling a rush of guilt as he spoke. He should absolutely not know how she felt about him.

"Fine, Your Grace. I—I did not sleep that much," she said, raising her eyes to his and allowing a small smile to cross her mouth.

He looked as though he wanted to laugh, but merely indulged in a raised eyebrow and a glint in his eye that made her shiver in a very interesting way.

"We are going where today?" he asked after a moment.

She picked up their itinerary. "The Right Way Railway."

"I should refuse to make an investment purely in protest of their asinine name," he declared in his normal high-handed voice. "But I am not so petty, so we will go see if theirs is, indeed, the Right Way." And then he did something even more surprising than kissing her in his library, or speaking to her so graphically when they were in bed, or even tickling her when she had made fun of him.

He winked at her.

And she nearly fell over onto the floor.

As though she weren't head over heels in love with him already—she had to admit that, because otherwise she wouldn't be being honest with herself—and then he had to go do something so—so different from his usual self, so *appealing*, as to wink.

She was sunk. She should just admit that now, that there would never be another man she loved quite like this one, all irascible, intelligent, and surprising male of him.

"What would you like this morning?" the innkeeper, the same one from the previous night, stood at their table, rubbing his hands together as he waited for their reply.

"Coffee for the lady, and I would like strong ale." He frowned, then looked at her. "Is there something else you'd like to eat?"

Now he was asking if she wanted something. As though he had suddenly developed a thoughtful streak that he was exercising only on her. She felt as though she was melting inside.

"Uh, yes. Bread and butter as well, please." She smiled as she spoke to the innkeeper, whose gaze darted back and forth between them, as though not entirely certain what their relationship was.

Edwina wished she could reassure him that she felt that way as well.

"Of course," the innkeeper said, beginning to turn away. "Oh, I forgot! A letter has arrived." He withdrew the letter, clearly written on high-quality paper, and handed it to the duke. He turned away as the duke read the address, and then held it out over the table to Edwina.

"This is for you," he said.

She took it, feeling a spark as their fingers touched. *Careful, Edwina*, she admonished herself. She slid her thumb under the fold of the envelope and undid it, shaking out two pieces of paper that had brightly colored writing on them.

And smiled as she recognized Gertrude's labored penmanship and enthusiastic doodling.

"She says she is doing just fine without me, that she has gone for ices twice already." Edwina lifted her head and looked at him in surprise. "Twice! This had to have been written a few days ago, does that mean she's gotten ices twice in one day already?" She shook her head. "My daughter certainly has a particular charm."

"No more charming than her mother," he said in a low voice meant only for her ears.

She felt those very same ears get hot as she turned pink. "Shh, you can't say those things in public."

"Hmph" was his only reply. "What else does she say?"

Edwina read the rest of the brief letter. "Just that she's the one taking Chester for walks now, even though William—that's the footman, in case you forgot—also goes, just to make sure she and Chester are safe."

"That dog is likely getting spoiled."

"Not more than my daughter is. It will be hard to get her to return to normal life after living at your house with your houseful of doting servants."

She heard him take a sharp breath. "Are you leaving my employ?" he asked in a terse tone.

"No, no, I have no plans to. I just assumed—"

"What? That I would have no need of a secretary? That I would suddenly be capable of managing all of the things that needed managing? You cannot leave." He spoke in his most autocratic voice, but it held a note of insecurity, which made her not quite as irritated as his words should have.

"At some point, Your Grace," she said deliberately, knowing it would annoy him for her to use his honorific when it was just them speaking, "you will be married. And it would not be appropriate for me to continue working for you when you have a wife."

The innkeeper returned with their drinks, setting them down on the wooden table. The duke waited until the man was well out of earshot, then leaned forward and spoke in a low, fierce tone. "You will not leave my employ until I allow it." He tapped the table. "I suppose I will marry at some point, but I have no plans to do so." Again, the contrast between his high-handed words and how much it seemed he wanted her made her both angry and pleased.

She was not doing a very good job of handling her feelings.

"When you do," she said again, knowing he had to understand, had to know what would happen, "I will leave your employ."

He leaned back, crossing his arms over his chest. "Fine."

Had she truly gotten him to agree to something?

"Because I have no plans to marry."

No, she hadn't. He was just reducing her words, her feelings, to semantics. It shouldn't hurt, that was how he dealt with things, but it did. It hurt that he would so summarily assume that this whatever they were doing could continue indefinitely, even though she knew it had to stop as soon as they returned home.

"When did you decide this?" Her words were sharp.

He shrugged, as though it wasn't important. She wanted to scream at him that it was, that this was her life, her future happiness, that he was toying with. He couldn't expect her to just—do what they were doing until he tired of her? Because she knew she would never tire of him. And she also knew he wouldn't even consider something so irresponsible as to marry her. It hurt, but it was the truth.

The innkeeper returned again, this time with her food, and laid it out on the table. "Is there anything else I can get for you?" he asked, glancing nervously at the duke.

"No."

Edwina resisted the urge to roll her eyes at his short tone, instead buttering her bread and taking a bite.

It was delicious; the bread was still warm and the butter melted just enough. It was a simple pleasure, the kind that would remain after the more complicated pleasures had become a distant memory. Like him, and their affair.

She sighed as she swallowed, wishing she could be content with the simple pleasures. Bread and butter, her daughter's smile, the times she felt as though she'd done good work for the day.

Although those were complicated also—her

daughter wouldn't be smiling if they were starving, and she wouldn't have done good work if she weren't employed.

She was doing a terrible job of cheering herself up, wasn't she?

"We should be on our way," she said, standing up before he could reply. He rose also, his expression still grim, as though he were thinking about how he might not get his way entirely.

Or perhaps that was just her interpretation of his expression. Maybe he had forgotten entirely, and was just anticipating having to deal with people who were less intelligent than he.

She had to remember who he was, and more importantly *what* he was, and that she was just another element of his complicated life. Nothing he would be concerned about, unless it seemed as though she was going to do something he didn't like. Such as leave his employ, or his bed, before he was prepared.

In the meantime, this was enjoyable, and she would just have to keep in mind that it was temporary enjoyment. And why shouldn't she have fun while she was in the midst of it?

Her words had unsettled him. The thought of her leaving, even though she had been with him for only a few weeks, made him want to shout and punch something.

Not at all the way he usually felt. About anybody. Not since his brother.

"Your Grace?"

She stood before him, holding her clutch of ubiquitous papers, her hair perfectly done up, her cloak buttoned tightly around her.

He much preferred her as she was in bed, her hair down, her glorious body uncovered where he could see it, touch it, slide against it.

"I am ready," he replied in a gruff voice. Damn it. He couldn't afford emotions. Not only were they not helpful, he didn't quite know what to do with them. He was comfortable with finding his dog a pleasant companion, but other than that?

"Excellent." She walked out of the inn, nodding at the innkeeper, who stood by the door.

"Thank you, Your Grace. I hope everything was suitable, Your Grace." The innkeeper spoke in that mixture of nervousness and obsequiousness that it seemed everyone adopted when talking to him.

Everyone, that is, except her. And her daughter.

Damn it.

"If you'll just step over here, Your Grace, you can see the area where we manufacture the smaller parts." The representative from the Right Way Railway was, thankfully, more cognizant of the workings of the factory than the man from the day before. But the factory itself was less tidy, and Michael sensed that the sloppiness extended to the company itself, even though he couldn't identify where.

Cheltam accompanied him on the tour, keeping herself a few steps behind him, in a properly secretarial way. Which annoyed him also.

Was this to be his life? To be annoyed at things that were entirely proper? Although that had happened long before he met her. It was just—now it felt like a slap, since he wanted to do things he'd never wanted before. In fact, he didn't think he'd ever wanted something so much. Damn it. This was getting far too complicated.

"Here is where we produce things such as the piston rod, the pistons, the brake shoes, and the coupling rods. Along with many of the other parts." The man was clearly enthusiastic about his work.

"Is this also where the eccentric crank is made?"

Michael glanced at her to find her looking at him, her eyes dancing with mischief.

"You know something about engines, Mrs. Cheltam?" The man sounded far more appreciative than Michael liked, and he stepped forward to place himself more directly in front of her before he realized what he was doing.

"Yes, I have picked up some knowledge in the course of working for the duke," she said, stepping out from behind him.

His arm almost—almost—reached out to keep her away, but he stopped himself just in time. It wasn't his place, even though it chafed at him to think that another man might find her as fascinating as he did.

"Yes, well, the eccentric crank is produced over there, along with some of the medium-sized parts." The man—if Michael were more interested in him he'd figure out what his name was—gestured to where a group of workers were laboring over a table, plumes of smoke whirling in the air above them while the steady drone of production was a constant hum in the background.

"Is the eccentric crank considered a medium-sized part, then?" The witch was definitely teasing him now, knowing he couldn't do anything to respond, not here in public.

But just wait until they were alone.

The man nodded. "Yes, it is. I'm interested in why you are so intrigued by this particular element of the engine?" he said, at which point Michael had to clamp his jaw shut not to yell at both of them. At least the Right Way Railway representative had no idea what he was saying.

But she did. The minx.

"I am not sure why I am so interested in the eccentric crank," she replied, darting another mischievous glance his way. "Maybe because of its eccentricism. Or the crankiness."

The man looked confused, as he should be, since she had just spouted nonsense.

"Oh, what I am saying? I just find all the parts fascinating." And then she lifted her eyebrow in his direction, as though to say, *I find all of you fascinating*, and goddamn if he didn't wish they were alone, and naked, and in bed.

He found himself stepping forward before he recalled where he was, actually, and that it would not be appropriate for him to throw her over his shoulder and take her somewhere to ravish her for her impudent words.

"I believe we have seen enough, thank you, Mr. . . ." he said, pausing because he still didn't know the man's name.

"Mr. Pierson, yes, thank you," she supplied, speaking so smoothly after his words it was barely noticeable he'd stumbled on the man's name.

"Thank you, Your Grace. Mrs. Cheltam." Mr. Pierson bowed to them in turn, bowing a bit lower for Cheltam, Michael noticed with a tinge of something in his chest. Jealousy? No, it couldn't be. He was never jealous.

They walked out to the carriage, Michael's long stride eating up the distance between the factory doors and where his footman waited at the door.

"Just you wait until we're safely inside, Cheltam," he said in a low growl. "I'll show you who's an eccentric crank."

"I cannot wait," she said in an equally low tone.

Which made him hasten his pace even more, so she was running to keep up with him.

Well, so this was what it felt like when one taunted a wild animal in its cage. If the animal was a tall, well-bred duke with a sharp temper. She had to admit she liked it. Even though she had no idea what to expect once they were alone in the carriage.

Although she had her suspicions, and she suspected they'd involve his mouth, his hands, and other parts of them in various iterations. Goodness, now that he'd shown her that the mouth could go elsewhere on the body, it opened up all sorts of possibilities.

She hoped she could discover more of them firsthand before this was all over.

The coachman held his hand out for her to assist her into the carriage, but the duke inserted himself so that it was his hand she took. As though he could not bear anyone else touching her.

The thought of that kind of possessiveness did, she had to admit, give her a certain kind of thrill.

She slid onto the seat, watching as he entered after her. She fluttered her hands on her lap, feeling nervous even though she had started this game. That, judging by the martial look in his eye, he had every intention of continuing.

"Eccentric crank, Cheltam?" His words were spoken in a suspiciously calm voice, and she licked her lips before replying.

"Yes, well, being in your employ has given me many new interests." She glanced over at him from underneath her lashes. Dear Lord, but he was handsome. And right now exuding a kind of sexual menace that shouldn't excite her, but absolutely did. Likely because she knew the man underneath the blunt, rough talk. The man who did unexpectedly kind things for her daughter, was egalitarian in his treatment of either gender, valued honesty and intelligence above any kind of sycophancy.

Was as blunt and rough in what he wanted in bed as he was out of it. She appreciated his consistency.

"Can you show me your . . . interest?" he said, leaning over to speak into her ear. Which made her shiver all over.

"If you can show me yours," she replied, sliding her hand onto his thigh. Not quite daring to go *there*, especially not in the carriage, but certainly willing to offer him the opportunity to move things to there, if that's what he wanted.

"Oh, I can show you," he said, twisting in his seat before wrapping her in his arms and kissing her senseless.

Or nearly senseless; she had enough sense to know that it was he who was kissing her, not some random man she'd accidentally stumbled into the carriage with; and she knew enough to realize that her hands were grabbing his shoulders to pull him closer, and she was leaning into the corner of the carriage, his body covering hers, his hands roaming over her body, seeming to want to find a spot of uncovered skin. He settled for placing his hands on her jaw, holding her still for his kiss while his tongue worked its magic. He really was a delightful kisser, not that she'd had much experience before.

Mr. Cheltam had contented himself with kissing her chastely on the mouth three times a year—on her birthday, their wedding anniversary, and Christmas. When he came to her bedroom to claim his husbandly rights, he didn't bother with kissing beyond a few halfhearted and messy passes of his mouth on hers. So perhaps the duke was a terrible kisser, but she had to doubt that, given how her whole body was reacting.

All too soon he drew back, his breath coming in short gasps, his eyes heavy-lidded and intense, his hands still gripping her, but his body not entirely on hers.

"How is that for an eccentric crank?" he asked at last, a sly grin stretching his mouth.

She found herself returning the smile. Who knew that this kind of activity could also be so humorous? "I can't imagine any other eccentric crank even comparing with that."

They smiled at each other, and she felt as though she were drowning in his eyes, forgetting entirely that they were in a carriage, that he was her employer, and almost what her own name was.

She shook her head after a few moments, lowering her gaze to the floor. "We should discuss our impressions. What did you think of the egregiously named Right Way Railway?"

He didn't speak for a moment, but his grip on her arm tightened. As though he didn't want to let this moment go.

I don't want that, either, she thought. But she couldn't tell him that, not without revealing how far she'd fallen in love with him. She, a widowed secretary with a daughter, only a few pounds away from penury, falling in love with a duke.

Every time she thought about it she got mournful. She should just not think about it any longer.

"I liked the gentleman's enthusiasm, even though I did not like his interest in you." He cleared his throat, as though embarrassed. "But I think some of the processes seemed overly complicated, and the factory was not as clean as the one we saw the day before."

"That was what I thought also. We should review the financials and keep that in mind as we make the next visits."

"Yes." He cleared his throat again, and now he slipped his hands down her arms to take her hands in his. "Thank you for—for all this. Coming on the trip, and being such a help, and . . ."

"And . . . ?" she prompted.

"You know what." It was odd, hearing him unable to say what he was thinking when he had been so bluntly, even crudely, honest in the most intimate situations. It also felt oddly touching, as though he were unable to find the words himself, words that weren't basic facts, that were more than statements of things. That were his feelings. Probably feelings he had never felt before, and wasn't quite sure what to do with.

"Yes," she said at last, and squeezed his hand. "Yes."

WHY DO DUKES FALL IN LOVE?

29. Love is the highest emotion, and dukes are the highest in every other place.

Chapter 20

They spent the rest of the short ride to that evening's inn in silence, still holding hands. It felt so comfortable. Yes, there were the remnants of the passion that had flared when they first got in the carriage, and she couldn't wait for the evening, but it also had the warmth of being settled. Of knowing who you were, and who he was, and how you worked together.

Even though what worked now could not always work.

They arrived at the inn, Edwina glancing out of the carriage window to see the innkeeper—fat where the one the night before was thin, a huge smile on his face—standing at the doorway, beckoning the carriage in.

"Until tonight," the duke said, drawing one of her hands up to his mouth to kiss.

She swallowed, unable to speak for a moment.

He descended first, then turned around to assist her out of the carriage.

She stepped down, glancing to the innkeeper,

who was waving a piece of paper at them. Another letter from Gertrude?

She walked forward eagerly, composing herself into her ducal secretary guise. "Is that correspondence for the Duke of Hadlow's party?" she asked. "I am his secretary, I can receive it."

The innkeeper frowned in confusion. "His . . . secretary?" Apparently the man hadn't realized a woman could be a secretary as well as a man could.

"Yes," Edwina replied in a terse tone of voice.

"If you say so," the man responded in a skeptical tone. His smile had dimmed, and Edwina found herself missing the anxious thin innkeeper from the previous night.

She soon forgot all about him, however, as soon as she read the letter.

Michael was just reaching the bar of the common area to ask for a drink when the door opened and Edwina burst in, her mouth open in a shocked O, her eyes wide and frightened.

"What is it?" he said, striding over to catch her in his arms. Although not enfold her entirely, he had to remember the boundaries between them. The necessary propriety of their relationship, even though he chafed at its constrictions.

"Look." She held a letter out to him, and he took it, scanning the lines quickly.

He raised his head and looked at her. "This says that your brother-in-law has taken Gertrude? But how? More importantly, why?"

She shook her head. "I don't know. I don't know the answer to any of those questions, just that I have to go back, I am sorry to have to leave you, but she is—"

"Do you really think I would let you go alone?" He was shaken, not just because of what had happened to Gertrude, but because she wouldn't just assume he would accompany her. What was he to her? Was he just an employer who happened to also be able to pleasure her in bed? What were they to each other?

Although this was not the time to be asking such questions.

"It is not your responsibility," she replied in a trembling voice. "She is under my care, and because I was here, I was not there to prevent—"

"You were doing your job," he interrupted. "Something I required, so if there is blame to be assigned, blame me." He folded his arms over his chest. "Although neither of us deserves any blame, it is that blackguard brother-in-law who is at fault." He took her arm and led her back outside. The coachman was already beginning to unhitch the horses, and Michael strode up to clamp his hand on the man's arm. "Change of plans. We are returning to London immediately."

"Yes, Your Grace." It said a lot—not all of it good—that his coachman didn't ask why, or even look confused by the sudden orders. Michael wasn't sure whether to be proud or ashamed his staff was so efficient.

"Inside," he said to Edwina, who was just standing in the courtyard, blinking away tears.

"The sooner we get home, the sooner we can retrieve Gertrude from the loathsome toad."

"Is that his name?" she asked, taking his hand and stepping up into the carriage.

Michael turned to one of the footmen who was standing nearby. "Have the second coach follow as soon as possible." The man nodded and dashed off, presumably to convey his orders. He leaped into the carriage, gathering Edwina into his embrace and drawing her head down into his chest. "It will be fine. There is nothing we can't handle."

She raised her head and looked at him, her dark eyes full of hurt. "That's why he did it, you know that. He wouldn't have bothered if it was just me, and we were still on our own. But now," she said, biting her lip as she spoke, "now he probably thinks you'll do something to help me get her back."

"And I will do anything to get her back. Is that wrong?" What was the point of being him if he couldn't use his power and wealth to get what he wanted?

Her breath came out in a short burst. "No, I don't want you to. That is, I do want you to, but I don't want him to have that kind of leverage. I'm not blaming you for it," which made his chest hurt less, because it had seemed as though she were holding him to blame, "but it just points out how our, how this"—she gesticulated between the two of them—"cannot continue."

Now he hurt even more. And he wanted to roar at her, to tell her that it absolutely could continue, they would retrieve Gertrude, and come to an understanding about what this was, and he would enjoy sexual relations with her at night while she worked with him during the day. He failed to see what her objection could be, beyond propriety. And they'd already dispensed with that over the past few days, and with some discretion, no one would be the wiser.

"Let's just get Gertrude back, and then we'll talk about everything," he said in what he hoped was a soothing voice. Since he didn't have any experience using one.

She paused, withdrawing from his arms. He felt suddenly bereft, and had to squelch the urge to tug her back. He did not have urges, usually, and he knew she would resist him anyway.

He hated how that made him feel. That it made him feel at all, actually. But he had to acknowledge that it appeared she'd unlocked a previously unknown treasure chest of feelings, all of which wanted to tumble out in a rush of emotion.

"I won't change my mind," she said in a low, firm voice. "But we can talk about it later, after Gertrude is back."

The trip back to London was so much worse than she could have imagined. Not just because she was worried about Gertrude, and just what her brother-in-law would demand for her return, but because this was it. Their affair was over, her heart was, if not broken, deeply bruised, and she would still have to deal with what she knew would be his stubbornness about accepting her decision.

She had hoped to have a few more days in his arms, in his bed, being able to glance across the table at him in the morning and think about what they had done the night before. Shared a few glances as they worked through his correspondence.

She didn't have any concern that things would be awkward—at least not for him—when he finally accepted the change. He valued her and her work, and he wouldn't let a minor thing like a romantic indiscretion interfere.

There was something to be said for being as remote as he was; there was no chance his heart was involved. Yes, there were other parts of him that would likely be upset about the change in their relationship, but he could find someone else for that outlet.

God, what if he set up a mistress? And she had to track the expenses, settle the rent, or see the bills that came in from jewelers and dressmakers?

You are getting ahead of yourself, Edwina. But still. It was a possibility she had to consider. He would no doubt say the same thing, if she were to ask him, because to him, planning and forethought were the only sensible things to do when considering a future situation.

"What are you thinking about?" His words interrupted her rising panic.

She couldn't answer honestly. Something he would likely be able to discern, which would perhaps make him want to end things with her, since he valued honesty above all things.

"I—nothing," she said, turning to look out the carriage window.

"We'll get her safe home again," he said in a nearly tender tone of voice. It almost made her cry, and rage against the injustice of it all—that she had found someone she loved, but she had to be the strong one and break it off—it just didn't seem fair.

But then again, life wasn't fair, was it? If it was fair, she wouldn't have been married to Mr. Cheltam, a man who only wanted her for her looks. She wouldn't have been left destitute at his not-very-mourned-by-her death. She wouldn't have the misfortune to have gained employment with an impossibly handsome, ridiculously intelligent gentleman who also spoke so—so *compellingly* in the bedroom.

Why couldn't she have found work with some older balding man with gas who needed assistance managing his various and sundry doctors' appointments? Or better yet, an imperious old lady who wanted assistance with her knitting?

But then she wouldn't have discovered how it felt to be with someone like him, even if it was just for such a short time. It was worth it, wasn't it? To know she could feel so intensely, could experience the heights of passion?

Could love someone like him. Could love *him*, in fact.

It was better than the alternative. So perhaps life was fair, but only in short bursts.

Meanwhile, she had to focus on figuring out what Robert wanted so she could retrieve Gertrude.

* * *

"We're here." His voice roused her from an uneasy sleep. She was leaning her head into the corner of the carriage, her neck bent oddly, her body twisted as though she were curled in around herself. She glanced at him and stretched her neck, feeling the pang of soreness.

The carriage slowed, and she leaned forward to look out the window, at the familiar sight of his house just ahead. The lights blazed, and she could see Hawkins on the step, his frown increasing as he saw them.

It hurt, but in a good way, to know that the duke's staff was affected by Gertrude's absence. That this had come, in just a few short weeks, to be their home, more homelike than Mr. Cheltam's house, even though Gertrude had been born there. She had been loved there, also, but here she was protected.

Even though the protection clearly wasn't enough.

The duke was out of the carriage before it came to a final stop, and turned to hold his hand out to her to help her down. He looked even more gorgeous with his unshaven stubble and unruly hair—as though he had just come from their bed, and been too engrossed in everything to maintain his appearance.

"Hawkins," he called over his shoulder, still holding Edwina's hand as she stepped onto the sidewalk, "please gather anybody with pertinent information and assemble in my office."

"Yes, Your Grace," Hawkins replied, relief in his tone. Edwina felt an easing of the tension she'd had since receiving the letter; he would make certain things were put back to rights, there was no other alternative that he would tolerate.

She swallowed as she entered the house, seeing Chester there waiting by the door. Waiting for Gertrude? His tail thumped on the floor when he saw them, and he let out a soft woof.

"Yes, boy, we'll get her back." The duke bent down to ruffle Chester's ears, then rose and strode into his office. "Come, Cheltam."

She followed, feeling like a tiny ship in his eddy, just another element in his massive, and massively important, life.

They would solve this, and then things would go back to the way they were before the kiss. When she was just Cheltam, and he was Hadlow, and he barked orders at her and she worked hard and there was no intimacy.

That was the way it had to be. Just as there was no question in her mind but that he would get Gertrude back, there was no question that whatever they'd shared was over. Forever. She couldn't afford it, in so many ways.

He didn't like how pale she looked. Even though he couldn't blame her; she'd told him, and he'd seen for himself, that her only concern was her daughter, so to find her gone must have been terrifying. That it was a reasonable reaction didn't make him feel better about it, however; not surprising, given that he was frequently unreasonable.

He had to control his fury at the situation, though. It wouldn't do anything but make him feel better, and that wasn't useful at this point. Even though making himself feel better was normally his objective in any situation.

He'd changed, he realized. He didn't first think of what was best for him, or what was most logical, or what would result in the least amount of tedious and unwanted emotion.

His first—and only—thought wasn't just about himself, and he was fairly certain he liked it.

Which was why it was unacceptable that she was planning on terminating their relationship.

But first things first. He had to help get her daughter back. That was the only logical course of action. Not to mention that he couldn't stand the thought of Gertrude being with the loathsome toad for a moment longer than necessary.

He waited in front of his desk as the various staff members filed in, Cheltam at his side. He heard her swallow, and had to resist the urge to put his fingers in the small of her back, a comforting caress that would be inappropriate and likely unwelcome at this time.

Mr. Hawkins stood in front of the crowd, looking nearly as implacable as usual. Nearly.

And then he cleared his throat.

"Where is Gertrude's governess?" Michael asked.

"Miss Clark," Cheltam murmured. "Her name is Miss Clark."

"I am here, Your Grace." The woman, who was

really little more than a girl, stepped forward, her hands knitted together in front of her. "I tried to keep him from taking her, but we were on a walk by ourselves, we were just stepping out to the park there, we wanted to get some flowers so Gertrude could paint them." She sounded agonized. Good.

"And he walked up to us as though he were waiting for us, and he took Gertrude's hand and said he was going to take her to see her cousins. I told him that we hadn't arranged that, and that we would visit at a mutually convenient time, and he—he told me, without Gertrude hearing, that he was taking her, no matter what I said, and I could tell you, Mrs. Cheltam, where she was."

"And that was when?" Michael asked.

"Three days ago. She's been gone three days," Miss Clark said, her voice faltering.

"Do not break down, Miss Clark, that is not what is required now." He tried to keep his tone from being sharp, but she flinched nonetheless. No doubt Cheltam would have something to say to him about that. He didn't bother looking at her to confirm it; he could tell by her sudden intake of breath.

Fine, he'd deal with that later.

"Of course not, Your Grace," Miss Clark said, her voice stronger. Good. That was what should happen.

"And you told Hawkins what had occurred, and he sent the letter. Has anything else happened? Have you heard from Mr. Cheltam since then?"

Miss Clark and Hawkins both shook their heads.

"He must have known Mrs. Cheltam was away from home." *Home.* It *was* her home, and Gertrude's, and it didn't feel right to be here, not without the little girl wandering about, asking questions and petting Chester and turning his staff from mere servants to caring, attentive people.

"It seems so, Your Grace." Hawkins looked shaken also. No doubt he felt responsible, not having insisted the footman—William?—accompany the governess and her charge on their visit to the park. Although it was hard to see what William could have done without upsetting Gertrude.

"Well. I will pay a visit to Mr. Cheltam and retrieve the girl." The sound of exhaled breaths echoed through the room. As though they were relieved. "You didn't think I would bother?" He couldn't help the irritated voice he spoke in. That they thought he would just allow someone who worked for him, never mind what relationship they might have had, suffer needlessly, when he could solve it—well, apparently they thought he was as self-absorbed as she seemed to have thought when she first arrived.

"Of course they know you would." Cheltam, of course, speaking in a soothing tone. When she should be the one most emotional, most agitated at this time. She was trying to soothe him. "It is merely that the staff—and I believe I speak for them, please do tell me if I am wrong, Mr. Hawkins—that the staff knows that if you say something will be taken care of, then it will be. It is as simple as that."

The various staff members around the room nodded their heads in agreement. Perhaps it wasn't an indictment of his callousness, then, but merely a tribute to his efficiency. He didn't feel quite as badly as he had a few moments ago, but then he would have to examine why he leaped to that conclusion.

Because he felt something was lacking in himself? Because he might have hesitated to do just what was so obviously required, because it also required effort?

He would examine it later. After Gertrude was safe. For now, he had a girl to reunite with her mother.

WHY DO DUKES FALL IN LOVE?

63. They have their reasons. Do not ask silly questions.

Chapter 21

"It is just a few streets away." Edwina sat beside him in the carriage, unable to stop twisting her hands together in her lap. He'd tried to take her hand when they first set out, but she'd just withdrawn it, shaking her head.

She wouldn't call what he was doing now sulking, precisely, but he had moved over into the far corner of the carriage, wedging his shoulders in and keeping himself away from her. If she had been less anxious, she would have laughed—only inside her head—at how much like Gertrude he was acting.

But he was here. And she didn't doubt but that he would get her daughter back, even though it chafed at her to know that Robert was going to get what he wanted—money, probably, and perhaps the promise of that investment. *I will do anything to get her back.* Michael had said that, and he didn't say anything he didn't intend to follow through on.

"Let me do the talking when we get there." He was using his duke-issuing-orders voice, only now it didn't irk her because she trusted that what he ordered would get done. And she'd seen another side of him, a softer side, even though that side was forever lost to her.

Her heart squeezed inside her chest, and she couldn't help but reach up and touch the painful part, right where it hurt.

"Are you all right?" He continued speaking before she had a chance to answer. "Of course you're not all right, that's a ridiculous question." He exhaled sharply. "What I meant to say is, how are you?"

She felt her heart turn over, the traitorous organ, at his words. Words she doubted he'd asked anyone before, given how little it seemed he cared for anybody else. She didn't think he had ever asked Chester how he was, and that was perhaps the closest thing he had to a friend.

That was sad, wasn't it? That in all the time she'd worked for him, he hadn't had a friend to dine, or done more than present himself in the House of Lords and then grouse about it afterward. He had no personal letters; she saw all his correspondence.

"You need a friend," she blurted out before she realized she'd spoken.

"A—never mind, it seems we're here," he replied, sounding relieved as the carriage drew to a stop.

He vaulted out, as was his custom, holding his hand out to her to descend. She took it because her knees were so shaky she wasn't sure she could remain standing on her own. But as soon as her feet hit the pavement, she snatched her hand away, wishing his touch didn't have the effect on her it did.

And while she was at it, perhaps she could wish she found him less handsome and rather stupid.

Rolling her eyes at her own inanity, she took a deep breath and walked up the stairs to Robert's house. Before, when she'd been married to his brother, she'd been impressed by the grandness of his abode, but it looked like a rundown shack compared to where she lived now.

No wonder Robert acted as he had after seeing where she was. And had seen how the duke had treated her in their brief conversation. Not that she excused him; it was a terrible thing to remove a child from a place where she was happy and cared for just to gouge funds out of someone. But having that envy of another's position, she knew the Cheltam brothers shared that. George certainly had had it, always wishing he could best another in business. Which was why he got himself a lovely wife, even though he and his lovely wife had nothing in common. Not even the commonality of valuing her loveliness.

It felt like a curse, usually. Unless—and there he was, at her side, looking down at her in the way that made her catch her breath, as though he was actually worried about her. Worried. About her. The Duke of Hadlow.

He rapped sharply on the door, grimacing as he shoved the hand that he'd been holding near hers behind his back. He could learn, then. Maybe this wouldn't be so hard.

"Hello?"

A suspicious-looking woman opened the door just enough to peer through. Edwina could see the woman had a dirty mobcap on her head, and her gown was spotted with grease. It seemed Robert had come down in the world; the last time she'd visited, before George died, a stuffy butler had greeted them, immaculate in his appearance and haughty demeanor. And if this was how the household was being run, where was Robert's wife?

"Mr. Cheltam is in." It wasn't a question, and he accompanied his words with a push of the door, forcing the woman to step back into the hallway.

"Here, you can't just be pushing your way in here, not without a proper introduction." Not only was the woman disheveled, she sounded as though she'd been drinking.

This was where Gertrude was? Edwina's throat tightened at the thought.

"I can, and I will. Mr. Cheltam!" the duke called, his commanding voice ringing through the empty hallway.

One of the doors opened, and Robert stepped out, his face a mixture of fear and bravado. "You're here about the girl." His gaze darted between them, and he appeared to swell up, the bravado winning out over the fear.

"Where is she?"

Robert waved his hand dismissively. "First we need to talk." He stepped into the hallway and beckoned to the room from which he'd just emerged. "In here."

The duke didn't answer, just strode down the hall as quickly as Edwina had ever seen him move.

She followed, glancing up the staircase in hopes she'd see Gertrude somewhere. Was she safe? Was she even here? Who was taking care of her?

Robert shut the door when all three of them were inside. They were in his office, which was nearly as disheveled as the woman who'd answered the door. Papers were scattered on every surface, some having fluttered to the floor, and there were blank spaces on the bookshelves, a layer of dust showing neither the books nor the shelves had been touched in some time.

"Please sit." Robert went to his side of the desk and sat without waiting for them to follow. The duke shook his head, as though sorry for Robert, and Edwina felt a twinge of fearful anticipation—was he going to kill him? Or just hurt him very badly? He was a duke, after all; he could get away with things other people could not.

"We won't be sitting. We will, however, be retrieving Mrs. Cheltam's daughter. What do you want?"

Robert blinked, as though surprised by the duke's directness. "I thought we could discuss that."

"We are discussing it. Tell me. Now."

Robert blinked again, as if trying to figure out what to say that would be to his advantage. Edwina wished she could tell him there was nothing he could say that would possibly make this better for him. And she better understood the duke's impatience with slower people, given how agitated she was for this all to be over.

"I am not certain Gertrude should be in your household." Robert spoke in a belligerent tone.

Edwina resisted the urge to close her eyes at what the duke's reaction would be.

"And why not?" His tone was deceptively soft.

Robert gestured between them. "It is clear that there are—are loose morals being displayed, and I owe it to my late brother to ensure Gertrude is raised in a good, Christian home."

Edwina nearly snorted. If the woman who answered the door was any indication, Robert was definitely not keeping a good home. She couldn't speak to the Christian element.

Never mind that it didn't seem that any of Robert's family was here any longer. The house felt still, as though it just housed Robert and the woman who'd answered the door. Where had they all gone?

But that didn't concern her nearly as much as where Gertrude was.

"I want to see her," she blurted. "I want to see how she is doing."

"As her guardian," Robert replied, his tone unctuous, "I believe I can accommodate that. But I will have to have your assurances you will not attempt to steal her away, not without—"

"Not without coming to some financial agreement," the duke interrupted in an impatient voice. "Yes, yes, we understand. What do you want?"

Robert consulted some of the papers on his desk. Had he already compiled a sheet of Things I Must Get from the Duke of Hadlow Before Returning My Niece? Edwina stifled a hysterical laugh at the thought.

"As you know, I am acquiring investors in the

Tea-rific Enterprise," and then Edwina did laugh; the name was as foolish as the idea behind it, "and when it is known the Duke of Hadlow is an investor, then—why, then it would be suitable for my niece to return to your home."

"You mean," Edwina said, hearing the words grind out of her mouth, "you will keep Gertrude in your possession until the duke has let enough people know he's invested in your ridiculous company?" Her voice rose continually as she spoke, so her final words were said in a shrill tone.

Then he did take her hand, as though to reassure her.

"Not acceptable. The girl comes with us today, and you can have my word as a gentleman that I will publicly support your venture, as well as invest—say a thousand pounds?—into the enterprise."

Robert pretended to consider it, then nodded his head. "Agreed. As a gentleman, I accept your promise." And then he looked at Edwina, and she felt the force of all of his jealousy, his dislike of her evident on his face, "but keep in mind that I am Gertrude's legal guardian, so if there is ever a question about where she is living, I will remove her."

Edwina's throat thickened at the obvious threat. She never thought he'd actually exercise his legal right to Gertrude. And even though they had both been left in charge, it could take years before the courts ruled on the matter. Years where Robert could retain custody.

"That will not be necessary."

She wanted to tell the duke to just shut up, don't

feed Robert's animosity any more than it was, but she couldn't speak, especially not to say something so familiar to her employer—Robert would seize on that as proof of their relationship, and would come demanding more soon. Or sooner than she thought he might otherwise. That this blackmail would continue until she was out from under the duke's roof, she had no doubt.

So not only did she have to sever her relationship with him, she had to leave his employ. Or he would have to continue to spend money on her behalf that would reveal just how close they'd become. Which would negate his spending money in the first place, since if it became known just what he'd done, everyone would speculate as to the nature of their relationship.

Michael was proud of himself he hadn't just walked in and beaten the loathsome toad. He'd been sorely tempted, especially when he was treating Gertrude as something to be bargained with, as if she weren't a person, likely a scared, small person who needed protecting from her purported guardian.

So it cost a thousand pounds. And he had no illusions that the toad would not return with more threats in the future. But what was money compared to human life? Compared to the look on Edwina's face when she saw her daughter?

Compared to how he felt when he thought about what it would be like to be taken away from someone you loved?

"Mama!" Gertrude cried as she spotted Edwina at the foot of the stairs. Michael waited behind, keeping himself between the toad and the ladies, just in case the man had second thoughts. He would have no hesitation then about beating him.

"My girl," Edwina said in what sounded like a strangled sob, pulling Gertrude into her arms and holding her tight.

Michael felt his throat tighten. He hoped he wasn't getting ill.

"We should leave," he said after a few moments.

"Yes, of course." Edwina rose from where she'd been kneeling, hugging Gertrude, a grateful look on her face as she regarded him. "Thank you," she said in a low murmur.

He shrugged. It was only money, and he had plenty of it. What he had in short supply was an efficient secretary and her lively daughter.

"Is there anything you need to bring with you?" Edwina asked Gertrude, who was already shaking her head.

"I just want to go home and see Chester," the girl replied. She narrowed her gaze at her uncle, and Michael wanted to crow about the obvious disdain evident in her expression. "You said you had a dog here, and you did not. You are a liar, Uncle Robert," she said, each word a scathing indictment of her uncle's lack of canine inhabitants.

Michael had never liked the girl more.

It was hours later, and Gertrude had been hugged by nearly every member of his staff, it seemed, and then she'd been put to bed, a still joyful Chester climbing up beside her. Edwina had tried to shoo him off, but Michael had stayed her hand.

"Let him be. He's missed her, too, you know." His fingers were on her wrist, right on her pulse, and she was looking up at him, her eyes wide and dark in the shadowy room, one candle flickering in a sconce against the wall.

She bit her lip, and glanced back at her daughter, whose eyes were closed, but her hands were still petting Chester. And then she nodded, and Michael saw the bright sparkle of tears in her eyes, and he felt his throat get tight.

"Let's go get you something to drink," he said in a low voice, still keeping hold of her wrist, hoping she wouldn't notice for another minute or so, another minute when he could touch her.

She nodded again, and withdrew her hand, preceding him through the door. One of the footman—not the William one, but another one— was seated on a chair in the hallway, standing up suddenly when he saw them.

"Thank you for staying here," Edwina said to the footman. She glanced up at Michael. "It is foolish, I know nothing can happen, but just—"

"Just for a few days until you both feel more comfortable." It *was* foolish, there was no way anybody would get to Gertrude here on the third floor, past the impenetrable mass of his staff, but if it made her less anxious, he'd do it. Hell, he'd hire a group of mercenaries if it would ease her mind.

What had happened to the remarkably logical

man he'd been? The first hasty decision he hadn't regretted—hiring her, having her and Gertrude come to live here—and all of a sudden he was tossing logic to the winds. Doing things because they would make someone else happy.

He was definitely different now. He was very afraid he might like it.

"Sit," he ordered, gesturing to the sofa in his study. The one where they'd kissed, it seemed so long ago, but it couldn't be that long.

She looked as though she wanted to rebuke him for his tone, but settled on a sly smirk instead.

He poured two healthy servings of brandy and walked to her, giving her the glass, holding his up to his nose to savor the aroma.

It didn't smell as good as she did when they were entangled together in bed.

He wished they were in bed right now.

"Your brother-in-law is not going to stop, you know." He sat down on the sofa next to her, the weight of his body on the seat making her shift toward him.

Yes. Come closer.

She looked down, at her glass, as though it was the most important thing in the room. *I am*, he wanted to shout, but then again, she knew that already. Was acutely aware of it, likely, which was why she wasn't meeting his gaze.

"I know that," she replied in a low voice. "I will pay you back, somehow, I just don't—"

"Marry me."

WHY DO DUKES FALL IN LOVE?

~~~***~~~

12. They have done everything else.

Chapter 22

"Pardon?" He couldn't have said, "Marry me." Maybe he said, "Carry me"? Although why would he need carrying? And how would he possibly think she could carry him anyway?

Maybe it was "very wee," only there wasn't anything all that small, and what was he doing talking about the size of anything anyway?

"Marry me."

Oh. He had said that. She took too large a sip from her glass, the brandy burning down her throat the way his words—

"Did you just say that?" she asked, when she was done sputtering.

He looked amused, damn him. As though marriage proposals and possible choking on strong beverages were something to chuckle about. *Oh, ha, ha, I've just asked the most unsuitable woman in the world to marry me, and then she expired because she was so startled she inhaled far too many spirits.*

"I did." He stretched one arm out across the sofa, his fingers coming to rest on her shoulder.

"Surely you cannot have failed to notice our mutual attraction."

He said the words as though that was all that was needed for a successful marriage. Not that she knew, she didn't even have the bare minimum of attraction in her one, and thus far only, marriage.

"There is a world of difference between—between what we were doing"—*and what we won't be doing any longer*—"and marriage. That is a permanent commitment," she said, her voice rising in outrage.

"I know what it is. I have successfully avoided it for thirty-four years." He spoke in a bored drawl, one that set her teeth on edge and made her want to fling something at his head. Not the brandy, she needed that.

She took another sip. This time, it didn't burn as much going down, instead settling a warmth into her stomach. "And why am I the one you should now marry?"

He looked at her for a moment, one eyebrow raised. She felt herself blushing.

"Not just because of that," she muttered.

"And why not?" He stroked her neck with his fingers, and she trembled. "We get along very well in bed, we get along tolerably well outside of it, and I imagine we will continue to do both things until we die."

Even George, when he'd proposed, had spoken of love.

Although George had lied. At least Michael—and she had to think of him as Michael now, now that they had done those things and now he was saying this thing—would never lie to her. Which was why he wasn't speaking of love, not at all, but of sexual congress and tolerable consanguinity. Maybe if she was lucky he would tell her that his house was very large so they needn't see each other *every* day.

"You cannot marry me."

This time, his raised eyebrow looked less amused. "And why not? I am the Duke of Hadlow, after all."

As though that would squelch the gossip, the chatter, the bloodlines, the family heritage, knowing how to be a duchess, how other children would treat Gertrude, and how she would always feel—always know—he had married beneath him. And he would know it, too.

"I am your secretary, Your Grace," and at that he frowned, his eyes narrowing. He looked fierce and mean, but she knew she had nothing to fear from him. Except for his anger, which would pass when he realized she was right.

If he realized she was right. The number of times he had been wrong about something was— well, she didn't know, but she suspected the number hovered around zero. There was always a first time, she thought, knowing she was on the verge of hysteria. Because she did love him, damn it, but he didn't love her, and she was not going to succumb to his offer, and suffer all the consequences, if it wasn't worth it. If his love wasn't the thing keeping her going when people were whispering about her and them, and making her feel uncomfortable.

"And as your secretary," she continued, willing her voice to stay steady, "it is my responsibility to advise you as to when you might be taking a misstep. Attending the wrong party, or investing in the wrong company, or—or marrying the wrong woman."

He withdrew his hand from the sofa and placed it on his knee. He downed his drink in one swallow, not choking at all, she noticed with envy. "Please do explain how you are the wrong woman."

Now he sounded offended. As though she had accused him of being wrong. Which she had done—he was likely more offended by that than by her not immediately saying yes to his inane proposal. Another reason she absolutely could not do this thing, even though she wished she could. She really did.

"I am the wrong woman, Your Grace," and this time she said it just so he would remember just who he was, and what responsibilities he had, "because I am not of your class. I don't know the first thing about moving in your world, being a duchess, nor do I care to. You know nothing of my family, and it is my belief that attraction and tolerating one another is not a good enough reason for people to marry." She paused. "Unless they are of the same class, and they both understand what they are getting into."

"So you're saying no?" She wanted to laugh at how astonished he sounded.

"I am. As your secretary," she said, wishing her damn heart wasn't almost audibly breaking, "I am saying that if you find yourself wishing for a wife, you should go find one among your own type of people. Someone that nobody would think twice about you marrying. Someone who knows all about how to run a vast household, who will be the appropriate mother for your children"—and then she nearly broke in front of him, thinking about what it would be like to bear his children, smart little things that would always get their way, and always be right—"whom you will also be able to tolerate. It shouldn't be that difficult, it is just that you likely haven't applied yourself."

His lips clamped together into a tight line, and she felt as though she were hanging on a wire suspended between them—if he said just one word about love, just one, she would submit and they could be together the rest of their lives. And her heart wouldn't break, and Gertrude would be secure, and she could explore his body and mind forever.

"Fine," he said at last. No talk of love. Nothing but acceptance. Did that mean he thought she was right? There was always a first time, after all.

"Fine," she repeated, placing her now empty—when did that happen?—glass onto the table beside her and standing on shaky legs.

She walked out without another word, unable to speak because she was concentrating so much on not falling to the floor in frustration. In heartbreak. In devastation at what could never be, and yet what could have been if she had just been willing to tolerate another unsatisfying marriage.

* * *

She'd said no. She'd said no. Michael paced in his room, his bedcovers turned invitingly down, him being appropriately garbed in his nightclothes, and yet he had no desire to sleep.

Because she'd said no.

When he'd thought of it, it had seemed like the perfect solution—he liked being with her, he definitely liked being in bed with her, and it would ensure her loathsome toad brother-in-law wouldn't ever be able to bother her again.

Perfect.

Except she'd said no.

Fine.

Now that he'd thought about marriage, it seemed . . . appealing. The idea of someone being his partner, of being the one to maneuver her way through the social niceties he didn't want to bother with, was something he had to consider.

So if it wasn't to be she, he would have to find someone else. Someone of his own class, as she'd suggested—she was an excellent secretary, after all—who was comfortable in his world, who was reasonably attractive, who didn't make him want to scream with her stupidity. It couldn't be that hard, could it?

Settled on that course, Michael climbed into bed, wishing he didn't feel so lonely—now that he knew what he'd been feeling all this time—wishing she hadn't thrown his own logic back in his face.

Fine. He'd go out, and he'd find himself a wife, someone who wouldn't say no.

Someone who wouldn't be her.

"Good morning, Gertrude." Edwina sat on the edge of her daughter's bed, unable to keep herself from touching her, the shape of her leg under the covers, a flung-out arm over her head. Anything to reassure her that her daughter was here, and was safe.

For now.

Gertrude opened her eyes, blinking dazedly. "Morning," she mumbled. Her daughter took a long time to wake up, just like her mother. Unlike her mother, however, she didn't have to be alert for anything her employer might throw at her.

Such as a marriage proposal.

She couldn't think about that, not now. Not when she'd spent most of the night thinking about just that thing, about how he'd looked, and what he'd said. And not said. Nothing about love, or caring, or being a family.

"What do you want to wear today? I'll help you dress." The weeks they'd been here, Edwina had let one of the maids come in to help Gertrude, since she was usually already working with the duke, and Gertrude was thrilled to have new people to talk to, but today she wanted to be the one to assist her daughter.

It might be just them soon enough anyway.

Because if he did find a wife, she would have

to leave. She couldn't bear to stay here, not with him spending his nights with another woman, not with her knowing what he looked like naked. What he looked like when he—well, then.

"I want the white one." Gertrude shifted to her side and pointed at the wardrobe where her gowns were kept. "Do I have to have lessons with Miss Clark today?" she said, her words already sulky.

Edwina smoothed her daughter's hair. "Yes, you haven't had lessons in a few days, you don't want to fall behind."

"Fine," Gertrude replied, and Edwina's heart hurt. *Fine.* Just what he'd said last night. Fine. Even though things were anything but, but at least she and Gertrude were together, and she would stay and work for him, saving her salary until she had to leave.

When he brought home someone else. Someone appropriate, and of good family, and most importantly, not her.

She blinked away the sudden tears, not wanting her daughter to notice and ask questions, questions she wouldn't be able to answer.

Why are you crying, Mama?

Because I acted improperly with my employer, and now I am suffering the consequences, and my heart is broken.

"Hop on out of bed, and let's get you dressed." Edwina swiped her fingers under her eyes to make sure there was no moisture there. This was going to be far more difficult than she'd imagined.

She'd have to go see Carolyn at the agency soon—she owed her a visit anyway, and she'd have to ask Carolyn to help find her another position.

Because things most definitely were not fine.

"Good morning, Cheltam." He sounded as he did every morning.

"Good morning, Hadlow." She stepped into the office, taking a deep breath as she walked toward him.

He was standing in front of his desk, his hands folded behind his back, his expression neutral. As though he hadn't proposed the night before.

As though it all hadn't mattered to him.

She lifted her chin as she sat. Well, if it didn't matter to him, she couldn't allow herself to show that it mattered to her. Even though of course it did. "What are we working on today?"

He frowned, then his features settled back into his usual expression. "The railway investments."

"Even though we haven't seen all the factories?" *Because we had to race home because I put my daughter in jeopardy by falling in love with you?*

He shrugged. "The factory tours aren't necessary to the decision." He looked at her, his gaze sharpening. "There were other factors in us going to visit them."

Oh. He'd wanted to get her alone—or relatively alone—and that was the best way to go about it. But now that it was all over, they could proceed as they would have normally, if she were a regular secretary and he were just her employer.

"Excellent." She reached forward to retrieve the stack of ever-present papers on the edge of his desk. *Her* edge. "So have you made your decision?"

Out of the corner of her eye she saw his hand draw up into a fist, then unclench slowly. "I think perhaps I have. The Powers and Smith Corporation, with smaller investments in the Better Engines Company and the Right Way Railway. Terrible name," he muttered, as though he couldn't help himself.

"Excellent."

His hand—now back into a fist—slammed onto the desk, making her jump. "Stop saying, 'Excellent.' "

"Of course." She kept her tone demure, her eyes lowered at the papers in her lap. No need to antagonize him, even though the earlier Edwina—the one prior to having her heart broken—wanted to smirk and say, *Excellent.*

"And review the invitations that arrived while we were away," he said, his tone stiff. "I wish to attend some events, but I don't want to be bothered with deciding which are best."

"Of course," she said again, and again, she saw his hand clench. She felt a fierce pride that she had been able to affect him at least a little bit. Was he now going to tell her not to say, "Of course"? What words would he leave her with, then?

Not yes. She'd already refused to say yes the night before.

And then what he'd said hit her like a punch to the heart. As though someone had hit her, just there.

He wanted to attend some events. Events where he would meet eligible ladies, women who weren't widows with canine-crazy children, who knew what to do when meeting the Queen, who had the right bloodlines and would likely accede to all of his requests.

Who would bore him utterly.

She rose and walked to the other side of his desk, the one where Hawkins had placed the various invitations that she and the duke both usually ignored. Because he was too busy, and what was more, he did not want to spend any time being with people who were only interested in parties, and gossip, and wanted nothing to do with eccentric cranks, either railroad or ducal.

"Do you have a preference for the type of event you attend?" Her voice sounded strained. Well, of course it would be; she was basically sending him off to another woman. To be chosen, by another woman.

"No. Just pick. No more than two a week, and only the ones where—" And then he stopped, and Edwina supplied the rest of the words for him.

"Where you will have the most chance of meeting eligible young ladies."

The silence hung between them. She bit her lip, turning her head to look in the corner of the room so that if she started to cry—damn it, when she started to cry—he wouldn't see it.

"Yes," he said at last. "Of course."

WHY DO DUKES FALL IN LOVE?

16. Because falling in hate is not ducal.

Chapter 23

Michael refrained from rolling his eyes as the butler stepped forward. "His Grace, the Duke of Hadlow," the man announced in a suitably respectful tone.

Michael walked past him, descending the stairs as he heard the murmur of more than a hundred of his reputed peers and their ladies begin. He shouldn't be annoyed; it wasn't as though he made a habit of attending such functions. It was natural that his arrival would cause nearly as much interest as if the Queen were to attend something.

He shouldn't be annoyed, but he was.

"Your Grace." His host, he presumed, stepped forward from the buzzing crowd and held his hand out. "I am so delighted you chose to attend our little party." Yes, his host. The Earl of Nibley, whom Michael had spoken with perhaps a year or so ago about implementing some law or another. The earl had wilted under the force of Michael's logic, which had made things easier, but had left

Michael with not a very good opinion of the man's strength of mind.

But what else was new?

Michael took the earl's hand, squeezing it perhaps a little too hard, judging by the man's wince. Was it his fault the earl's handshake was as weak as his opinions?

"May I introduce my wife, the countess?" The earl beckoned a woman forward, a woman whose sycophantic expression made Michael's skin crawl.

He really was not in a good frame of mind to be doing this, but he wasn't sure he ever would be. And now that he'd decided to take a wife, he had to just get on with it.

"Good evening, Your Grace." The countess's expression was even more beatific after she'd spoken. "Allow me to present my daughters." She made a quick gesture, and two women—girls, really—stepped forward, both of them clothed in startlingly white gowns, the only distinction between the two being that one looked terrified, while the other looked vaguely amused.

"Lady Elizabeth Nibley and Lady Lucinda Nibley."

"It is a pleasure to meet you," Michael said, taking each of their hands in turn. The terrified one turned an unattractive shade of red, and if he had been anyone other than himself, he would have felt sympathy toward her, given how obviously awkward she was at the introduction.

"My oldest"—and the countess gestured to the red daughter—"is betrothed to the Viscount Langley's son."

Ah. So she was off the table, marriage-wise. Not

a problem, since he did not want to be married to someone who was in danger of bursting into flames if he looked at her. Much less touched her.

Not that he wanted to do that, either.

"Could I persuade Lady Lucinda to grant me the honor of a dance?" He might as well begin this whole unpleasant process, and at least this girl didn't seem to need a glass of water just because he'd looked at her.

"Certainly, Your Grace." The girl's voice was low, and he found himself nearly bending over to hear her. Not good, either. He would develop a crick in his neck if he married her.

And why was he so quick to decide?

Oh, because he always made the right decision, and never had cause to doubt himself. Like when he had decided to focus on growing his family's wealth rather than just letting it be, or when he had helped to change the work laws for poor families in various factories.

Or when he had hired Cheltam as his secretary.

Before he could continue to pursue that line of thinking—thank God—Lady Lucinda's hand was in his, and he was guiding her onto the floor. It felt as though everyone was watching them, holding their respective aristocratic breath as the music started.

They danced in silence, Michael counting off the steps as he usually did. The music was tolerable, but he'd never felt as though he were immersed in it, so when he danced, he spent far more time ensuring he performed the steps adequately rather than just enjoying himself.

Although immersing oneself in music didn't seem as though it were something he would ever be prone to. The only time he'd felt immersed, the only time he'd ever felt as though he were more than the sum of his brain was—

He couldn't think about that. He would not. He shut the door firmly on that part of his mind, instead returning his focus to Lady Lucinda.

"The party is well attended." He glanced over the woman's head at the other guests. They all looked generally the same—well-to-do people dressed in their best finery chattering and drinking and ensuring they were posing in the most attractive positions they could muster.

Boring.

"Yes, it is." She bit her lip, like she—

Not thinking about her or any of that now.

"Do you like parties, Your Grace?"

That was an asinine question. Because he never attended parties, in general, so one would presume he didn't like them. But he could not answer honestly, despite his first impulse to do so, because this party was being hosted by her father, and he did not want her reporting back to her parents that the Duke of Hadlow did not like the entertainment and then the word would spread and there would be talk.

He hated having the weight of the world's approbation on his shoulders.

Why couldn't they want his opinion on something that actually mattered to him? Like innovations in industry, or the best way to ensure that everyone who resided in England was properly fed and taken care of?

It wasn't logical.

But meanwhile, he hadn't answered the question. "Certainly I do, when I am in a humor for it."

That was relatively close to the truth. He had never yet been in the humor for a party, so it wasn't precisely a lie.

"The music is pleasant, is it not?"

How could he answer that? If he lied, and said it was pleasant, he would be lying. It wasn't unpleasant, but he wasn't enjoying it. If he told the truth, they were returning to that problem where he was inadvertently insulting her family because of his opinion.

He expelled a breath, wishing it were as easy as breathing to be himself.

"It is." And now he was lying, and he hated lying.

"Have you been enjoying the temperate weather, Your Grace?"

Was she going to ask him questions for the entire duration of the dance? It wasn't difficult for him to maintain one part of his brain with counting the steps of the dance and the other one for inane questions, but he would prefer not to.

"It has been temperate," he replied. He had no idea if it had been or not, he seldom paid attention to the weather, but at least he wasn't strictly lying.

If he were to marry—an idea that was rapidly losing favor in the court of his mind—would this be his everyday interaction with his wife?

Did you enjoy the lovemaking, Your Grace?

Again, not something he would likely be able to answer honestly.

The music sounded as though it were winding

to a close, and he felt an emotion he wasn't sure he could name—not surprising, given how few emotions he usually had—sweep over him. Relief that the dance was ending?

"Thank you, Your Grace." Lady Lucinda curtseyed, her expression seeming to mirror his feeling— relief at being finished with dancing with him?

And then he was piqued, but he could not allow his irkedness to color his actions.

"It was my pleasure." And then he shut his eyes, knowing that if he were to do this, he was going to be setting on a course of lying for the rest of his life.

"Cheltam!"

Edwina jumped in her chair, startled. She had put Gertrude to bed a few hours earlier, and should be asleep herself, but wasn't able to. So she had found the most boring book in the duke's library—something about proper tilling practices—and was attempting to read it, hoping it would make her sleepy.

Thus far, all it had done was to make her fascinated by how many different theories on tilling seemed to exist. She'd never thought about the topic at all, which now seemed like a failure on her part.

She placed the book down on the table and stood, wishing the duke's library held something more pertinent to her interests. *How to Stop Inappropriately Lusting After Your Employer*, perhaps, or *Living Within Your Means When Your Means Add Up to Ten Pounds for the Rest of Your Life*.

"There you are," the duke said, striding into the library still garbed in his evening wear.

It simply was not fair that he managed to look so handsome all the time. Tonight he was breathtaking—dressed in severe black, with his white shirt the only relief from the all-imposing blackness. His cravat was tied simply around his neck, since he didn't need the fussiness that most men seemed to require to make them look intriguing.

He was just intrinsically intriguing, damn it.

"Yes, here I am," Edwina said, then resisted the urge to wince at how stupid the sentence was. "I hope you had a pleasant evening?" she continued, lacing her hands in front of her. Resisting the urge to walk forward and touch him, to slide her fingers down the lapel of his coat, to place her hands on his chest and lean up for a kiss.

He did not reply; instead, his lips turned down as though he were contemplating something he did not care for.

She wished she were high-minded enough not to feel happy about that, but unfortunately she was not. She was definitely low-minded, especially when it came to him.

The highest aristocrat in England. The irony was not lost on her.

"Dance with me." His words came out in a short, demanding burst.

"Pardon?"

His jaw clenched. "Dance with me," he said again, through gritted teeth.

She glanced around the library, as though musicians were going to suddenly appear.

He didn't wait for her—or for the imaginary musicians, for that matter—and stepped forward, placing his hand at her waist, gathering her into his arms, holding her other hand in his.

"You are aware there is no music."

He gazed down at her, his green eyes showing a spark of humor. "I am, Cheltam." He raised an eyebrow. "Were you not aware it is within a secretary's duties to hum a tune when her employer demands it?" He sounded so arrogant, so completely sure of himself she nearly apologized for not knowing that secretaries were, indeed, required to hum.

And then felt a bubble of laughter in her chest. This was the man she had come to know. The man only she knew. The man she had to give up. But she could dance with him, couldn't she?

She placed her hand on his shoulder and nodded. "I will rectify my shortcoming, Your Grace." At which he frowned, of course, since she had just addressed him by his honorific.

She began to hum a tune she'd heard when she'd first arrived in London from her parents' house, one of the first pieces of music she'd danced to. It felt so long ago, before marrying George, before Gertrude, and definitely before him. His mouth relaxed, and he nearly smiled, although "smile" would be too generous a word for what his lips were doing.

Oh, his mouth. She had to stop looking at it, instead closing her eyes to concentrate on her humming.

Although that was nearly worse. With her eyes closed, she could feel that they were just alone together without any kind of obligation, as though they were merely man and woman dancing to-gether. No impediment to their touching, nothing to keep them apart.

She allowed herself to get lost in the moment for a few minutes, his long legs so close to hers, his body exuding a palpable heat that warmed her far more than it should.

"This is . . . pleasant," he said at last, in such a wondering tone that she nearly laughed. He sounded so discomfited by the fact, which then repudiated his words, although she would have to agree that it was pleasant.

She opened her eyes, and her breath caught all over again at how his mere appearance affected her.

There was no possible way she could stay in his employ, whether or not he found a woman to become the Duchess of Hadlow. She bit her lip and swallowed, anticipating the visit to Caro-lyn. That she would tell her friend all about it she knew; whether she could do it without bursting into tears wasn't as clear to her.

Meanwhile, she could just enjoy this dance. This moment, held in his arms one last time.

Tomorrow she would set about changing her life. And not for the better, but it would definitely be less painful.

She kept humming long after the song would normally be finished. Unwilling to let this go. Knowing she had to.

WHY DO DUKES FALL IN LOVE?

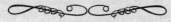

93. Because the heart is governed by no one.

Chapter 24

"Good morning," Edwina called as she stepped into the agency. The duke had gone out for a ride and allowed her to make a visit while he was otherwise occupied. Gertrude was grouchy about lessons with Miss Clark, but brightened when the duke told her she could help him walk Chester after her lessons. Everyone thus taken care of, Edwina had gone off to see Carolyn, to see if she could implement the changes she needed to make to her life.

She heard the sound of steps, then Carolyn walked into the room, a wide smile on her face.

"It's my favorite duke's secretary," she exclaimed, taking both of Edwina's hands in hers.

Edwina felt her expression tighten, and Carolyn gazed at her, a puzzled look on her face. "What is wrong? You're not my favorite secretary?"

Edwina expelled a breath. "It is complicated, my friend."

Carolyn frowned. "Do sit down and tell me all about it."

Edwina allowed Carolyn to sit her down on the small sofa at one end of the room and then her friend plopped down beside her. "So?"

Edwina felt the tears welling up in her eyes. So much for keeping herself from crying. She hadn't even said anything yet.

"Oh no, dear, it can't be that bad," Carolyn said, leaning over to envelop Edwina in a hug. And then Carolyn drew back, staring intently in her face. "Can it?"

Edwina shook her head. "No, it's not that, thank goodness, but I have to find another position. I can't stay there any longer than I have to."

She told Carolyn everything—well, nearly everything—as they sat together on the sofa, alternating her words with tears. Carolyn, true to how wonderful she was, just patted her arm and listened.

Until Edwina came to the end of the sadly abrupt story and stopped talking.

"I wish your case were unique," Carolyn said at last. She shook her head. "But it's not, unsuitable men engage in inappropriate activities with wonderful ladies all the time."

Edwina blinked a few times as she digested what her friend had said. And then she laughed. Bless Carolyn for remaining staunchly in her corner. "You forget he is the most suitable man, it is me who is inappropriate."

Carolyn held her hand up. "I know you are only trying to protect the reputation of your employer, Edwina, but the duke is quite unsuitable. It sounds as though he is far too arrogant to be a suitable mate, not to mention he is scrupulously honest. From what I know of marriage, there needs to be a certain amount of prevarication." She sniffed. "Besides which, you need someone who will know what an honor it is to be married to you. Not just one who proposes to save some trouble."

Edwina knew her friend was just trying to make her feel better by making light of the whole thing, but she felt her heart sinking. If she did marry him—not that she was going to, especially since he'd been so cavalier about her refusal— they would both always be conscious he had married beneath him. Why couldn't she have fallen in love with someone closer to her station? Hawkins, perhaps?

And then she did have to laugh again at the thought of falling in love with the duke's absolutely correct and somewhat stiff butler.

"You know I'm right," Carolyn said in a smug tone.

Edwina nodded. "Absolutely. It is unfortunate you are not in the husband-providing business; it would be so much easier if I could just give you a list of the attributes I require and have you find a much more appropriate man." *Must be intelligent, tall, handsome, confident, incisive, and brutally honest.*

And then she wanted to cry since that exactly described the duke.

"I will find you something else," Carolyn said. "It will be difficult, because there is Gertrude to consider as well, but I will find something for you," her friend promised. But instead of feeling relief at having her friend so assured about her abilities, Edwina merely wanted to cry. Again.

"Where tonight, Cheltam?" Michael leaned back in his chair and watched her under hooded eyes. She'd been unusually subdued today, and he wondered where she had gone when she'd left that morning. Did she have someone else she was seeing?

His chest tightened with an inexplicable emotion. Jealousy. Claiming. She was his, damn it, even if she didn't know that herself.

Even if he didn't know how he could keep her.

"The Queen is attending some function at Court."

"I don't want to go there," he said, cutting her off.

She grimaced, then continued speaking. "As I was saying. The Queen is attending a Court function, and the Viscount of Marlsby is hosting an event after for the appropriate people." She raised an eyebrow. "And you, of course, are appropriate."

He nodded, even though he wanted to argue with her—he was only appropriate because he was the duke, not because of who he was. Of who he had shaped himself to be—someone who was confident, aggressive, always looking for something new.

Never settling.

But he'd have to settle sometime, wouldn't he? It was only logical to take a wife, someone who would be his hostess as he continued to press for innovation in the House of Lords, someone who would provide ease of access for sexual relations, someone who could run his household.

And, as she'd pointed out so bluntly—something he had to admire, even though he rebelled against it—he needed someone who was appropriate for a duke. Any duke, but in this case he was the duke.

It all felt rather . . . cold. Which was what he wanted, he assured himself.

"So it is the Viscount of Marlsby's tonight, then." He tried not to think about how much more he wished he could stay home and perhaps invite her and Gertrude to dine with him. As he had before—before everything had happened.

He knew she'd decline, though. She'd made it clear there was to be nothing that wasn't entirely appropriate—he was beginning to hate that word—between them. Except for that one evening when he'd burst into the library and danced while she hummed a never-ending tune. It felt as though his fingers could still feel her, his body acutely aware of hers just a waltz's distance away.

And then she had stopped humming, and there had been an awkward moment when he tried to find the words to coerce her into his bed, only he couldn't do that to her. Or to himself—he wouldn't ever beg for anything like that. He never had before. He never would.

The Viscount of Marlsby's. Hopefully there would be a female there who was both appropriate and relatively interesting.

* * *

Five hours later, and Michael thought he could safely say there was no female who was both appropriate and relatively interesting. There weren't even any inappropriate ladies to liven things up.

"Yes, Your Grace." *Lower gaze to floor. Look up from under lashes. Offer a slight smile.* "Of course, Your Grace." *Pretend to be fascinated by everything he said.*

He had danced with no fewer than half a dozen young ladies, all of whom did precisely the same thing in nearly the same order. Did they get taught that by their governesses? If not, the lack of imagination was remarkable.

"Your Grace." His host, who'd told Michael to call him Marl, touched him on the shoulder, rousing him from his very appropriate, and boring, thoughts.

"Yes?" Michael couldn't help the supercilious tone. He was proud of himself for recognizing it was supercilious. Before, he would have just thought it was his normal tone of voice. Which, for him, was always supercilious.

Cheltam had pointed out so many of his faults, it was rather astonishing she'd been as inappropriate with him as she had. Did she even like him?

That was not something about which he should be thinking at this moment.

"Your Grace, may I present Miss Emily Dougherty? Of the Sussex Doughertys, of course."

"Of course," Michael echoed as he took the lady's hand. This one didn't do the under-lash gazing at him, at least. She looked him direct in the face, even raising her chin at him as though in challenge.

He felt a stirring of interest.

"Miss Emily is here with her older sister, who is betrothed to my own son. Isn't that correct, my dear?"

He could have sworn she rolled her eyes. Did appropriate young ladies even roll their eyes? "That is correct, my lord. Your son asked the most important of questions and Amanda replied in the affirmative." Her tone was not supercilious, not at all, but there was something mocking about it he couldn't help but be intrigued by.

"Miss Emily, might I ask if you have a partner for this dance?" He might as well discover if she had more conversation than temperate weather and the good fortune of her sister to be marrying Marl's offspring.

Although if said offspring was as dim-witted as Marl seemed to be, perhaps it wasn't good fortune at all.

Now you're just being cruel, a voice that sounded suspiciously like Edwina's said in his head.

"It would be my pleasure, Your Grace." Miss Emily curtseyed and waited as he placed his hand appropriately at her waist and gathered her other hand in his.

The music began, and Michael recognized it immediately as the tune Edwina had hummed that other night. Curse it to hell. Was he always going to be wandering around being reminded of the damn woman?

"Is something wrong, Your Grace?" Miss Emily

asked. She didn't sound worried that something was wrong, merely curious. More intriguing than any of her fellow young ladies, that was for certain.

"Nothing," he said in a curt tone. And then felt—did he feel *apologetic*?—so he hastened to add, "I am merely distracted."

"Yes, it is . . . distracting to be dancing with a stranger, isn't it?" Her tone was dry, nearly acerbic, and he took a better look at her. She was pleasant-looking enough, not ravishing, but not an eyesore, either. She was of moderate height, could apparently dance well enough not to step on his toes, and did not seem to have gotten the same lessons about conversation every other female in the room had.

His mouth twisted as he considered just how low his standards were. Not that he was about to propose marriage to this Miss Emily or anything, but that she was the best of the group based on three minutes' worth of conversation was ridiculous. If he applied the same measurement tactics to his business investments, he would have given money to Cheltam's brother-in-law and his Tea-rific enterprise without being coerced into it.

"Why do I get the feeling, Your Grace, that you would rather be anywhere else but here?" She didn't sound offended, although the words implied she should be.

"No, of course I would like to be here. That is," Michael continued, wanting to keep himself as honest as he could without being offensive—a skill he had not yet mastered—"I suppose there are places that would be worse to be. A muddy ditch, for example, or freezing at the North Pole."

"So what you're saying is that being here is preferable to being doused in dirt or close to frozen? That is hardly a ringing endorsement." It sounded as though she wanted to laugh, and he nearly did as well. Perhaps—

"And so why are you here?" She raised one finger off his shoulder to gesture at the room. "Surely it is not because the company is so enthralling." And then she definitely rolled her eyes, blowing out a breath that revealed her aggravation. "Not that I am fishing for you to say I am so enthralling. I am perfectly aware I am not."

"Actually, Miss Emily, you are more enthralling than anyone else I have met here." Michael felt his lips curl into what might have been a smile. He was enjoying himself, as much as he was able to, given where he was and what he was doing. Only—only this Miss Emily, while intriguing, was not nearly as intriguing as Cheltam. Not because she wasn't intriguing, she was, but because she wasn't Cheltam.

Damn it. Was now, after he'd messed it all up, when he was to realize that only Cheltam would do as a wife for him?

"Now you look as though you did something horrible. I assure you, you have not stepped on my toe, or said anything untoward."

"No, only—only if you will excuse me," and Michael made a quick bow, then made his way to the door, for once not sure even he could solve this problem.

WHY DO DUKES FALL IN LOVE?

6. Why wouldn't they?

Chapter 25

Unlike the other evening, she wasn't awake when he returned. Hawkins, after taking his hat and coat, informed Michael that Mrs. Cheltam had retired some hours ago, apparently not feeling that well.

Michael had to wonder how much he had to do with how she felt. Then immediately thought he heard Cheltam's voice in his head—*Not everything is about you, Hadlow*—only things generally *were* about him. But he couldn't very well go wake her up, no matter how she was feeling, to tell her she had to reconsider his proposal because he just didn't think any other woman would do.

He waved Hawkins away and went into his study, pouring himself a large glass of brandy and walking to look out the window.

The street was empty and dark. If he were less pragmatic, he could say the same about his life. But he wouldn't fall victim to weak flights of fancy, not when he had so much to do. Such as propose marriage. Again.

For the first time perhaps ever, he wasn't certain he could be persuasive enough. He took a healthy swallow of his brandy, feeling the burn slide down his throat. She wasn't impressed by his title—in fact, it was an impediment—and he knew her well enough to know she wouldn't settle just because he had enough money to support her. She'd done that with her last husband. All he could offer her was what he had offered her before, plus his own stronger feelings on the subject.

She wasn't going to say yes.

A sick feeling spread over him, made his skin prickle, and his insides tighten. He knew she would never say yes, not after pointing out how his proposal was illogical because of who she was and what he was. How she wouldn't be able to bear being a duchess, and being whispered about. He wouldn't care about the whispering—he never had—but she would. And if she cared, he would end up caring as well.

But even so, he wasn't going to compromise by offering marriage to anyone who wasn't her.

He shrugged, finishing the glass. What did it matter if he was to be on his own for the rest of his life? He hadn't found the need to alter his circumstances until now, so there was no reason he should feel bereft. But he did.

Perhaps he should consider Cheltam's advice to find a friend. If Miss Emily were a man, he could see being friends with her. She was appropriately honest, intelligent, and possessed a dry wit he appreciated. But given his position, he wasn't allowed to be mere friends with a female—there would always be whispers, intimations of what he really intended. And if he didn't end up marrying her, she'd wind up with a tarnished reputation because he hadn't found her worthy enough to propose to.

He found himself pouring another glass of brandy. And wishing he wasn't so acutely aware of just why he felt so miserable.

"Mrs. Cheltam?" Hawkins stepped into the duke's study and regarded her with an expectant air.

"Yes, Mr. Hawkins?" Edwina hadn't slept well the night before, despite having taken herself to bed earlier than usual. She could have blamed it on thinking about the work she'd done that day— she'd sent letters to all the engine companies, letting them know of the duke's final decision regarding investments—but she wasn't going to lie to herself. And she wasn't sick, even though she'd allowed Hawkins to believe so. Unless being heartsick counted as actually being sick, which she doubted.

She'd noted the time the duke had returned home—well after midnight—and spent far longer than she should have contemplating if he had met anyone who would pique his interest.

Hawkins cleared his throat. Right, she hadn't replied yet. Because she was too immersed in her own thoughts, thoughts of the duke and his future. Which would not include her.

"Thank you, Mr. Hawkins. If you will excuse

me, Your Grace?" She didn't wait for his reply but rose and walked out of the study. Hawkins would have said if the visitor was her brother-in-law, so she wasn't anxious about who it might be, merely curious.

"The lady is in here, Mrs. Cheltam," Hawkins said, opening the door to the library. Where she had danced with the duke that evening.

Carolyn leaped to her feet as Edwina entered, a smile on her face.

"Good afternoon, Carolyn." Edwina gave her friend a hug, then sat down on the sofa and beckoned to Carolyn to sit beside her. "You must have something for me to make the visit. I hadn't expected anything quite so soon, especially with Gertrude to consider. But then again the agency is getting more well-known, so perhaps there are more positions open than I would have thought, and—"

"You're babbling," Carolyn pointed out.

"Yes," Edwina admitted. "So I am. Tell me what it is you came to say before I get a chance to babble again."

"Well," Carolyn said, reaching over to take Edwina's hand, "it appears that I have found something for you, something where Gertrude will be welcome also. The Dowager Countess of Feltington is in need of a companion. Her daughter lives with her as well, a widow, and she has a daughter who also, it seems, is in need of companionship."

"Why isn't her daughter the dowager countess's companion?"

Carolyn paused. "From what I understand,

the daughter is a bit of a loose screw, and her mother is determined to watch over her granddaughter, but also wants someone around who is trustworthy."

"Ah. And where is the position?"

"Well out of London, nearly fifty miles to the west. There is no chance you will encounter the duke again." Carolyn spoke as though this was a good thing, which Edwina supposed it was, even though her heart felt even sicker at the thought of never seeing him again.

She wished, not for the first time, that she was more willing to settle and had said yes when he'd asked. Only she knew that that way inevitably led to unhappiness, as she would continue to love him, and he would continue not to love her, and likely eventually grow bored of her.

"And Her Ladyship wants someone immediately, so the sooner you can get there, the better."

"I don't need to meet with her?"

Carolyn shook her head. "No, it's all settled. I went ahead and accepted the position for you, the salary isn't quite what you are making here, but it is something that will be adequate for your needs."

"Oh." Edwina wished it didn't hurt so much. And then wanted to smack herself. Because if it didn't hurt so much she wouldn't have to leave in the first place.

"You are ready to leave, aren't you?" Carolyn squeezed her hand.

"Of course. It is just sudden. I will need a few days to sort things out so I don't leave the duke unprepared." *And so I can prepare myself for never seeing him.*

"I expected that, so I informed Her Ladyship you would arrive within the week. That will be sufficient time."

At which Edwina wanted to protest—forever wouldn't be sufficient time, but she couldn't tell her friend that. She could scarcely admit it to herself.

"Thank you," she said instead. "Thank you so much for this; you cannot know what it means to me."

Carolyn's smile was wistful. "I do know, Edwina." She patted Edwina's hand. "I do."

"Well?" The duke's tone was impatient as Edwina returned to the room. It appeared that he'd been pacing since she'd left—his chair was pushed carelessly back, his hair showed signs of having been raked through, and there was a wary gleam in his eye that made her heart hurt.

"Well." She raised her chin and took a deep breath. "My visitor was my friend Carolyn, the woman who runs the Quality Employment Agency. She has found me another position, one which I will be taking straightaway."

He strode to stand directly in front of her, so close she swore she could see the spark of anger in his gaze. "So this is your solution? To leave me?"

His words were sharp, as was his expression. She shouldn't have expected anything else; this was something he did not want, since it would inconvenience him.

But he could find another secretary. She couldn't find her heart again, not until she wasn't near him anymore.

"It is not a solution," she replied, concentrating on keeping her voice steady. "It is a necessity. I cannot stay here any longer, not with—with—" and then she felt her eyes tickle as the tears started to well up. She could not cry. She could not.

"With us no longer being involved? That was your choice, not mine," he said, his tone almost sounding hurt.

And apparently she could cry, because she realized the tears were streaming down her cheeks, and she was gulping, trying to stop the flow as she looked anywhere but his face. Because if she looked at him, and there was a softening in his expression, she might soften as well, and stay here, and be with him, even though she knew it was wrong.

Even though it would feel incredibly right. At least for the short term.

"So that is it then." His tone was flat. Cold. "Can I"—and now his tone did sound softer, and she felt another rush of tears—"will you give me one more night before you leave? Just one?"

The temptation was too much for her. Another chance to be in his arms, kiss him, have his full attention on her, and how she felt, and how he could make her feel. It wouldn't be so wrong, would it, if they both knew it was the last time? Forever?

She knew it was wrong, but she just couldn't say no. "Yes." She spoke in a whisper, but it appeared he heard it, since he gripped her upper arms and drew her into his body, resting his chin on her head.

"Thank you." Had he sounded cold before? Now he sounded passionate, earnest, thankful. Things she didn't think he had ever sounded like before.

"Not tonight, though," she murmured. "Not until the last night. Just a few days from now."

She felt his body stiffen. "So soon."

"Yes." Because even that time felt too long for her to stay here, with him, knowing he could never be hers, that she could love him as much as she wanted to but he wouldn't love her back.

He released her and put his finger under her chin, raising her face to his. His gaze was intense, so strong it felt as though it might scorch her. Which was how she felt with him most of the time anyway—as though he could burn her with his intensity, his touch.

He had burned her. She would never be the same after knowing him, but that didn't mean she wouldn't recover. She would, but she knew she would never be the same.

Michael urged his horse to go faster, even though he was already moving at a pace that was quicker than what was expected of a gentleman's ride in the park. He'd been seething with a fury he didn't even understand himself since Cheltam had told him she was leaving. How dare she? How dare she turn her back on what he offered her, knowing what they were together?

Thank God he'd gotten her promise for another night, because if he had to bid her goodbye without that—he didn't know what he'd do.

He'd never felt this—this *lost* before at the end of an affair. Of course he'd always been the one to end it before, so perhaps that was the cause of this new, strange emotion. And Cheltam was different from any of the other women whom he'd had before. He would miss her. And her daughter. Gertrude had been adamant about spending every possible moment she could with Chester, which meant by default she'd been spending time with him—they'd taken to walking for an hour or two in the late afternoon, right after tea, and Michael found he looked forward to their time together. Even if her conversation was primarily about what Chester was looking at, and smelling, and doing other things to.

He'd gone out to a few more social events, where he always made sure he at least greeted Miss Emily, even though she couldn't be his friend, and he definitely did not want her as a wife. She amused him, at least, and it seemed he amused her. He danced with a few under-lash fluttering debutantes, repressing his normally blunt opinions so he wouldn't scare the ladies.

That was no way to be. It was far better to be on his own, he assured himself, than to have to compromise his viewpoints to accommodate someone who couldn't handle who he was, even though they were more than happy to accommodate what he was—namely, a duke with wealth, lands, and responsibilities.

But the days were ticking by, and as long as she hadn't changed her mind, tonight they would be together for one last time. The last time. And she and Gertrude would leave tomorrow, and he would be on his own again, a duke without a secretary.

A man without a lover.

A man without a friend.

"You are all ready, Mrs. Cheltam?" Miss Clark glanced at the trunks Edwina had packed. Edwina had had to get an additional one since the household staff had insisted on purchasing new toys for Gertrude and the duke had insisted she take the books Gertrude had used for her studies. "It is not as though they will be useful after you've gone," he said flatly. She'd nearly opened her mouth to tell him that they could be useful if he had a wife, and had children, but she couldn't; she knew her heart would crack if she mentioned his future.

And now, tonight, she would be with him. One last time. The last time for her, she knew, since even if she healed, and her heart eventually mended, she would never fall out of love with him, and she was done with compromising herself when it came to her choice of partner. It would be enough that she'd had this love, albeit for a short period of time. She could concentrate on raising Gertrude, and finding some measure of comfort in doing the right thing for her daughter. The right thing for her, as well, even though it felt like absolutely the wrong thing right now.

"We are ready, yes, Miss Clark." Carolyn had found a position for Gertrude's governess, as well, and Miss Clark would be leaving for her new post the day after Edwina and Gertrude had gone. Edwina hadn't even thought of what their leaving would do to Miss Clark, and she was grateful for Carolyn's forethought.

"I will miss you," Miss Clark said, a glint of moisture in her eyes. Edwina gathered the younger woman into her arms for a hug, swallowing against the lump in her throat. Miss Clark was too young to have to deal with Edwina's emotions—it wouldn't be fair to collapse in her arms just because she'd done the stupidest thing of falling in love with her employer.

"I will miss you, too." Edwina stepped back, keeping her hands on the other woman's shoulders. "You will promise to write and let me know how you are? I will do the same."

"Yes, it will be a pleasure. I never thought I would find a friend in my first position, and yet here I have." Miss Clark spoke wonderingly, and Edwina's heart hurt all over again at how open and honest she was. She'd been like that, too, but so long ago she could barely remember. Now she felt as though she were battle-scarred, the nicks and hurts from her marriage written on her skin, the anguish and loss of Michael taking residence in her heart.

But she had to put all that aside, at least for a short time. It wouldn't do to spend her last evening as Michael's lover sobbing all over his chest, much as she might feel the urge to. She wanted something she could look back on, not something she would regret.

So she would lose herself in the moment, in his arms, savoring every touch so she would have nothing to regret. Besides the whole falling-in-love-with-an-unattainable-man thing.

"Mama says we're to live in the country." Gertrude's expression showed what she thought of that. "But she said there would probably be a dog there, so it won't be all bad." She did not sound convinced.

Michael speared another piece of meat onto his fork, wishing he could stab Edwina's plans as easily. They hadn't dined together since before, before the time she'd come to his bed. He hadn't asked her to since then, either, since he knew she would just decline.

But she couldn't refuse tonight, not when it meant her daughter could spend a few more hours in his company, or more accurately, in his dog's company. Chester was not normally allowed into the dining room, of course, but Michael had made an exception for tonight, much to Hawkins's dismay.

Chester sat to the right of Gertrude, rousing every time she "accidentally" let a piece of food drop. He roused quite frequently.

"It will be different, certainly," Michael began, "but you will find friends"—*unlike me*—"and soon you'll wonder how you ever lived anywhere else." He didn't have much—that is to say any—experience with trying to make someone feel better, but judging by Edwina's approving look, he'd done all right for his first time.

"And there will be lots more room to run around, and it won't be as smoky and loud."

"I like smoke and loud," Gertrude said grumpily, if not grammatically.

Michael stifled a snort.

"And you will be taking lessons with the dowager countess's granddaughter; you can show her everything you learned with Miss Clark."

"That might be all right," Gertrude conceded.

"And you will write me letters all about it, won't you?" Michael surprised himself with his request, not to mention his desire to have Gertrude write him letters in the first place. When had he ever thought corresponding with a child would be something he would want? The answer was never. And yet he found he did want it, wanted to keep that connection even though they were far away. Where he would likely never see them.

"I will, as long as you write back. Since Chester can't," Gertrude added, lest Michael think she actually wanted to correspond with him.

"I will," he promised, taking a not too large sip of wine and meeting Edwina's gaze. She smiled at him, and he felt the shock of her smile through his whole body. It wasn't a smile that said. *We'll be naked together later on*, although he would have been fine with that smile as well; it was a smile that said, *Thank you for being so kind to my daughter, you're not nearly as uncaring as you think you are.*

Edwina broke the gaze and looked at her daughter, her eyes narrowing. "Gertrude, concentrate on your dinner, now." Gertrude's hand halted in its journey down to Chester, some sort of food in her hand. While Chester was not the most intelligent of dogs, he was smart enough to know when he should pay attention, so he stood up and snagged the morsel from Gertrude's hand.

She drew it back into her lap and picked up her fork, staring assiduously at her plate.

Michael tried not to laugh. It wouldn't do to undermine Edwina's authority, especially since they were to be on their own again. Tomorrow.

Suddenly, he didn't have the stomach for any more dinner. He picked up his wineglass instead and took a swallow, conscious of not wishing to have anything tamper with his memories of the night to come. Memories that would have to last him, since he would never see Edwina again.

What was this odd feeling he had? He'd never experienced its like before. Something as though there was a band across his chest tightening by the minute.

"Are you all right?" Gertrude was looking at him with a puzzled expression.

"Fine." He heard how curt he sounded, and knew that wasn't fair. "Thank you for asking. I am fine, I was just thinking."

"About what?"

He definitely could not answer that, not even

if it wasn't a young girl asking. He didn't know what he was thinking—just that it was bothering him, and he didn't like to be bothered. Hadn't he structured his whole life so that would never happen? And yet here he was, at his own dinner table, filled with bother.

"Nothing in particular." He put his elbows on the table and leaned forward, drawing a look of ire from Edwina and a delighted look from Gertrude. "What are you thinking about?"

Gertrude glanced down at where Chester lay. "About leaving. I'm going to miss Chester." She glanced up. "And you, too."

"I am going to miss you as well," Michael replied, his throat closing up as he spoke.

"We should get you into bed," Edwina said. Unfortunately not speaking to him. "We have a long journey tomorrow. I don't want you to be too tired."

"Can Chester come, too?"

Michael smiled at her. "As if I could keep him away. Of course he can." It would be the last time for all of them. He wouldn't deny her the treat, nor did he think Chester would allow it anyway.

Edwina rose, gesturing to Gertrude to do the same. He felt a moment of panic—did she remember that they were to be together?—and then she looked his way and nodded, mouthing, *Later* as she placed a hand on her daughter's back to guide her out of the room. Michael stood and bowed to both of them as they left, his fingers reaching out toward Edwina's sleeve, but not touching her. Just hanging suspended there for a moment, as lost and adrift as he felt inside.

He was at the door as soon as he heard the soft knock, flinging it open so fast her hand was still raised.

"You came." Until he saw her, he hadn't been certain she would come after all. What if Gertrude had a nightmare? Or she had a change of heart?

But she was here.

"Come," he said, taking her arm and drawing her inside. He shut the door firmly, then took her in his arms, lowering his mouth to hers as he pushed her against the door.

It had been so long. Too long.

Her mouth opened for him, and her arms wrapped around his body, pulling him in close. She was warm, and soft, and he wanted to bury himself inside her—not just his cock, though he wanted that, but his whole self. He wanted to burrow under her skin, find and claim the solace he knew only when he was with her.

She wore only her night rail and dressing gown, and he could feel her hardening nipples against his chest. One hand went to wrap itself in her hair, while the other grasped her lovely, heavy breast. So warm and full in his hand.

He was erect against her, and he thrust forward gently, letting her know just what he was feeling. She moaned into his mouth, and he twisted them so she was walking backward, toward the bed. As she walked, he pushed her wrapper off her shoulders, then drew the night rail up and pulled it over her head so she was completely naked.

He withdrew his mouth from hers just long enough to coax her onto the bed, then shed his clothing as quickly as he could and got onto the bed as well, caging her with his body, returning his mouth to kiss her with a passion, with a need he didn't think he'd ever felt before. No, that he knew he'd never felt before.

Her hands gripped the back of his head, her fingers caressing his skull, holding him to her. Her body arched up between them and he felt her mons against his cock, rubbing and pressing.

He withdrew his mouth and stared down at her, noting her heavy eyes and her moist, red lips. "What do you want?" he asked softly, his hand sliding down her body to wander between her legs. And placed his hand on her, cupping her there.

"What do you think I want?" Her voice was husky with desire.

He grinned, then lowered his mouth to her ear. "I think you want me to put my hard cock inside you and make you scream." He slid his fingers inside her wetness. "I can feel how much you want me." He nipped the lobe of her ear, causing her to jump. "Just tell me, Edwina."

She moaned as his fingers worked inside her, her body writhing on his bed. "I want you to—I want you to fuck me, Michael."

His eyes slid closed as she spoke, his whole body reacting to her words. He withdrew his fingers and reached for the condom he'd optimistically placed near his bed, sliding it onto his throbbing shaft. He rose up on his knees and gazed down at her, at her pale body lying against his sheets, at her dark hair spread out on his pillow. Looking as lovely and delicious as he'd ever seen.

He took himself in hand and pushed at her entrance, her legs falling to the side as she let him in.

"God, you're so tight," he said as he eased himself in. She bit her lip, her eyes on where they were joined, her hands holding his arms, then reaching to his back to pull him closer to her.

And then he was all the way inside, his balls snug against her skin, his cock pulsing inside her.

"Oh yes," she murmured, and began to wriggle against him, her hands clamped on his arse.

"Tell me what feels good," he said, licking her neck. She flung her head back, her eyes closed, and her breasts pushed into his chest, her whole body warm and soft and just what he wanted.

"Just like that," she replied, biting her lip as he began to move in and out. He watched her face, gauging her reaction, and he sped up just slightly as her eyes fluttered open. "Yes, God, Michael, yes," she moaned, and her fingers dug into his buttocks so sharply he imagined he would have bruises the next day. He'd welcome them—a tangible reminder that this had happened.

She began to moan, her head turning on his pillow, her eyes shut again, and he felt her pussy spasm as she came.

He didn't last more than a minute after her, his climax hitting hard, feeling as though his entire body was absorbed in this moment.

He collapsed on top of her, knowing she could handle his weight. Knowing, actually, that she could take whatever he could give her, no matter what it was.

His short temper, his bitter acerbity, his wit, his humor, his—no, not that. He didn't. He couldn't.

And wanted to groan, in pain this time, as he realized he did, and he could, and it was too late.

WHY DO DUKES FALL IN LOVE?

8. If they don't, then they're idiots. Don't be an idiotic duke.

Chapter 26

"Mrs. Cheltam! Over here, please, I need your fingers."

Edwina smiled as she heard the dowager countess from the other room. "Excuse me, ladies," she said to Gertrude and Molly—Molly was the dowager countess's granddaughter, younger than Gertrude, who treated Gertrude as though she were a goddess sent to walk among the humans. A position Gertrude had no problem accepting.

Molly's mother—the dowager countess's wayward daughter—had taken herself off only a few days after Edwina and Gertrude had arrived, liberating herself from her duties as mother and daughter with an alacrity that was nearly palpable.

"Yes, my lady?" Edwina walked into the dowager countess's sitting room, really a converted library that was now festooned with all the projects the dowager countess found herself engaged in—and, Edwina soon found, just as immediately disinterested in.

Currently, Edwina's employer was busily knitting scarves for the poor, big, lumpy snarls of yarn that would probably keep someone's neck warm, even if they weren't precisely attractive.

An older woman with kind eyes and an even kinder smile, the dowager countess was an easy person to work for. Certainly nothing like her last employer, Edwina thought.

She and Gertrude had been here for nearly a month already, and Gertrude, at least, had settled in well—she went roaming around the nearby acreage with Molly and various dogs that hung around the kitchens.

Edwina wished she could say she had settled in well, but she felt as though she'd left a part of her, a heart-shaped part of her, back in London. Where he was, no doubt cursing her name as he searched for a new secretary.

Or maybe he'd found one, and maybe it was another woman, and he was even now wooing her with his brusque humor and dry wit.

She should not be thinking about that. If he were wooing anyone at all it would be a woman of his own class, one whom he could marry and have children with, and—

"Are you all right, dear?" the dowager countess asked in a worried voice.

Edwina started, realizing she hadn't moved past the entrance of the room and was just staring at the tangle of yarn in her employer's hand. "Yes, I am sorry, my lady, I was woolgathering," and then both of them laughed as they realized what she had said.

"I need your help untangling this, dear," the

dowager countess said, holding her hands, now covered in yarn, out to Edwina.

Edwina took a seat near her and began to work through the threads, her head bent over the work. She made an effort to lose herself in small tasks like this one, since it took her mind off him and how her whole self hurt when she thought about him.

Gertrude had sent him a letter when they first arrived, mostly extolling the virtues of the resident dogs, but he hadn't replied yet. Edwina tried not to envy her daughter's ability to correspond so casually with him; if she herself sent him a letter, it would be entirely shocking, and all the servants in her new position would comment, with word leading inevitably to the dowager countess. And Edwina would have nothing to say in her defense, so she just hoped he would reply to her daughter so she could get a glimpse of his life.

Though if he wrote to say he was betrothed, she might just take herself off to one of the distant hills and howl for a few hours.

"Next month I thought we would go visit my friend Lady Patten," the dowager countess said. "Now that you're here, and it makes it so much easier to travel. Martha"—the dowager countess's maid, a nervous woman who jumped when anyone spoke her name—"has been wishing to visit her sister, and it seems like it would be the perfect time."

"Of course, my lady," Edwina murmured. More things to distract her from the heartache she knew would ebb at some point. Perhaps by the time Gertrude's own children were grown up. If she were being optimistic, as well as melodramatic.

"Does Lady Patten live far from here?"

The dowager countess screwed up her face in concentration. "Perhaps just an hour's drive? I'm not certain. I usually fall asleep on the journey, you know," she confided, as though it were a secret that she fell asleep many times during the day.

Edwina smiled in reply. "It sounds lovely."

"We can leave the girls here under Diana's care." Diana was Molly's nurse, Molly not yet having a governess, which delighted Gertrude, who was not much for lessons. The dowager countess promised that she would find a governess as soon as Molly turned five, so Gertrude only had a few more months of freedom. "And then you and I and Lady Patten can go shopping—she lives near a nice little village, they often have fairs and the like, we should see if we can find some ribbons for your hat." The dowager countess looked at Edwina with a mischievous look. "I don't wish to say goodbye to you so soon, but I do think you should find yourself another husband."

It was something she'd been saying since the second day Edwina had arrived, so by now, Edwina knew just to smile and nod, as though it were something she agreed with.

The thought of being with a man other than Michael was an unpleasant one, an idea that felt like a burr under her skin. She knew that it was likely that, if she stayed here, the dowager countess would wear her down and she would find herself married again, likely to a nice-enough person, someone who could be a father to Gertrude.

But every fiber in her being rebelled against the image so soon after being with him. Having him touch her skin, come inside her body, talk to her in such shocking language.

Maybe someday. When she had deadened enough inside to forget him, when she just longed for comfort, or a kiss now and then, not longing for his touch, the fiery passion only he had inspired in her.

"We should go visit your friend soon," Edwina said, surprising even herself with how urgent she sounded. If she could just distract herself enough from her thoughts, maybe one day it wouldn't be so agonizingly painful. She didn't think visiting an equally elderly lady with the prospect of purchasing new ribbons for her hat would eradicate him from her thoughts entirely—far from it—but it would take her mind off him, off the ache his absence left, for a few moments, perhaps.

"It's not getting better," Michael informed a disinterested Chester. He picked up his glass of wine and drained it, then frowned at the empty glass. He strode to the bellpull and yanked it, hearing the immediate cadence of footsteps.

"Yes, Your Grace?" Hawkins stepped inside, his expression retaining its normal placidity. It was only when he thought Michael wasn't watching that his expression drooped, as though he, too, were missing the Cheltam ladies.

"More wine." Michael picked up the empty wine bottle and waved it in the air. "Better yet, bring two."

Hawkins cleared his throat.

"Now," Michael added. His butler swallowed, then bowed and stepped out of the room, leaving Michael holding the empty bottle and his constant companion of loneliness.

He hadn't expected to miss them quite so much. Naturally he missed the physical elements of being with her, any man would, but contrarily, he didn't feel the urge to go find another woman. Even for just that. It seemed, in his ridiculous brain, that only she would do, and to do that with another would be to betray her.

"Your wine, Your Grace." Hawkins had returned sooner than Michael expected; perhaps he'd learned from the past few nights and laid in some bottles close by? Hawkins brought the bottles to the small table in the corner and bowed as he took the empty wine bottle from Michael's hand.

"If that will be all, Your Grace?" Thank goodness Hawkins didn't sniff, even though his glance did dart to where the wine bottles rested. As though gauging just how much liquid was inside, and how much would soon be inside Michael.

He probably shouldn't be drinking this much wine, but he hadn't found anything else that even came close to making him lose the ache in his chest. And even when he was drinking wine, the ache remained, just a bit less.

One and a half bottles later, he'd figured it out. He'd applied his brain to it, and reviewed all the evidence at his command, and he knew. He absolutely knew for certain.

Not that he hadn't known before. But he'd been lying to himself—him, lying!—and it took all this anguish for him to figure it out.

"I think—no, I know I am in love with her," he told a bored Chester. "Damn it, how did I manage to fall in love? Of all the illogical things to do, I had to do the most illogical one." He drained his glass and contemplated the rest of the bottle.

He probably shouldn't; he didn't want to have a bursting head tomorrow.

But that was logical. He was tired of logic. Logic said he shouldn't fall in love with her, logic said he shouldn't have even proposed the first time, logic said he should just find another woman who would suit just as well, and be far more suitable.

He was damn tired of logic.

He poured the remainder of the bottle into his glass, then pointed an accusatory finger at his dog. "Why didn't you warn me?"

Chester raised his head to look at him, but saw there was no food, so put it down on the carpet.

"How could I have been such an idiot?"

No answer.

"I love her." It felt true, and honest, even though he'd never thought he would ever say those words in his entire life. But he couldn't lie to himself, not anymore. He'd been trying to figure out just what was wrong in his life, in his brain, how it felt as though there was an Edwina-shaped space in his life, and if he could just fill it with work, or wine, or—or something, he would be fine.

He was not fine.

"And I've totally and entirely messed it up." He swallowed against the lump in his throat. "I offered her marriage, but she didn't—doesn't—want that. I let her go without fighting for her because I was too much of an arrogant, logical idiot to figure out I was hopelessly and madly in love with her."

Chester offered no suggestions.

Michael drank the rest of the wine, knowing he would have the devil of a headache tomorrow, but not caring. Even though it was illogical not to care.

He was done with logic. If this was where logic got him—alone, drinking wine while he talked to his only friend, who couldn't reply because he didn't speak—then he was going to go ahead and do illogical things now.

Starting tomorrow. And, hopefully, for the rest of his life.

"My lady?" Edwina tapped her employer on the arm. They'd been traveling for an hour, and she could see they were about to enter a village, the one where the dowager countess's friend lived.

"Wh-what?" The dowager countess awoke with a start. "Are we there?"

"Nearly so, I believe." Edwina gestured out the window. "That is our destination?"

The dowager countess leaned forward and looked out the window, glancing back at Edwina with a delighted smile. Edwina couldn't help but return the smile; at least her employer seemed happy, and settled, despite having had—from what Edwina could gather—a not altogether happy marriage, along with a troubled daughter. There was hope for her, then. If she could just last another couple of decades being miserable, maybe she would eventually achieve the kind of peace the dowager countess had.

"Lady Patten's house is just beyond the dressmaker's shop." The dowager countess wagged a reproving finger at Edwina. "And don't think I've forgotten about those ribbons, that will be the first place we go after we have some tea. I am famished," she said, even though she had eaten most of the muffins her cook had packed for her.

The coach slowed, and Edwina saw a woman somewhere in age between her and the dowager countess standing outside a tidy-looking house.

"That is Lady Patten?" Edwina asked.

"Yes, and doesn't she look wonderful." Honestly, if Edwina could just borrow some of her employer's joy in simple things she would be so much happier. As it was, she could feel that someday, perhaps earlier than a few decades from now, her heart would heal. She thanked Carolyn for the thousandth time that she had found Edwina such a suitable position, far away from the source of her unsuitable feelings.

"Mrs. Cheltam is . . . not here?" Michael gaped at the woman, apparently a housekeeper, who had just told him that Mrs. Cheltam was not at home. Was not expected back for hours, even.

"No, Your Grace." The woman looked terrified, and Michael couldn't blame her; he hadn't wanted to bother with waiting for his coach and all his usual accompaniments to travel to impede his speed, so he'd ridden here over the course of a few days, changing horses as he went, spending the minimum amount of time sleeping, and definitely no time shaving or worrying overly much about his clothing.

He knew he looked even more intimidating than usual, and then he'd informed the woman of his name, and he had worried for a moment that she would faint dead away at having a disheveled duke at the door.

And now Cheltam wasn't here anyway, which rendered his speed in traveling a debatable point.

"Would you—would you like to come in?" At least the housekeeper had recovered enough to offer a measure of politeness.

"No." He, however, had no such compunction about politeness. Should he just leave? It was a fool's errand anyway—she wasn't going to say yes, she'd already made her choices, and they hadn't included him.

If it were the old he, the old logical he, he would have left immediately without even bothering to leave a note.

"Where did she go?" he asked instead.

The housekeeper paused, as though wondering if she should share the information. She shrugged. "She and the mistress went to the next town over."

"Which way over?" he asked, trying to subdue his natural impatience.

She raised her arm and pointed. "That way. You can't miss it, it's the only town on that road."

Michael glanced in the direction she'd pointed and sighed. Being illogical meant going to so much more trouble than just doing what made sense. But doing what made sense wouldn't make him happy.

"Thank you for your help," he said, and strode back down the path to where his horse stood grazing on the grass.

The dowager countess was sleeping again. It had been a busy day, visiting Lady Patten, talking about every single thing that had happened to the two of the ladies in the two months since they'd seen each other. Going to the dressmaker's shop where ribbons were bought, fabric was exclaimed over, and a new hat was found that would sit nicely on the dowager countess's gray curls.

They had been on the road for perhaps thirty minutes when Edwina felt the coach slowing. Too soon for them to be home, and as far as she knew, they hadn't planned on making any more stops.

The coach came to a complete stop and Edwina opened the carriage door, wincing as her eyes adjusted to the sun.

"Cheltam."

Oh my God. Was she hallucinating? Her vision cleared, and she saw him, standing next to his horse in the middle of the road. Gazing at her with an intense expression on his face.

"Move along, we got places to be," the dowager countess's coachman said. "Miss, you might want to get back inside, we'll be starting up again once this gentleman gets out of the way."

"I won't be getting out of the way." He didn't take his eyes off her, and she felt his scrutiny throughout her entire body. "Not unless you get out of the way with me."

He ran a hand over his face as though frustrated. "That is, that isn't what I mean."

She didn't think she'd ever hear him admit to saying something wrong again.

"Come walk with me?"

Nor had she ever heard him ask something in such a hesitant, wanting tone.

"What is it, Edwina?"

Edwina turned her head to see the dowager countess's head poking out of the carriage window. "Who is that?"

"I am the Duke of Hadlow, my lady," Michael said. "I wish to speak with Mrs. Cheltam, if you might spare her the time."

The dowager countess beamed. Of course she did. "Of course, we are in no hurry. Do go on and hear what the duke has to say, Edwina."

Edwina turned back to him. He was still staring at her with a passionate intensity that unnerved her.

"Well? Will you hear what I have to say?" His voice was pitched low, nearly too soft for her to hear. But she did.

"Yes," she replied, walking toward him.

He walked as well, reaching his hand out as though to take hers, then dropping it, a grimace twisting his mouth.

"Let's go over there," Edwina said, gesturing to the side of the road where a few trees offered respite from the sun. As well as being distant enough so the dowager countess wouldn't overhear.

They walked in silence, Edwina hearing her heart pounding through her body. What was he doing here? How had he found her? Why did he have to be so handsome still, even though he clearly hadn't shaved, and he was dressed in simple traveling clothes?

Most importantly, why was that what she noticed?

"Why are you here?"

He appeared to take a deep breath, then held his hands out in front of him. "I'm shaking," he said in wonderment. Edwina looked down, and yes, his hands were shaking.

Something must be terribly wrong.

"What is it? Is someone hurt?"

He shook his head. "No, not—well, yes." He took her hands in his and she nearly gasped aloud at how it felt to have his skin touching hers— neither of them wore gloves, and the bare contact was almost more than she could stand.

"Are you hurt?" she asked in a softer voice.

He regarded her with a look in his eyes she had never seen before. Something vulnerable, wanting, and yes, hurt.

"I hurt myself," he said at last. His gaze didn't

leave her face. "I need to tell you this, to explain everything, to tell you what an idiot I am."

Her face must have shown shock, since he chuckled dryly. "I know, not anything you—or I, for matter—ever expected to say. I'll say it again. I am an idiot."

"Why?" It was a whisper.

"Because I—" and then he did the most surprising thing, dropping to his knees onto the grass. Still holding her hands.

"Because I love you."

"That's why you're an idiot?"

He snorted. "No, and may I point out I am doing this terribly?"

"I don't think you have to," Edwina said in a voice that trembled only slightly.

"I am an idiot," he said in a return to his normal arrogant tone, "because I didn't see past my own image of myself and who I thought I was to see who I could become. Who I was, with you." He squeezed her hands. "I always thought that to be the best person I could, I'd be reasoned, logical, and practical. That any hint of love, of the possibility of more, died with my brother." A pause. "But it turns out that the best person I can be—the happiest person I can be—is when I am with you, loving you so intensely I can't imagine life without you, even though it makes absolutely no sense for me to be in love with you. To marry you."

Her heart felt as though it had gotten stuck in her throat.

"But I want to be that person. I want to forget reason, and logic, and intelligence—"

"By marrying me?" Edwina interrupted.

"You did hear the part where I said I was doing this terribly, didn't you?" he asked in a dry voice. "Yes, by marrying you. It isn't practical, you said that yourself. I should find a woman of my own class who can fit into my world. But I don't want to. I don't want to live in my world without you. I want to make my world one where you are. All the time. With me," he said, as though he hadn't just said basically the same thing a multitude of ways.

"You want to marry me . . . because you love me?"

Apparently she was just as idiotic as he, since she hadn't understood precisely what he was saying in all the ways he was saying it.

"Yes. I love you, Edwina. I want you and your daughter in my life, and I don't give a damn if it's not practical. If you want, I will promise to do at least one poorly thought-out thing a day to prove my love."

She couldn't suppress the burst of laughter that emerged. He really was terrible at this, and yet—and yet, illogically, it only proved his sincerity. His honesty in confessing his feelings to her.

"Well?" he said in an anxious tone. "Do you have anything to say?"

She nodded. "I do. That is, I will. I will say I do."

And now who was being overexplanatory?

It didn't matter, though, since he leaped to his feet and swept her into his arms in one motion, his mouth claiming hers in welcome possession.

In the distance, Edwina heard the dowager countess emit a huzzah as she kissed him back.

If he loved her, none of the problems she'd mentioned before would matter. It would be enough to deal with the comments, the difficulties, the glances that would imply he had married beneath him—she knew full well what she was about to do, and none of it mattered. If he loved her, if he loved Gertrude—which she knew he did—it didn't matter.

Love really could overcome logic.

WHY DO DUKES FALL IN LOVE?

18. There is no logical answer.

Epilogue

"But that doesn't make any sense," Gertrude said, frowning.

Michael smiled in satisfaction. "Exactly." They were all sitting outside in the duke's gardens, the rain starting to fall. Dark clouds scudded across the sky, and yet Michael had said they would stay outdoors for just a bit longer.

Chester didn't seem to mind, having chased a squirrel up a tree and then dug up some of Edwina's flower beds.

"We're going to get rained on," Gertrude continued in exasperation.

"You can go inside, dear, if you like," Edwina replied. "The duke and I will stay outside for just a bit, just to enjoy the unreasonable weather."

She gave him a secret smile, one that lit him up as unreasonably as the weather.

He'd kept his promise, having done one nonsensical thing a day, at least, since they'd gotten married. It felt so freeing to be able to just do something because one wanted to, or one knew one shouldn't. It was getting to be a habit, nearly as addictive as having Edwina in his bed every night, seated at his breakfast table every morning.

They'd hired a new secretary together, a meek young man who nonetheless told the duke—to his face—when he was making a mistake. That had happened once in the month since he'd been hired, but still, it was impressive.

Gertrude was delighted to be reunited with Chester, not to mention the duke's staff, who welcomed her like a long-lost hero on her return.

And his wife—his lovely, intelligent, passionate wife—told him every day how much she loved him, and his height, and his position, and his influence, and his power, and his money. Only being practical, she assured him.

Dear Aunt Sophia,

How are you? ~~I am desperate.~~ I am doing well. As you know, I am now the Duchess of Blakesley. Don't ask me to explain how an unmarried woman could inherit such a title. The solicitors explained it four times, and from the little I understand, it seems my ancestors received some special dispensation to allow any direct heir to inherit, regardless of gender. Since that ridiculous scenario has occurred, I am at the London townhouse preparing to take on my new position ~~for which I was never prepared~~. I am writing you to ask if you have any advice for navigating Societal waters; I am quite adept at swimming (the second footman taught me when I was twelve), but this is a very different kind of pond. A veritable ocean, one might say. ~~And I am drowning.~~

If you would be so kind, please send along any recommendations for ~~anything~~ hiring staff, assembling a proper wardrobe, ~~how not to annoy the Queen~~, manage several country estates, and any other thing I might have overlooked ~~in my desperation. Have I mentioned I have no idea what I am doing?~~.

Normally I would consult a book if I were at a loss in any situation, but there don't appear to be any manuals on what to do if you are an unexpected duchess.
Sincerely,
~~Genevieve~~ Duchess

P.S. If there is such a book, please do share the title!

Chapter 1

"There's only one solution," Lady Sophia said, holding the letter in her hand as Archie felt his stomach drop. "You'll have to go to London to sort my niece out." She embellished her point by squeezing her tiny dog Truffles, who emitted a squeak and glared at Archie. As if it was his fault.

"But there is work to be done here," Archie replied, hoping to appeal to his employer's sensible side. He had left the Queen's Own Hussars over a year ago, and had been working for Lady Sophia for nearly all that time since.

During which he had come to realize his employer didn't really *have* a sensible side, so what was he hoping to accomplish?

"Didn't you tell me Mr. McCready could do everything you could?" Lady Sophia asked. "You pointed out that if you were to get ill, or busy with other matters that your assistant steward could handle things just as well as you."

That was when I was trying to get one of my men work, Archie thought in frustration. *To help him get back on his feet after the rigors of war.* And Bob had proven himself to be a remarkably able assistant, allowing Archie to dive into Lady Sophia's woefully neglected accounts and seeing into her investments, neither of which she paid any attention to.

Despite his protestations to Lady Sophia, however, he had to admit he couldn't resist the letter-writer's plea; he knew what it was like to be in need of guidance, even if he didn't understand how a female could inherit a duchy. He'd found a mentor when he'd first joined up, a man who made sure he understood what was expected, and what he was capable of. That man had perished in battle, and Archie had made it his purpose in life to help others who needed it.

But he did not want to ever return to London—there was a chance, in fact a distinct possibility, that his family would be there, and he did not want to see them. But he owed it to his colonel.

This duchess would be just like one of his young soldiers, although hopefully she was not armed.

He took a deep breath, recognizing his duty, even though it chafed. Even though the memories of his familial estrangement were still too tender six years later. "Yes. Bob is more than capable of taking care of things while I am gone advising your niece."

Lady Sophia placed Truffles on the rug before lifting her head to look at Archie.

"She is not my actual niece, you understand,"

Lady Sophia explained. "She is the daughter of my goddaughter, who married the duke, the duchess's father."

"Who?" Archie had yet to untangle the skeins of Lady Sophia's conversation. Thankfully she was more than happy to continue talking. And talking.

"Genevieve," she exclaimed, gesturing to the letter. "The duchess. It is quite unusual for a woman to inherit the duchy."

"Quite," Archie echoed, feeling his head start to spin.

"But it happened, somehow, and now she needs help, and since I don't know anything about being a duchess . . ."

Because I do? Archie wondered. But there wasn't anybody else. She wouldn't have asked Lady Sophia, of all people, unless there was anybody else.

Or if she was as flighty and confident as her faux-aunt.

". . . You'll have to go. It's all settled." She punctuated her words with a nod of her head, sending a few gray curls flying in the air. "I have every confidence you will be able to take care of her as ably as you do me. Mr. McCready will assist me while you are away."

She leaned over to the floor to offer Truffles the end of her biscuit. "The only thing Mr. McCready can't do is attract as much feminine interest as you do, Mr. Salisbury." She sat back up and regarded him. "Which might make him more productive," she added.

Archie opened his mouth to object, but closed it when he realized she was right. He wasn't vain, but he did recognize that ladies tended to find his appearance attractive. Lady Sophia received many more visitors, she'd told him in an irritated tone, now that he'd been hired.

Bob, damn his eyes, smirked knowingly every time Archie was summoned to Lady Sophia's drawing room to answer yet another question about estate management posed by a lady who'd likely never had such a question in her life.

Archie responded by making Bob personally in charge of the fertilizer. It didn't stop Bob's smirking, but it did make Archie feel better.

"And you will return in a month's time."

"Sooner if I can, my lady." If this duchess needed more time than a month, there would be no hope for her anyway, and he could depart London without seeing any of his family. Plus he'd discovered country life suited him; he liked its quiet and regularity. It was a vast change from life in battle, or even being just on duty, but it was far more interesting than being the third son from a viscount's family. A viscount who disowned his third boy when said boy was determined to join the army.

Meanwhile, however, he had to pack to head off to a new kind of battle—that of preparing a completely unprepared woman, likely a woman as flighty and often confused as Lady Sophia, to hold a position that she was entirely unsuited for.

Very much like working with raw recruits, in fact.

Dear Duchess:

You are probably surprised to receive correspondence from a gentleman you've never met. ~~I assure you, I am not in the habit of addressing strange women, either.~~ Your aunt Lady Sophia shared your letter with me, and asked that I pen a reply, since your aunt is ~~scattered~~ naturally quite busy.

I am your aunt's steward, and my duties include assisting Lady Sophia with any planning and business dealings. I am on my way to London to see how I might be of assistance.

You can expect me in three days' time.

Respectfully,

Mr. Archibald Salisbury, Capt. (Ret.)

"Three days' time?" Genevieve heard herself squeak. When did she start *squeaking*? Squeaking was not something she had ever done before.

Then again, she'd never been a duchess before. Maybe it was some understood thing that duchesses squeaked, and now that she was one, she did as well. And if that was the case, then she wouldn't need Mr. Archibald Salisbury, Capt. (Ret.), after all. It would just be intuitive. Rather like when she just knew that choosing to read *The Miser's Daughter* was far preferable to *Threshing and Other Exciting Farm Things* or whatever other boring tomes resided in the library.

"What is happening in three days' time, dear?"

Genevieve turned and smiled at her grandmother, who was sitting in what was now referred to as the Duchess's Sitting Room, even though it had been her father's Study. Apparently female dukes—also known as duchesses—didn't need to Study.

But she would. She did wish there was some sort of book she could just read on the subject. *Duchessing and Other Very Specific Occupations*, or perhaps *How to Duchess Without Being a Dullard*.

"A Mr. Archibald Salisbury," *Captain, Retired*, she added in her head, "is Aunt Sophia's steward. And she is sending him here to answer some questions I have."

"I can answer questions," her grandmother said indignantly. "Why just this morning Byron asked for breakfast and I gave it to him."

Byron looked up from her grandmother's lap and regarded Genevieve sleepily, one paw stretched out.

"If only it were that simple, Gran," Genevieve replied in a fond tone. She looked back at Mr. Salisbury's letter. "We will have to see if this gentleman can be of assistance." And if he couldn't, she would just have to blunder along as she had been.

Her grandmother lifted her head in Genevieve's general direction. Her grandmother was almost completely blind, which made it difficult to ask her opinion about anything Genevieve might wear. Among other things. "You will know best, I am sure." She accompanied her words with a warm smile and a pat on Byron's head.

It was heartening, if also terrifying, that her grandmother had such confidence in her. That the staff back at home in Traffordshire—where she had spent the first twenty years of her life— were also so confident, even though she had had no training in how to be a duchess beyond having Cook address her as Your Highness during the two weeks Genevieve had insisted she was a princess from the country of Snowland.

She should have spent less time imagining that cold possibility and more time facing the reality that she would be inheriting the duchy.

But it hadn't seemed real. And that was the problem. Nobody had thought it would happen, even though theirs was an ancient peerage that granted any heir (not just a son) the title. A bit of royal legerdemain that allowed women to become duchesses in their own right provided there was no male heir. Her father had remarried after Genevieve's mother's death, and it seemed certain that her father would have a son to inherit the title. But he had not, and then his wife had died, and now he was gone, too. The only ones who had paid her any type of attention were the servants in the house she'd grown up in. Who'd loved her, and been kind to her, and who'd brought her books, and biscuits, and smiled as she explained the intricate plot of the novel she'd just read.

But who didn't have any clue of what it would take to be a successful duchess.

Although she should be grateful she hadn't learned how to be any kind of ducal entity from her father, who had apparently been terrible at the whole thing.

He was far more interested in sampling London life to pay attention to pesky things like estate management. Genevieve's strongest memory of her father was of him kissing her cheek and making some sort of inarticulate approving noise at her.

Which reminded her that she was about to get some help in the form of the unknown Mr. Salisbury. Help that she sorely needed, even though apparently it also made her squeak.

She rang the bell, making both her grandmother and Byron jump. She heard footsteps, then the door opened to admit her butler.

"Your Grace?"

Thus far, Chandler had treated her with the utmost external respect, but Genevieve had caught an expression of disbelief on his face at times he'd thought she hadn't been looking at him.

She couldn't fault him for it; it was the same expression that she had when she looked at herself in the mirror.

She pretended she was the princess of Snowland again. It was easier than dealing with the reality of who she was now. "A Mr. Archibald Salisbury is arriving in a few days," she said in what she hoped was a suitable tone. "He is my aunt Sophia's steward, and he will be attending to my affairs until we locate a suitable person for the position." Was she explaining too much to him? Not enough? Why didn't she know? Oh, of course, because she hadn't been raised to become a duchess. It had been thrust onto her, through a variety of mishaps and unfortunate demises.

"Yes, Your Grace. I will place your guest," and was it Genevieve's imagination, or did the butler seem to sneer the last two words, "in one of the guest rooms on the third floor."

"Excellent. Oh, and," she added, as though it was an afterthought, "Mr. Salisbury is not precisely a guest. But he is to be treated as one for the duration of his stay."

"Yes, Your Grace," he replied, bowing. She thought there was a tinge more of a thaw in his manner—because she was behaving as a duchess ought? And since when did she care so for the opinion of people she'd just met, and who worked for her?

Of course. Since she recognized that even the barest hint of talk would undermine her position and her ability to carry out her duties. Since then.

She hoped Mr. Salisbury was as stuffy, appropriate, and efficient, not to mention boring, as his letters implied. The last thing she needed was someone else to upset her peace of mind.

"Your Grace?"

Genevieve paused in the act of dropping a bit of cheese for Byron, whose expression of expectation turned to disgust as Genevieve's hand stilled in mid-air.

"Yes?"

She and her grandmother were in the Duchess's sitting room again, since her grandmother was most comfortable navigating her way around the furniture here. Genevieve knew she would have to redecorate eventually, all the furnishings were worn, or old, or both, but she was hoping to be able to keep everything in the same basic location so her grandmother wouldn't fall.

"Your Mr. Salisbury is here." Chandler's sharp eyes focused on Byron, and his gaze narrowed. He had not said so in so many words, but he did not have to—it was clear he did not approve of Byron's being in the household. Of course, he probably didn't approve of Genevieve, either, so she couldn't pay heed to his opinion on either of them.

"Do show him in, Chandler."

She took a deep breath and settled her hands in her lap, her thumb and index finger rolling the crumb of cheese into a ball as Byron continued to glare at her. Drat, and her hair was likely untidy. She'd felt it unwinding when she came to the room, but then her grandmother had needed help with some yarn, and then Byron came begging, and now the likely very proper and properly dull Mr. Salisbury, Capt. (Ret.) was about to come in, and he would be shocked at her impropriety. And her hair.

Although as far as impropriety went, an unmarried duchess living on her own with only her grandmother and a hungry cat as companionship was far worse than untidy hair.

"Mr. Salisbury," Chandler said, then stepped aside to let the gentleman in.

Oh goodness.

The man was so tall it seemed he filled up the entire doorway, blocking out the light that streamed from the large windows in the hall. All she saw was an enormous shape that looked vaguely man-like. And then he came into the room and Genevieve was able to focus, and then it felt as though he'd blocked out all the air from her lungs. Even though he hadn't, he was just standing there holding his hat in his no doubt equally compelling hands.

But the rest of him seemed so improper it really did take her breath away, now that she could see him. Properly. He was so ruggedly good-looking it seemed impossible, and yet here he was—dark hair with just a hint of a curl, a strong blade of a nose over a full mouth, blue eyes that gazed at her unrelentingly. As though he could see inside her soul.

Which Genevieve knew perfectly well could be characterized with the word "confused."

And his build was—well, *impressive* was one word for it. Genevieve imagined there were other words, far less proper words, words that deliberately untidy-haired women would know. He was tall and also broad-shouldered and lean-hipped, and he stood in her sitting room with an easy grace that nonetheless seemed as though he could move at any time. To attack, to defend, to—

Not that. She could not even think that.

"Your Grace?" His eyebrows had drawn together, and he was looking at her as though she were an oddity he had run across, and wasn't certain he liked.

That was the expression she'd seen on most people's faces since inheriting. It shouldn't discomfit her; on a less impressive gentleman it wouldn't. But him, with his height, and his looks, and his general (no, *Captain!* her mind corrected hysterically) air of command—well. Well, it seemed as though she could be discomfited after all.

And here she thought the worst part about being a duchess was the whole inability to handle anything part.

"Yes, Mr. Salisbury," she said, keeping her voice low so it wouldn't tremble. Or squeak. "Thank you so much for arriving, and so promptly, too." She glanced toward Chandler and nodded. "That will be all."

Her butler withdrew, closing the door behind him. Leaving her with him and—"Oh, goodness, please allow me to introduce my grandmother."

"The dowager duchess?" he said, walking forward to bow in her grandmother's direction.

Gran giggled and held her hand out. "Heavens, no, I am Lady Halbard. My daughter was the Duchess's mother."

How, in goodness' name, could Gran tell that he was so good-looking? Because she was preening, at least as much as a sixty-year-old woman could. Which is to say she was wriggling in her seat and smiling in a nearly coquettish way.

The only time Genevieve had seen her grandmother behave that way before was in the presence of the butcher, who had apparently been quite comely in his youth, when Gran had much better eyesight.

"It is a pleasure to meet you."

Gran wriggled some more, and Genevieve found herself almost wishing she were ten years old again, and could roll her eyes with impunity.

"Would you excuse us, Gran? Mr. Salisbury and I have some business to discuss."

Her grandmother began to rise, and Mr. Salisbury reached out to hold her elbow as she stood, a delighted smile on her face. "Byron and I will leave you alone. Byron!" she called, even though the cat had yet to acknowledge it had a name, much less that anyone was in authority over it.

"Byron?" Mr. Salisbury asked, that look of confusion on his face again.

"Byron. Named after the poet. *Childe Harold's Pilgrimage*?" Gran replied.

"Ah. Of course," Mr. Salisbury replied, even though he still looked confused.

"The cat," Genevieve explained.

"Ah!" The look of confusion cleared somewhat.

"I spoke with him once," Gran said dreamily.

"The poet, not the cat," Genevieve said hastily.

"He was the most handsome man," Gran continued. Apparently Gran had long been a connoisseur of masculine beauty.

"Let me help you, Gran," Genevieve said, going to her grandmother's other side. The one not currently occupied by the handsome observant man. Not Byron, but Mr. Salisbury. And now she was doing it. She shook her head at herself as she began to walk.

"Thank you, dear." Gran patted Mr. Salisbury's arm. "It is such a pleasure to meet you, I am hoping you will be able to help my granddaughter with whatever she needs." And then to make matters worse, she punctuated her vague and somewhat leading words with a knowing chuckle.

Genevieve felt her face start to burn in embarrassment. Gran wouldn't see it, of course, but he likely would. The realization of which only made her face burn brighter.

They waited until the door shut behind Gran, as Genevieve tried frantically to get her face to cool.

"Well Your Grace," Mr. Salisbury said, regarding her with an intense gaze. "How may I be of service?"

Oh dear, Genevieve thought. That was certainly an open-ended question. Where should she begin?